"Every page seduced me, every passage was poetic and provocative, this is Jasinda Wilder at her absolute, steamiest best! *Madame X* . . . invited me into a sensual world where I was one of the wicked participants. This isn't just a sizzling hot read, it's an exhilarating, unforgettable experience."

—Katy Evans, *New York Times* bestselling author

"Jasinda Wilder like you've never seen her before. *Madame X* draws you in from the first page and doesn't let go until long after the last."

—K. Bromberg, *New York Times* bestselling author of the Driven series

"Jasinda outdid herself! Every word, every line in this book was a treat and I savored every bite. Sensual, intelligent, and well-paced, I am on the edge of my seat and needing more!"

—Alessandra Torre, *New York Times* bestselling author

"Wilder . . . pulls out all the stops for this spellbinding novel of identity, passion, and fear . . . The intense, violent, erotic story is told in the first-person voice of X herself, with impressively well-handled second-person passages directed at her often odious clients . . . Once readers fall into X's story, they'll be desperate for the next installments."

—*Publishers Weekly* (starred review)

BERKLEY TITLES BY JASINDA WILDER

Madame X
Exposed

eXposed

A MADAME X NOVEL

JASINDA WILDER

BERKLEY BOOKS, NEW YORK

BERKLEY

An imprint of Penguin Random House LLC
375 Hudson Street, New York, New York 10014

This book is an original publication of the Berkley Publishing Group.

EXPOSED

Library of Congress Cataloging-in-Publication Data

Names: Wilder, Jasinda, author.
Title: Exposed : a Madame X novel / Jasinda Wilder.
Description: New York : Berkley Books, [2016] I Series: A Madame X novel ; 2
Identifiers: LCCN 2015039286 I ISBN 9781101986899 (paperback)
Subjects: LCSH: Man-woman relationships—Fiction. I Sexual dominance and
submission—Fiction. I BISAC: FICTION / Romance / Contemporary. I FICTION /
Contemporary Women. I FICTION / Romance / Suspense. I GSAFD: Romantic
suspense fiction. I Erotic fiction.
Classification: LCC PS3623.15386 E97 2016 I DDC 813/.6—dc23
LC record available at http://lccn.loc.gov/2015039286

PUBLISHING HISTORY
Berkley trade paperback edition / March 2016

PRINTED IN THE UNITED STATES OF AMERICA

10 9 8 7 6 5 4 3 2 1

Cover photographs: *Woman* © Mayer George / Shutterstock;
Bridge © Sean Pavone / Shutterstock.
Cover design by Sarah Hansen.
Interior text design by Laura K. Corless.

Penguin
Random
House

ONE

am naked; you are clothed.

The way it always is, it seems. Do you keep me naked merely because you enjoy the sight of my nude body? Or is it another form of control, of manipulation? A way of keeping me contained, keeping me captive? Some of both, I think. When I am naked—which is often, now that I live with you in your cavernous tower-top home— your eyes flit and float to me, rake over me, absorb my dusky flesh and athletic curves. Your eyes are always on me, even when you are working. Your eyes move from your laptop to me, pause on the elegant column of my throat, slip and slide down to the valley between my heavy breasts, to the flat plain of my belly, the juncture between my thighs, and then you, somewhat reluctantly, it sometimes seems, force your gaze back to your work.

Life with Caleb Indigo: a concerto of keyboard keys clicking and clacking, an overture of gazes and glances. You are always working. Always. I wake at midnight to the sound of your phone ringing—your ringer is a plain, old-fashioned bleating of a rotary-style phone—and you answer it with a curt "Indigo," and you listen carefully, intently, and then respond in as few syllables as possible, end the call, toss the phone onto the nightstand close to hand, and tug me roughly up against your chest. Four A.M.: You jab your legs into slacks, shrug into a button-down, fingers nimble on the buttons, announce that you have business to see to, and then you do not return till three in the morning or four or even six, when you appear looking haggard and unshaven with dark circles under your eyes. But then, I, anticipating your return, am awake. And you know this.

And you stand at my side of the bed, staring down at me, waiting. I roll over, gaze up at you. Slowly, you divest yourself of your clothing. Your gaze will not leave me, and perhaps you slide the flat sheet away to bare my form. I cannot help but notice the way the zipper of your slacks tents and tautens as you gaze at me. And I am, in that moment, flushed with desire.

I cannot help it.

And I do try. Just to see if I have found some new source of self-control where you are concerned.

But the result is always the same: I see you, watch you peel the shirt off, unbutton it quickly, swing your arms back to pinch your shoulder blades together, and the shirt falls away. Your torso is bare, magnificent, a sculpture of tanned, muscled perfection. My throat will tighten and I am compelled to swallow again and again, as if I could swallow down my need for you. And then my gaze will rake down your furrowed eight-pack abdomen to your groin, to your bulging zipper, and my thighs clench around the gush of heated need. My breath comes in panting gasps.

I don't need to say anything.

You unhook the clasp of your trousers, pinch the zipper tab in your big thumb and long forefinger, slowly draw it down. Free your erection. It will sway in front of my face, tall and hard and perfect.

And I am undone.

Any will I possess is eradicated.

Your hands will be rough on my flesh, scraping, teasing, possessing. And I will revel in that roughness, in the clutch of hard hands on my buttocks, tugging me to the end of the bed and holding me aloft as you plunge into me, eliciting a whimper.

And I will come apart for you, watching the tendons in your neck pulse and tighten, watching your abdomen flex, watching your hips drive, watching your biceps ripple as you keep me held effortlessly where you want me.

And you will come, too, but never quickly. Never until I have reached my own climax. And sometimes not until I have reached it twice. If I do not find that release with the driving and thrust of your body, you press that big thumb to my clitoris and force me to it with gentle, skillful, insistent circles as if you somehow just *know* precisely how to pleasure me.

When you do find your own release, it is quiet, an intense groan, perhaps a bead of sweat trickling down your temple, as if even your sweat obeys the rule of artfulness that seems to dictate your existence.

And then, done with me, you will brush a thumb over my temple, sweep flyaway locks of raven-black hair aside, grant me a moment of eye contact, a moment of personal connection. Just a moment, only a fragment of time. But *something*, at least. As if you know I need those moments to continue this . . . game.

This ruse.

This deception.

This faux-domestic relationship.

Without those moments of intimacy granted in that postcoital gaze, I would combust. Detonate.

And even with them, I am discontent. Disturbed.

You know it.

I know it.

But we do not speak of it. I try, and you brush it aside, sweep the conversation away like so much dust from a corner. Answer a phone call, claim to have a meeting to scurry off to, an e-mail to answer, a deal to broker.

An apprentice to train. Although you are smart enough to not ever mention your "apprentices" to me.

But I know you go to them. I know you "examine" them and "train" them, when you leave me.

I know.

I wish I didn't, but I do. And I cannot un-know it. I've tried that, too.

You slip the second-from-the-top button of your crisp, never-wrinkled button-down shirt through the loop, tuck and blouse it just so, align the silver buckle of your slim black leather belt with the line of buttons and the zipper. You roll the sleeves to your elbow in precise fourths, brush your hand through your dark hair, and then you leave. Not a word of good-bye, not a hint of where you're going or when you might return.

Just a glance at me, a moment of intimacy, that thumb through my hair, sweeping it back around my ear. And then you're gone.

And I know where you go.

You don't go to broker a deal. You don't go to negotiate terms with other businessmen. You don't go to sign a contract, or to scout a new location, or investigate potential real estate investments. These are all things a businessman would do—I know, I've researched it. You're president, CEO, and chairman of the board of Indigo Services, LLC, as well as a dozen other businesses both private and publicly traded. You should be sitting in a corner office, with a landline phone pressed to your ear, a computer monitor in front of you, discussing P-and-L statements—profit and loss, that means—and quarterly returns, and who isn't performing up to par.

Par is a golf term, meaning minimum number of strokes to complete a hole, but it often is used colloquially to mean a minimum standard; I'm always learning new things, now that I have access to the Internet.

You should be doing these things. I've learned what a CEO does, what a businessman does. From TV, from books, from the Internet.

And I don't think you do any of those things. Or, at least, not when I would expect you to do them.

You answer e-mails at four in the morning. You wake me at six for sex, exercise from six thirty or so until eight thirty, shower, eat a quick breakfast, and then you go to sleep at nine and wake at noon. Wake, answer e-mails, return phone calls, do things involving spreadsheets and graphs, and then you leave.

Or, sometimes, after sex with me in the morning, you skip the shower, and just leave.

And when you return, you avoid me. You work out. Shower. Avoid me. Work. Avoid me.

Finally, you might sit with me, eat with me, take me to dinner or to the theater.

And Caleb?

I know what you do when you leave, why you avoid me.

You're "training" your "apprentices."

Translated, that means fucking.

Teaching ex-prostitutes and ex-drug addicts and ex-homeless girls how to pleasure a man. How to give a proper blow job. How to take anal. How to take a come-shot to the face and look sexy and grateful and seductive while doing it. How to beg for sex without actually saying a word.

You teach them this by showing them.

By fucking them.

They put their mouths on your cock, and you instruct them on proper fellatio technique.

You bend them forward over the bed and put your cock in their bottom, and you tell them how to make sure they don't get hurt in the process, how to make sure it feels good for them.

You pull your cock out of their mouths and you come all over their faces, and claim it's for their sake, because some clients like that, although *you* don't. Oh no.

How do I know all this?

I am friends with Rachel. Down on the third floor, in apartment three. Rachel, formerly known as Apprentice Number Six-nine-seven-one-three, or just Three for short. An apprentice in your street-to-Bride program. After you've left for the day, after your three hours of sleep, after I watch your sleek white Maybach slide elegantly toward Fifth Avenue, I take the elevator to the third floor and knock on door number three, a bottle of white wine in one hand.

Rachel pours the entire bottle into two glasses—not wineglasses, because she doesn't own any of those, but rather into large cylindrical juice glasses—and we drink it sitting on her bed, and we talk. She tells me things. About her former life, which she isn't allowed to talk about but does with me for some reason. About her current life as a Bride-in-training. She tells me everything. Sometimes *too* much.

"Sorry, TMI?" she often asks.

TMI: too much information.

Yes, I tell her. That you were just there—in the very bed upon which I sit—fucking her in the ass, that is too much information. That you pulled out and came on her back is also too much information.

Yet still she tells me. As if I am her priest, her confessor. It's girl talk, I think she thinks.

Education for me, is how I see it. It's how I learn terms like *come-shot*, which I probably would have been better off not knowing.

I find it strange, however, that you do none of these things with me. That you never have.

You don't fuck me in the ass. You don't come on my back, or my face.

I try to imagine how I would feel if you did. Would I like it? Would I hate it? Would I feel degraded . . . or turned on? Some days I think one way, some days the other. I don't have the courage to ask you about this. I don't think I want to find out how I feel about it.

Rachel likes pain with her sex. She likes to be spanked. Hard. She likes it when you tie her hands behind her back with a necktie and fuck her from behind and spank her with your belt while you're balls-deep inside her. That's verbatim what she tells me.

I don't want to know that.

I also can't stop going down to talk to her, knowing that she'll tell me all these things.

I want to know, and I hate that I want to know.

She also tells me about her fellow apprentices' predilections. Four has a thing for having a vibrator in her anus while you have sex with her. Five is a blow job aficionado and does actually like taking come-shots to the face. Seven, Eight, and Nine don't like any one thing in particular that Rachel knows about, and Two likes autoerotic asphyxiation, meaning she likes it when you choke her while fucking her.

I know more about the sexual goings-on of Floor Three than I think is healthy.

It also tells me that you have an unnatural and possibly superhuman sex drive. At least once a day with me. Rachel claims you visit her once a week, usually. Plus girls Two and Four through Nine. Including me, that's ten women. A different woman every day, with an extra three you can rotate to have more than one a day. Which, honestly, is just one possible permutation based on the available information, variables, and my skill with mathematics.

Your life is sex, I think.

And work.

You sleep with me, though. Like, actually sleep. Three hours in the morning, from nine to noon, and usually, unless "work" intervenes, another three hours from ten at night to one in the morning. Strange hours. You're always on the move, always going. You wake suddenly, completely, and immediately. Your eyes flick open, you blink twice, and then you get up and dress. No stretching, no rubbing of your eyes, no yawning. No hesitating on the edge of the bed, rubbing your stubbled jaw with a palm. Just . . . awake, totally. It's eerie.

Living with you is bizarre, that's what I'm learning.

I'm never bored anymore.

I still work. But now I go down to what was once my apartment, which has been converted into an office, and meet my clients there. My bedroom now has a computer, and there's a large flat screen TV in the living room. It is my space. If I have a "home," it is there, not really the penthouse with you.

There is no evidence, visually, that I live with you. I do not know if this is unusual or not. I have not changed any of the decor. I have a section of your closet for my clothes; by "closet" I mean two thousand square feet dedicated to clothing storage. Your home—which is the entire upper floor of the building—is open plan, certain areas sectioned off with movable screens. The closet, then, is a very cleverly designed area, screened off so as to be invisible from anywhere else in the apartment, built-in racks to hang suits, slacks, and button-downs, shelves for T-shirts and underwear and socks. And my clothes. But apart from the shelves and hangers of my clothing, a casual visitor—of which there are none, not ever—wouldn't know I'm a resident. There are no pictures of you, of me, of your family, of anyone. Just abstract art by unknown artists. Macro photographs of a leaf or an insect head, the surface of a lake so still it could be a mirror, splotches and swaths of color, textured paintings using glops of paint an inch thick, an elaborate line drawing of tree. Weird, impersonal, beautiful.

Like you, in many ways.

My space is my old apartment. I still stand at my window and make up stories for passersby on the sidewalk below.

My life is the same, really. Except now I live in the penthouse, and I watch TV and surf the Internet and you have access to my body whenever you are home. Ostensibly, I suppose I could leave the building if I wanted.

But I still have no money of my own. I never see a check or a single dollar bill. I have no identification.

I still have no control over my clientele.

I have no name but Madame X.

No further knowledge of my past, other than that I'm Spanish . . . or so you say.

They sniff a tumbler of scotch, nostrils flaring, eyes narrowed, lips pursed. Assessing.

"What kind of whisky is this?" comes the question.

"It's scotch, actually," I answer. "Macallan 1939."

Their hands clutch the crystal tumbler, thin lips touch the rim, golden liquid slides. Tongues taste, a pink smear visible through the distortion of the crystal. "Damn. That's fuckin' amazing."

"For ten thousand dollars a bottle, it had better be very good," I answer.

They do not flinch at the number. Of course not. Today they are a rich boy of the highest caliber. Family homes in the Caribbean,

Mediterranean, in the south of France, even a ranch on the pampas of Argentina. They are used to absurdly expensive goods, watches, liquors, cars, private jets. A ten-thousand-dollar bottle of scotch is de rigueur.

This does not, however, mean they are possessed of a refined palate or discerning taste.

Or manners.

Of course not.

I struggle to remember the name from the dossier; this is their first appointment.

Clint? Flint? Something like that. Bland. Like them. Tall, but not too tall. Flat brown eyes. Average brown hair, albeit expensively cut and coiffured. High, sharp cheekbones, at least. Not too well muscled or defined, no extravagant amounts of time in the gym for them, it would seem. A kind of throaty voice, as if they speak through a bubble of phlegm. It is maddening, actually.

Clint. That's their name.

"So, Madame X." Doc Martens rest on my coffee table, rudely, barbarically. "How's this work, exactly?"

I inhale sharply, for patience and for effect. "First, Clint, you remove your feet from my furniture. Then, you tell me whether you read the pamphlet and the contract."

"I skimmed the pamphlet. Sounds like a modern version of Emily Post etiquette lessons for men, except you charge a grand an hour." A sip of the scotch. "And yeah, I read the contract. I mean, no shit. Who doesn't read a contract like that before signing it? It's not like online terms and conditions or whatever. So I get it. No touching you, no hitting on you. Whatever. I've got a girlfriend, and I don't cheat, so that's not a problem. I just want to get this bullshit over with, to be honest."

"Why are you here, Clint?"

"'Cause Daddy holds the purse strings for now, and Daddy says I need my edges smoothed out." This is said with extreme sarcasm, virulent bitterness.

"And you disagree?"

A shrug. "No shit. I mean, I don't see the point. What are you gonna do, tell me to stop swearing and teach me which fork to use at black-tie dinners? Fuck that."

I am very tired of this whole ruse, suddenly.

"That's precisely what I'm supposed to do. Tell you to clean up your language. Tell you to keep your stupid, dirty boots off other people's furniture when you're in their home. And yes, I'm supposed to smooth out your edges, teach you how to behave in polite society as if you have a single well-mannered bone in your entire uncouth, barbaric body." I let out a breath, rub the bridge of my nose. "But, honestly, Clint, I don't see the point. You are probably irredeemable."

"What the fuck is that supposed to mean?"

"It means you are a grotesque barbarian with no manners whatsoever. It means that you have no charm. No poise. It means, furthermore, that I don't really believe you even have the potential to learn any of that. It means, Clint, that you are a waste of my time."

"Well Jesus, you're a real bitch, you know that?" They stand up, brown eyes blazing with hate. "Fuck you. I don't have to take this from you."

"Indeed you do not." I gesture at the door. "How does that phrase go? Oh yes: don't let the door hit you on the way out."

They leave, and I am relieved.

I really don't know how much longer I can do this.

Pretend that what I do is "work." That it holds any value. That I like it. That it means anything whatsoever. To me, to the clients, to Caleb. To anyone. It's just . . . emptiness. Time wasted. A game. All of us playing pretend.

I can't do it anymore.

I am suddenly overwhelmed, overcome. Anxious. Restless.

Angry.

I have this feeling inside me that defies description. A yawning chasm, a metaphysical hunger. A need to go somewhere, to do something, but I don't know where, or what. A need for an intangible *something*. The need borders on panic, a feeling that if I don't leave this condo, leave this building right now I might explode, might devolve into arm-flapping, screaming, gibbering insanity.

I stand up suddenly, try to force a measure of calm into myself by smoothing my white Valentino Crepe Couture dress over my hips. Wiggle my foot in my lavender Manolo Blahnik sandals. As if such physical gestures could soothe the disquiet within me.

I'm in the elevator, suddenly, and the *ding* of the car arriving drags with it a host of memories. I have the key now. Or a copy of it, at least. I can insert the key myself, turn it to whichever floor I want. The doors slide open and I'm shaking as I step into the elevator car. Fighting hyperventilation.

I need to go.

I need out.

I need to breathe.

I cannot.

Cannot.

I clench my fists and squeeze my eyes shut and stand in the center of the elevator and force my lungs to expand and contract. Compel my hand to extend and my fingers to fit the key to the slot, compel my fingers to twist the key. I don't pay attention to which floor I have chosen. It doesn't matter. Anywhere but here.

Ground floor. The lobby. Hushed conversation between a man in a suit and a woman behind a massive marble desk. The lobby is an expanse of black marble, three-foot-by-three-foot tiles veined with gold streaks. Soaring ceilings, easily fifty feet high. Thirty-foot-tall cypress trees rooted under the floor itself lining the walls on either side of the lobby. It is a space designed to intimidate. The reception desk is a continent unto itself, the receptionists on pedestals behind it, literally looking down at visitors. It reminds me of a judge's podium from centuries past, when the judge literally sat several feet above you, thus engendering the phrase "to look down upon" someone in arrogance.

My heels *click-clack-click-clack* across the floor, each step echoing like the report of a rifle. Stares follow me. Eyes watch me.

I am beautiful.

I look expensive.

Because I am.

I did not know this, before.

Before I made the naked journey from my condo prison up to the penthouse, thus making a choice for my life.

After that, I began learning.

That my beloved crimson Jimmy Choo stilettos cost two thousand dollars. That my Valentino dress, the one I have on right now, cost nearly three thousand dollars. That each article of clothing I own, down to my underwear, is the most expensive of its kind there could be.

I discovered this, and didn't know what to do with the knowledge. I still don't. I didn't pay for them. I didn't choose them.

I allow my thoughts to wander as I cross the vast lobby, forcing myself to walk as if I am confident, arrogant. I let my hips sway and keep my shoulders back and my chin high. Focus my gaze on the revolving doors miles and miles in the distance, across acres of black marble. Acknowledge none of the stares. In the center of the lobby there are twelve large black leather couches arranged in a wide square, three couches to a side, each separated by small tables. People wait and converse and perhaps do business deals, and they all watch me cross the lobby. Surreptitiously, I count them. Fourteen.

Fourteen people watch me cross the lobby, as if I am utterly unexpected, a rare sighting.

A leopard stalking down Fifth Avenue, perhaps.

I try to capture that essence, pretend that I am a predator rather than prey.

It gets me through the revolving glass doors and outside. It is late August, hot, the air thick. The sun bright, beating down on me from between skyscrapers. The noise of Manhattan assaults me in a physical wave: sirens, a police car zipping past me, howling. An ambulance in pursuit. A garbage truck groaning around a corner, engine grumbling. Dozens of motors revving as the light turns green twenty feet to my right.

I force myself to walk. Refuse to let my knees fold in, refuse to let my lungs seize. The panic is a knife in my throat, a blade in my chest, hot wires constricting my breath. I am clutched by talons of panic. The sirens did it, the sounds of sirens howling like wild beasts, howling in my ear.

Tires squeal somewhere and I cannot see, my eyes are squeezed shut, and hot dark marble burns my bicep as I lean against the side of the building, succumbing to panic.

I hear questions, someone asking if I'm all right.

Clearly I am not, but I am beyond answering.

Until I feel a hand on my shoulder.

Hear a voice in my ear.

Heat from a big body crowding against me, blocking the world and the noises and the questions.

"Hey. Breathe, okay? Breathe. Breathe, X." That voice, like the warmth of the sun made sonic. "It's me. I've got you."

No. It cannot be.

Cannot be.

I look up.

It is.

Logan.

TWO

W hat—what are you—" I cough, clear my throat, try again. "What are you doing here, Logan?"

His palm touches my cheek, and I can breathe. "Stalking you, obviously."

"Logan." I manage to sound scolding. It is a feat of will.

I hear the grin in his voice, but also the strain. "Actually, I wasn't kidding. I really am stalking you. I mean, I've been looking for you. Hoping to get a glimpse of you. Talk to you, even just for a second."

"Why?" This is weak, small, confused.

"Because I can't stop thinking about you, X. I've tried, and I suck at it. I'm really good at thinking about you, it seems, and not so good at *not* thinking about you."

This brings a smile to my lips. "You must be a glutton for punishment then."

"I am, though. I love punishment." His hands weave into mine, help me to my feet. "The real truth is, I have business on this end of town, the next building over. I couldn't help passing by this building and wondering if you were up there. If you're happy. I never thought I'd actually get to see you, though."

Now I'm confused. Which of his statements is the truth? "You're contradicting yourself, Logan."

"I know. I'm trying to obfuscate how debilitated I am at running into you like this."

"Obfuscate. That's a wonderful word." What I don't ask is why he's so debilitated. I don't think the answer would do me good.

"Are you obfuscated, X?"

"Completely." Am I gazing up at him? I am. Very much so. I am faint. My heart is pitter-pattering. I want to feel his hands in mine again.

"Good," he says. "Then my work here is done."

"Jokes do not suit this situation, Logan."

"No?" He sounds serious, suddenly. His voice smooth, too smooth. Too featureless. A little cold. "What am I supposed to say then? That I'm still absurdly, childishly hurt by the fact that you chose him over me? Or that I legit just *cannot* stop thinking about you? Wanting you? That I keep wanting to show up at your door again and literally carry you off over my shoulder like a fucking Viking? What is the right etiquette for a situation like this, Madame X?"

"Don't, Logan. Please don't." I don't mind begging.

"I can still feel you, your bare legs around my waist." His voice is in my ear, murmuring. Intimate. Sensuous. "I can feel the heat from your tight pussy against my stomach. I can smell you. I can feel how wet you are for me. For *me*. You wanted me, X. I could have done anything I wanted with you. I had you *naked*, in my arms. Wet and wanting and desperate and *all over* me. I could have laid you down on the carpet right there in the hallway and fucked you senseless, and I guarantee you, if I had, you wouldn't have walked away from me."

"Then why didn't you?" Oh, I am damned.

"Because you weren't ready, and you still aren't. You were scared, and you still are. You were like a frightened little rabbit out of its hole for the first time, blinking in the sunlight. There's a lioness inside you, X, you just have to find it and become it."

"I didn't even make it ten feet from the door on my own, Logan," I whisper against the soft cotton of his T-shirt.

"But you walked out, didn't you? Baby steps to the elevator, Bob."

"What?"

"*What About Bob?*" he asks, expectant. "No? Nothing? Okay, never mind. It's a movie reference."

I sigh. "Total amnesia, remember? Movies are not exactly a common feature in my life, Logan."

"Well, that'll be the first thing I'll rectify. You and me, we'll stay naked in my bed for a month, having hot, wild monkey sex and watching movies. Catch you up on all the great cinema you're missing out on. *What About Bob?* is a classic. *Fear and Loathing in Las Vegas. Goodfellas, The Godfather*, shit, I'll even throw in some rom-com for you. *Notting Hill* is a great one, or *How to Lose a Guy in Ten Days.* Or, wait, wait, *Love Actually.* God, that movie is awesome, although I know some people hate it. I love it. It's real."

"Hot and wild monkey sex, Logan? Really?"

He laughs in my ear, pulling me to his chest, arms wrapping around me. "Yes, X. Hot and wild monkey sex. It's the greatest thing on earth. No inhibitions, no time, no responsibilities, nothing but both of us taking as much pleasure from each other as we can, for hours and hours and hours until we're too exhausted to even move."

"And watching movies."

"And watching movies. And drinking beer by the case, and ordering pizza and Chinese takeout."

"I've never had either," I admit.

"You're not for real, are you?" He is utterly incredulous.

"And you're not *still* surprised at my lack of experience with things you deem normal, are you?"

"It just seems wrong," he says. "Beer and pizza . . . it's like—a basic, elemental part of life. Seriously. Without beer and pizza and movies, you're not really living."

"I certainly feel alive."

"X . . . you are alive, yes, but are you *living*? Not just existing, not just continuing to be physically present in the world day by day, but . . . *enjoying* life. Making a difference. Being totally *you*. Owning who you are and choosing a life that fulfills you. Because from where I'm standing . . . it doesn't seem that way."

"And beer, pizza, and movies is a part of that, is it?" His words hit too close to bull's-eye, and my defenses are engaging.

A sigh. "No, X. It is for me, yes. But in the context of this conversation, beer, pizza, and movies are a stand-in for you having the freedom to make your own choices. You're still wearing designer clothes, I notice. Probably designer lingerie underneath, too. When I took you shopping, I bought you basic clothes. Basic comfortable jeans, a T-shirt, basic bra and underwear. Nothing fancy. And you seemed . . . I don't know, more *you* in them. This is still you, this designer-clothes-fancy Madame X. But that's *Madame* X. Not X, just X. And I don't think you're free to choose that. Not while you're with him."

"Logan—"

"All I'm going to say here is that to me, you deserve more. More than just fancy clothes and a penthouse prison."

"It's not a prison, Logan." I say this because something inside me insists I do, even though his words yet again strike hard and accurate.

"I want you to leave him and be with me," he murmurs. "I have absolutely no problem saying it in so many words, right here, right now. That's what I want. I want you. I want *us*. But I also want you to have a choice. I want you to be able to decide what you want out of life. Even if that isn't me. Which means I'll help you find what you want, regardless of the outcome for me."

We're standing in the middle of the sidewalk not ten feet from the front door of Caleb's tower. This feels dangerous, somehow.

"Logan . . . why?" I really do not understand. "Why do you care so much?"

He shrugs. "I honestly don't know, X. I wish I did. It'd be a fuck of a lot easier for me if I could just walk away, if I could stay away. But I *can't*. I've tried." He gestures up at the tower. "He's not what you think, X. You have to see that much, at least."

"Then what is he, Logan?"

A frustrated groan. "Not a good person. Not who you think."

"What proof do you have, Logan?" I hear myself ask.

Do I need proof? More than the evidence of the third floor? Yet still I persist. I do not know why.

I do, though. Don't I?

Because Logan scares me. He challenges my conceptions, my worldview. Makes me want things I'm not sure I can have. Things I never thought I could have. He makes me feel like choices I never even knew existed are suddenly possible.

Logan turns away, stares into nothingness, scrubs his hand through his hair. "None. Not yet, at least."

A long, low, sleek, white vehicle slides up to the curb. It is a Maybach Landaulet 62. Worth somewhere between half a million and a million dollars. I've ridden in that exact vehicle. I know who is about to emerge.

"Shit," Logan murmurs. He glances at me, eyes searching mine. Whatever he finds leaves him unhappy. "I'll find proof, X. I'll show you."

I have no words; there is nothing to say. I can only watch him turn away, and feel a pang of sadness, a spear of distress. Something in him calls to me, speaks to my soul. The intensity of it frightens me. I do not know how to handle the power of what merely being near Logan does to me.

The rear passenger-side door of the Maybach opens, disgorging a god of the tall, dark, and handsome variety.

A displeased god. "Logan." This, in a deep, cold voice. "She made her choice."

"Yeah. Doesn't mean it was the right one, though." Logan walks away then. Doesn't turn back.

Something in me fractures.

Why were you speaking to him, X? And what are you doing out here?" Your voice is low and calm. Too low, too calm.

"He was passing by. I ran into him."

"What are you doing out here, X?" You repeat the question.

I find a seed of courage. "Am I not allowed outside, Caleb?"

Your eyes narrow. "Of course you are. You're not a prisoner. I just worry for you. The streets are unsafe, and you're prone to panic attacks."

Prone to panic attacks. Yes. I am. But something about Logan soothes me. Makes me forget my panic. Makes it all okay.

I do not say this, of course.

"Sometimes I wonder if perhaps you don't want me to really get over them, though," I find myself saying. Unwisely. Foolishly. Courageously—the seed has germinated, perhaps. "I wonder if perhaps you just want me to stay up there in your tower, at your disposal."

Your hand closes around my arm. "I'm not having this discussion with you out here."

You pull me through the revolving door, back across the expansive marble lobby, and for some reason, I let you. I am outside myself, watching as I allow you to haul me into the private elevator, up and up and up back to the penthouse. Watching as you release my arm and pace in circles around me. You are, suddenly, a lion pacing in its cage, feral and furious, and I am a little lamb somehow stuck in the cage with the predator.

"I worry for you, X," you repeat.

"I know you do." I stand my ground, watch you pace. "Perhaps you don't need to. Not as much."

"Of course I do," you insist. "Your understanding of the world beyond these walls is . . . limited."

"And perhaps that is something I wish to rectify."

"Why?" you ask. You cease pacing, stand inches from me, staring down at me, dark eyes icy with suspicion. "Why the sudden change?"

"It's not sudden, Caleb—"

"It's him, isn't it?" This from you sounds almost . . . petulant.

Jealousy? It is unbecoming, Caleb. It does not suit you.

"It isn't about Logan." I pause, blink, thinking, and then take a breath to nudge the seedling of courage to grow a little stronger. "Or, not entirely."

"What does that mean, X? 'Not entirely'?"

I hesitate, seeking a neutral but true answer. "It means . . . the brief time I spent with Logan did make me curious about the outside world. It didn't start with him, though, and it doesn't end with him." I try a placation. "You can't keep me locked in here forever, Caleb. I am not a possession. I am woman. A person."

"I'm just trying to protect you." You are closer, your hard chest pressing against my breasts, your hands coming to rest on my hips.

"I know."

"You may not be a possession, X," you say, your voice a buzzing rumble, "but you are *mine*."

This statement twists me up. Part of me knows it's true, and likes it. And part of me hates it. Part of me knows as long as I am yours, I will never be my own.

My thoughts are smashed by your lips on mine, sudden and crushing. A little clumsy. Impulsive, even. Not with the usual mastery of your body over mine.

As you kiss me, I am struck by a question: how often do you kiss me?

The answer is immediate: not often. Almost never. Not your mouth on mine, not your lips against mine. Not like this, not with this intimacy. You kiss my body, my breasts, between my thighs, but my lips? Never.

I do not know what that means.

You kiss me slowly, and as you kiss, your skill grows.

It isn't until your hands begin scouring my body, however, that my will is swept away as it usually is. It isn't until your hands are tugging at the zipper of my dress and nudging it off my shoulders that heat suffuses me, that my stomach tenses and my core tightens. When I am standing before you in nothing but lingerie—and yes, the lingerie is Carine Gilson, and you told me when you gave it to me that it was handmade by the designer herself specifically for me—that is when my heart rate spikes to a frantic hammering and my hands shake and I am weak in the knees.

Your eyes rake over me. "You look ravishing, X. That set really suits you. Carine outdid herself when she made it for me."

"For you?"

A brief, uncharacteristic smile. "Well, yes. Lingerie, at the heart of it, is about the viewer rather than the wearer, isn't it?"

This tolls within me, a truth I do not like. It is not just true for lingerie, I think. But for all of my clothes.

It is true about me, as an entity.

I would say "individual," but I fear I am not an individual so much as an entity. A possession. Like a fine vase, or an original painting.

A piece in your collection.

You somehow have placed me on a couch, sitting down on the edge. Your fingers are brushing across the delicate Lyon silk over my core. I cannot help but feel the rush of heat at your touch. I watch, and part of me feels disconnected. Impartial, somehow.

As when you hauled me up here, I watched almost as if from above, as if I could see myself and you, see us. Me, on the black leather couch nearest the elevator. I am leaned back, my shoulders touching the upright part of the couch. My knees are splayed wide. Pale peach silk covers my core, Chantilly lace demi-cup bra over my breasts, propping them up, making what are already large appear even larger. For you.

Not for me, but for you.

You kneel on the glistening dark hardwood floor, broad shoulders between my knees. Still in your suit. Dark pinstripes stretched across perfect muscles, crisp white button-down, a thin gray tie. Two-tone oxford dress shoes. Your hands on the insides of my thighs, your mouth now brushing over my skin, over my hip, across my stomach. I watch as your hands tug down the silk, and I watch as my bottom lifts, allowing you to slide the underwear away, leaving me bare.

I watch as your fingers brush over me. Thick fingers, strong. Hard. Not quite gentle as they stroke between my nether lips. Insistent, knowing. Familiar.

My body is utterly known by you.

The passive grammatical construction of my thoughts seems apropos.

I am curious, in a strange way. My voice responds to your touch, my body rises and writhes as your tongue laps at me and sends thrills of pleasure through me. It feels good. Of course it does. You are a master of pleasure. I am curious, though. What will you do? What will you want from me? And will I give it to you?

When I have spasmed, spine straight, backside lifting off the couch cushions, you finally reach to my back and unclasp the bra, set it aside, and I am, once again, naked while you are clothed.

You will remain clothed until the last possible moment. I know this, from experience.

But somehow I'm just now realizing it.

You lift me in your arms and turn me so I face the back of the couch, kneeling upright. I feel your weight on the couch behind me. I feel you lower your zipper. You won't even disrobe for this. Just unbutton, unzip, lower your slacks and black Armani briefs.

Slide into me.

I gasp, of course. Because you fill me and strike within me just so, and know how to thrust so I feel it perfectly, so I cannot help but gasp, and your fingers pinch my nipples and reach around to touch my clitoris and I am undone. Undone.

Watching, numb within.

Gasping, aching, coming apart.

But numb.

How is this possible?

What is happening to me?

When you have finished, you step away. Button and zip. Present-able within seconds, unruffled. Not a hair out of place.

You lean over me. I am still bent forward over the back of the couch, thighs quaking with the effort of holding myself upright while you take your pleasure in me. I felt it too, oh yes. I must give you your due: You do not take without giving as well. But now, finished, with your essence still inside me, still warm, you lean over me, chin brushing the top of my left shoulder, stubble scratching.

Your voice is distant thunder in my ear. "Mine, X. Don't for-get it."

Ah. That's what this was about. Reminding me.

Don't worry, Caleb. I am reminded.

I think of Rachel then. Of the things you do to her. The things that should be degrading, but somehow aren't.

And yet, I do not have the courage to ask you to do any of them to me.

And then you're gone. Just like that.

I shower, again. Scrub your touch and your essence away.

I still feel as if I am outside myself, and I do not like it.

I watch as I dress again, this time in the plainest lingerie I own—*you* own, really—and the least sexy, least revealing dress. Flat shoes, no jewelry. Hair in simple twist, pinned up.

Once again, take the elevator down. I think I am going to the lobby, but for reasons I do not understand, I am on the third floor.

Knocking on the door marked 3.

THREE

Madame X," Rachel says. "Come on in."

"I didn't bring wine this time," I say.

A shrug. "No problem. I shouldn't drink right now anyway. Caleb's been on me about my figure." Eyes flit to mine, assessing. "You're upset."

I sweep through the doorway, cross the living room, rest my forehead against the glass of the window, stare down. "I feel lost, Rachel."

"About what?"

"Everything."

A silence, as Rachel hunts for something to say to this. "He has that effect, sometimes."

I shake my head. "No, it's not like that. He's different with me than he is with you." I glance at Rachel. "Has he ever had sex with you while he was still clothed?"

A shrug. "No, I don't think so."

"He does with me. More often than he's naked."

A frown. "That's kind of weird."

"That's what I was wondering." A pause. I glance at Rachel: reddish-blond hair, lovely, heart-shaped face, expressive brown eyes full of conflicting emotion, hope, fear, despair, anger, defiance. "Can I ask you something?"

"Sure. Of course."

"I will apologize now if what I ask offends you, but . . . the things you've told me, that Caleb does to you, to the other girls on this floor . . . do you ever feel . . . ashamed of them? Or degraded by them? Do you do those things because you want to, or because he expects it?"

"I ain't—I'm not offended. It's a reasonable question, I guess. No, I'm not ashamed of any of it. Degraded? I don't know. Not really. I don't mind it. Do I want it, like, do I *like* it? Does it make me feel good? No, not really. It's not for me. It's for him. He likes it. He says it's to teach me. But I know better. He's different with each of us. He ain't the same with me as he is with Five next door. He's rough with her. Not the way he is with me, though, because I like to feel a little pain. I told you this before. With Five it's . . . just *rough*. He shoves her around, pushes her where he wants her, jerks on her hair. Things like that. Never actually hurts her, though, just . . . acts rough." A glance at me. "You curious, X?"

"No," I immediately protest. Then think better of the lie. "Yes. I don't know."

A knowing grin. "You are. But you're afraid of it. Ain'tcha?"

I shrug. "A little, yes." A breath. "That's a lie. I'm very afraid. Today, just now, actually, I went outside. I met someone I used to know, and Caleb was jealous." I find myself telling the story, and feeling lighter as each word leaves my lips. "He stripped me naked, and he performed cunnilingus on me—"

Rachel laughs. "Jesus, you're so fucking uptight and formal. Just say he went down on you. Ate you out."

I try it. "He . . . he went down on me. And then he put me on my knees on a couch and knelt behind me and—and fucked me. And he never even took his pants off. Just left them partway down. And then he just left."

Rachel blinks. "That's harsh. He just . . . left? Like, he didn't say *any*thing?"

"He reminded me that I was his."

"Marking his territory, I guess." Rachel glances at the ceiling. "I think it'd be hot to have him fuck me like that, still clothed. Like it's . . . illicit. Is that the right word? Like we ain't supposed to be doing it?"

"Like he's ashamed of me." That's how it feels.

A shake of the head. "Nah, I don't think that's it. He ain't the type to be ashamed. Not of himself or anything he does, or of anyone he's with."

"Then what could it be? Why would he be that way with me? That's how it's always been with us. In the dead of the night, sometimes he'll take his clothes off, but he always puts them back on as soon as he's done. And he always leaves right after."

"I don't know. I really don't. It's weird. He's not that way with any of us. He always leaves after, yeah, but he's busy."

"Is he, though? Busy doing what? Us, that's what."

"You're not one of us. I don't say that to, like, exclude you. It's just that you're not what we are. You're not like us, either. You're better." A duck of the head, eyes down.

"I'm not, Rachel. Different, perhaps, but better? No. I'm still just one of ten for Caleb. And he doesn't even bother to take off his clothes with me."

"Try asking him, sometime? Try to take the initiative. See what he does."

I don't address the suggestion, but I do file it away to think about later. "Does it bother you, knowing you're just one of many for him?"

Another careless shrug. "No. No way. I don't give a shit. I hear him with the others all the time. Five's a screamer, so I can't exactly ignore it. Plus, I used to be a hooker. I guess I just don't think about sex like normal people do. It ain't no big thing for me. And I'll be out of this program soon. About to make the next level, which is just one step closer to becoming a Bride, becoming someone who matters."

There's a fallacy somewhere in Rachel's statement, a heartbreaking assumption, but I'm not sure I want to dwell on it. I have my own problems.

"I should go," I say.

"All right." A grin as Rachel opens the door for me. "And you know, you ever want to hide under my bed again and listen, just let me know. Could be fun."

I think of this as I board the elevator. Do I want to listen to that, again?

I think maybe I do. Morbidly, perhaps.

'm in Rachel's closet.

I should be working, I have a client in fifteen minutes. I am finding I do not care about clients anymore.

Rachel's closet is sparse, so there is plenty of room for me. The door is cracked just slightly, allowing me to see out. I am nervous. Scared. Excited. Worried that what I'm about to do is going to backfire.

I'm not just going to listen, I'm going to watch.

Am I a fool?

Yes. Undoubtedly.

I hear the door open, and soft leather soles pad across hardwood. I hear voices.

Rachel's. "Caleb. Hi. How are you?"

"Well enough, thank you." A pause, sounds of movement. "You are due for an examination soon, yes?"

"Yeah. Yes. For Companion."

"Lisa says you've been doing excellently in your assignments as an Escort. She has been receiving requests for you specifically."

"I'm trying hard. I want to make Bride."

A pause. "I confess, Rachel, that I will be a little unhappy to see you enter the Bride pool. I enjoy our time together."

"Me too."

"Do you?" This is delivered sharply.

"Of course!" Rachel protests. "I never enjoyed sex until you. It was just something I did to survive. With you, it feels good."

He rarely just *talks* to me, the way he does with her.

Oh yes, I am jealous.

All I see through the crack in the door is the doorway to Rachel's room, and a slice of the bed. If I pivot to the side, I can see the rest of the bed. Watching through the crack now, I see Rachel precede you through the door. She is fully dressed, in a pair of jeans, a pink flowery blouse, bare feet. You lift your chin, and Rachel peels the blouse off, baring pale, slight breasts, pink areolae and darker nipples. No bra. And then something shocking: Rachel reaches with both hands and unbuttons your shirt. Leaves it open but still on. Unfastens your slacks, lowers the zipper. You are not wearing underwear. Stranger yet.

Your erection sways free.

My heart hammers in my chest and I worry you can hear it, it beats so loudly. I am utterly still and not breathing.

You step out of your trousers and shrug the shirt off, and you are naked. It is broad daylight and the blinds are open. You tug Rachel's jeans off, and she too is not wearing underwear. I cannot fathom that, how it would feel to not wear panties or a bra.

You are both naked.

Together.

Standing in the sun, facing each other.

Rachel grasps your erection, fingers sliding down, and your lips tighten, your eyes narrow, your nostrils flare. You remain still as a pale hand pumps down your erection and back up. Faster, and faster.

You begin breathing heavily.

"Enough." You pull away abruptly, and I watch your abs tighten. You are holding back, I realize.

I am turned on, and disgusted with myself.

But fascinated.

Rapt.

You reach out, slide your hand into Rachel's hair, pull, and then the kiss becomes a wild and stormy thing. I am never kissed by you this way, with such heat. It is brief, and then you push Rachel down. Kneeling, eyes up on yours. A smile. That smile, is it real? The hunger, the eagerness? The way lips part, eyes remaining on yours, fingers around your base, bringing your erection between those pale, plump lips.

You sigh, and your eyes close. I watch you, more than Rachel. You urge for more, pulling Rachel toward you, thrusting your hips forward. A gagging sound as your long erection reaches the back of Rachel's throat. Leaning forward, taking more. Eyes water, nostrils flare, and you do not see. Rachel's hands are busy, cupping your testicles, gripping your erection as you pull back. Clutching at your backside as you thrust roughly.

"Take it on your face," you order.

Rachel pulls back and lets your erection pop free, a string of saliva connecting lip to shaft. Rachel sinks down lower, grips your erection in both hands, pumps hard and fast. At the end, you take your own erection in your hands and Rachel just waits, mouth open, eyes on yours, eager.

You come, streams of white semen spurting out of you and splashing onto Rachel's face. Between parted lips, onto blinking eyes. Rachel sweeps out her tongue and tastes it, licks it away, and you keep coming.

I watch, equal parts horrified and aroused, as you orgasm onto Rachel's face, over and over and over, jets of thick seed dripping onto pale skin. And through it all, Rachel's expression is seductive, aroused, pleased with the glops of thick come sliding down her face.

What would that feel like?

This, then, becomes the strangest part of the scene: you vanish into the en suite bathroom, return with a washcloth, and oh-so-gently wipe away your semen.

I am expected to clean myself when you're done with me.

And then . . . ?

And then you press Rachel to the bed and bury your face between those thin white thighs, and I do know how this feels, how your tongue feels against my labia, against my clitoris, and I throb thinking of it. I throb, watching your dark head move between thin creamy white thighs so unlike my thick, muscular, darkly complected ones. Watching you eat Rachel out, to use a newly acquired phrase. It is an apropos phrase, too. It looks like you are attempting to devour something hidden in her cleft, head moving side to side, up and down, in circles, and then I watch you slide your fingers under your chin and move them in thrusting motions over and over. Rachel gasps, arches, cries out, and you reach up with your free hand and twist Rachel's small rosebud nipple so hard I cringe in sympathy.

Rachel screams then, a cry of raw pleasure.

You elicit screams for long minutes more, and then straighten, and you are erect once more. You grip Rachel's slim hips and roughly twist her belly-down so you are standing with those hips in your hands, and you do not show any mercy at all as you thrust in, hard. Flesh slaps against flesh, and Rachel cries out. Your hand flashes—*crack!*—and smacks hard, so hard. White flesh pinks rosy, and then you do the same to the other buttock, and now you alternate. Thrust, smack, thrust, smack.

And then you happen to glance to your left.

Your thrust falters.

My heart stops in my chest.

Fear bolts through me.

I am frozen.

You have seen me.

"X." It is a guttural command.

I am motionless, paralyzed.

"Out here. *Now.*"

I push open the closet door. "Hello, Caleb."

"I did not take you for a voyeur." You are still buried inside Rachel.

"Neither did I."

"Yet here you are, watching us."

I have no answer. I will not argue.

Us. That word stings.

You smack Rachel's buttock, pulling your arm back, swinging it in a vicious horizontal arc. The impact against already rosy flesh is brutally hard, must hurt so badly. Rachel's head hangs between trembling shoulders, body rocked forward as you thrust.

"You want to watch, X?" Your voice is quiet with fury. "Then watch." You point at the bed. "Up there."

I climb on the bed, and now Rachel's eyes meet mine. There is no shame in that brown gaze. Excitement, rather.

You resume fucking.

Your eyes pin me, never waver. You spank Rachel's buttocks harder than ever, and the girl only rocks into you all the more and cries out in bliss and now glances up at me with sex-glazed eyes and winks at me.

I alternate watching you, and Rachel.

Both sets of eyes are on me, and I am excruciatingly aware that I am affected by this scene. I press my thighs together as I kneel on the bed and watch you fuck Rachel.

When Rachel comes yet again, it is while staring up at me, mouth gaping open, breathless, body jolting forward with each of your brutally hard thrusts, and it is bizarre, so strange, far too intimate a thing to watch another woman come, to see your erection inside a body not mine, to watch you fuck another woman to orgasm. I am torn apart with disgust. I hate this.

Yet also,

I am ablaze with arousal.

I watch you come.

At the last moment, you pull out, and your eyes are dark orbs of ice as you release your orgasm onto Rachel's back. I watch that, watch the white stream leave the tip of your penis and watch it hit pale, pale skin, watch your face as you orgasm.

You smack Rachel's bottom once more, almost affectionately, and then slide off the bed.

I am off the bed, darting past you.

"Come back here, X." It is a command.

I disobey. Run. Run. Slam into the silver door of the elevator, slam a palm against the call button. I hear your step down the hall.

"X, I said *come back* here!"

I do not reply. I am breathless, chest aching, lungs burning. I cannot breathe.

I am dizzy.

The elevator arrives, and I lurch onto it, stab at the button that will take me to the lobby. As the doors slide closed, I see you.

Bare from the waist up, wearing only slacks. Your chest glistens with sweat. Your hair is in disarray. You are furious.

Your hands stop the door from closing, and panic seizes me. But instead of freezing me, this time, it spurs me to action.

"Why do you never treat me the way you treat her?" I hear my voice say, breathless, shrill, nearly sobbing. "Why don't you fuck me the way you do her?"

"She's an apprentice—" you start.

I see Rachel behind you, peeking around the corner. Shamelessly naked, still. Curious.

"So?"

"You're worth more than she is. She'll only ever be a Bride. You're . . . You are Madame X."

Rachel, behind you, is livid. Tears fill brown eyes. "You *bastard*." This is hissed.

You whirl. "Rachel, wait."

You seem almost human, suddenly. Caught between Rachel and me.

"But I'm not worth being naked with. Not worth behaving as if you *want* to be with me. As if you enjoy *fucking* me, like you obviously do her." I cannot stop the words. It is an avalanche. "I am just a possession to you, Caleb. You keep me because you like owning me, not because you *like* me. Not because you *enjoy* me."

None of this makes any sense. I am jealous, but I hate you. Yet I also need you, want you, desire to be treated by you the way you treat Rachel. I want—

I do not know.

Nothing I want makes any damned sense.

I do not understand myself.

What do I want?

Freedom.

I shove you. Hard. Surprised, you stumble backward, and I hear Rachel gasp in surprise.

The elevator door closes.

"God fucking damn it!" I hear you shout this louder than I've ever heard you speak before.

I am cognizant of nothing but my own gasping, ragged breath as I cross the lobby, and I know I'm sobbing, but I don't care.

For once, the noise of Manhattan does not paralyze me.

In four-inch Gucci heels, I run.

In a custom couture dress, I flee.

There is only one place in this city that I know, and somehow I find it.

The Metropolitan Museum of Art.

I have no money for the admission fee. But when I arrive at the ticket counter, there is a little old black woman behind the desk.

She recognizes me. "Oh, it's you! I haven't seen you in . . . oh, years!"

"Hi . . ." I don't know her name. But I know her, it feels like. "It has been a long time."

"Where's Mr. Indigo?"

"I . . . I came without him."

A look crosses her face. "Oh." She tilts her head sideways. "Honey, you all right?"

I shake my head, unable to summon a lie. "No. No. I need . . . I need to go in, but I forgot money. I don't have any money. And I need—I *need* to go in."

"It's pay what you want here," she says. "Even if you got a dollar I can let you in."

"I have nothing. Not a penny."

A moment of hesitation. Then she reaches into her back pocket, withdraws some crumpled green bills, stuffs two into her register drawer, and hands me a ticket. "On me today, sweetie. You used to love this place. You was here all the time, back then. Every day."

"Thank you. Thank you so much."

She waves her hand. "Ain't nothin'."

"You don't know what this means to me."

Neither do I, I don't think. But I go in, and discover that I know the way. My feet carry me to the painting.

There is a bench, low lighting. White walls. My painting is not prominently displayed, just one of many, and not an important one. I take a seat on the bench, ankles crossed beneath me.

I stare at her.

Portrait of Madame X.

She possesses such poise, such effortless strength. The curve of her neck, the strength in her arm, the calm expression on her face.

I stare for a long, long time. Find calm in the painting, finding some measure of strength.

There is one more to see. I wander the halls, and somehow cannot find it.

There is a guard, tall, black skin so dark it glistens. "Excuse me, sir," I ask. "Where is the *Starry Night*?"

I receive a blank stare. A shrug.

A nearby visitor glances at me, a middle-aged woman. "Honey, you're at the Met. *Starry Night* is at the MOMA, the Museum of Modern Art. Just down the road a bit, in Midtown."

I thank the woman and return to the bench in front of the Sargent. Thinking.

I have memories, distinct memories of being here with you, and you wheeled me from this to the *Starry Night*.

But how can that be? They aren't at the same museum.

I've distracted myself well enough, thankfully. I am no longer seeing over and over Rachel with you, your eyes on mine, no longer feeling my arousal and disgust and sense of betrayal.

I have pushed those emotions down, deep down where I won't have to deal with them just yet.

And then I feel you.

"I knew I'd find you here." Your voice is quiet, like the rumble of a subway train below the streets.

"I have nothing to say to you." I do not look at you. Scoot to my left so there is a foot of space between us.

"Too bad. I have a lot to say to you."

"That would be new."

A sigh. "X, you don't understand—"

"If you say that to me *one* more *fucking* time, I will scream," I hiss. I like cursing. It makes me feel powerful and free.

"Why did you spy on me?"

"I do not know. I wish I hadn't, yet also I am glad I did." I struggle to breathe past the subtle power of your cologne and your presence. "I understand now what I mean to you."

"You mean more to me than you can possibly comprehend, X."

"Which is why you never even bother to take off your clothes when you're with me? Why you never stay with me, afterward? Why you treat me like I'm . . . delicate?"

"What, X? You want me to do that shit to you?" You say this a little too loud, glance around, and lower your voice so it is barely audible. "You want me to treat you like I treat the girls? You want me to come on your face? You want me to pull your hair and hurt you? Is that what you want, X?"

I shake my head. "I don't know. I don't know if I want that. I don't know, Caleb! I just know, watching you with her, I felt jealous.

And angry. I felt . . . as if you enjoy her more than you do me. I don't want to be just another girl among many for you."

"I can't give you what you're asking for, X. You don't—I know you hate it when I say this, and I'm sorry, but you really don't understand."

I groan in frustration, loudly enough that other visitors stop and stare at me. "Then help me understand!"

"How, X? What am I supposed to say to you?"

"The truth?"

"What is the truth? The truth about what?"

"About me? About us? Why you keep me locked up in that fucking tower like . . . like Rapunzel."

You do not answer for a long time, staring at the Sargent painting for which I am named. "How many hours have we both sat in this spot, staring at this painting?"

Apropos of nothing, that. But also . . . relevant. I am here of my own volition.

"Many indeed." I hesitate, and then continue. "My memories are faulty, it seems. I distinctly remember being here, in the wheelchair, with you. Looking at the Sargent, and then you'd push me through the museum and we'd look at the Van Gogh together. I *remember* this, Caleb. As clearly as I am standing here, I can feel it, see it. But now that I'm actually here, I've discovered that what I remember isn't possible. Because the Van Gogh is at a different museum entirely. And I . . . I don't understand. How can I remember something falsely?"

You breathe out through pursed lips. "I did some research on memory, while you were in rehab, learning to walk and talk again. The storage and recall of memory is a subject we understand very little about. But one thing I remember reading was that most of our memories, from childhood and things like that, we aren't actually remembering the event itself, we're remembering a memory of a memory. Make sense? And the farther we are away from the core event, the more distorted the actual memory becomes, so what we are remembering might actually be very inaccurate when compared to what really happened."

This rocks me. I have to remember to breathe, remember to stay upright. "So . . . the few memories I do have, they may not even be real?"

I cannot trust my own memories? How is this possible? Yet what you say makes far too much sense.

"That's what scientists say, at least." A shrug, as if it's inconsequential.

"I have so few memories. You, Logan, Rachel and the other apprentices, Len . . . you all have lifetimes of memories. A linear identity that you can hold on to. I do not have this. I have six years of memories. That is all. My identity is not . . . linear. It is . . . fractal. It is disrupted. False. Created. I am not me. I am a me that you created."

"X, that's not fair—"

"It *is* fair, Caleb. It is the truth. You created me. You gave me my name. You gave me my home, my apartment on the thirteenth floor. You bought all my books, and if I have any identity of my own, it is in those pages. You taught me manners and poise, bearing and comportment. You asserted upon me my identity as Madame X, the woman who schools idle, entitled rich boys. What have I chosen for myself, Caleb? Nothing. You buy my clothes. You buy my food. You structured my exercise routine. I exist entirely within the sphere of your influence."

"What are you saying?" You speak carefully, slowly.

"I'm saying you created my identity. And I'm beginning to feel as if it doesn't fit. As I'm wearing a dress that is either too tight or too loose. Too tight in one place and too loose in another." I pause to breathe, and it is a difficult task. "I am . . . unraveling, Caleb."

A long silence.

And then: "You are Madame X. I am Caleb Indigo. I saved you. You're safe with me."

My outbreath becomes a tremor. "Damn you, Caleb Indigo."

"I saved you from a bad man. I won't let anything bad happen to you ever again." Your hand twines into mine. There is sorcery in your touch and in your voice, weaving a palpable spell over me.

You pull me to my feet and lead me out of the museum.

Into your Maybach. Classical music plays softly, a cello solo wavering gently. I focus on the strains of music, seize it like a lifeline as Len slithers the long car through the sludge of traffic, taking us back to your tower.

Your hand rests on my lower back as we stand in the elevator. You twist the key to the *P*, for *penthouse*. We rise, rise, and I can't breathe. The higher we go, the more constricted become my lungs.

At the penthouse, I am greeted by the black couch, upon which and over which you have fucked me so impersonally, more than once, and I am panicking, gagging on my trapped, rotten breath, on the slamming knot of my pulse in my throat.

You step out, expecting me to follow, but I spin the key abruptly. Not for the lobby or the garage or the third floor or the thirteenth floor. Any floor, at random. You sigh and watch me, let me go. One hand in the hip pocket of your perfect suit, the other passing through your thick black hair. A gesture of frustration, irritation, resignation.

I do not even know which floor I get off on. I find a staircase leading up, and I climb. Climb. Until my legs ache and I'm sweating in my three-thousand-dollar dress, I climb. A door appears where the stairs finally end. I can climb no more, my legs turned to jelly. I twist the silver knob, push. The door sticks, unused to being opened, and then suddenly flies ajar. I stumble, lurch out onto the roof of the tower.

My breath is stolen, and I take a few slow, awed steps farther out onto the roof.

The city is spread out around me in the darkness of night. Squares of light glow from high-rises across the street and across the city. The sky above is dark, charcoal gray, a crescent moon shining low on the horizon.

When did it become night?

How long was I at the museum, alone, staring at the portrait? That long? I have no memory of the car ride back here, only the sensation of movement and blurred faces passing and cars, yellow taxis and black SUVs, and the cello playing quietly.

I move to the edge of the building, a long walk across white stones scattered on the roof. A silver dome twists off to my right, and to my left a fan spins in a large concrete block, roaring loudly.

Stare down, fifty-nine stories down at the sidewalk. The people are specks, the cars like toys. Vertigo grips me and shakes me until I'm dizzy, and I back away.

Collapse to my bottom, knees splayed out, unladylike.

I weep.

Uncontrollably, endlessly.

Until I pass out, until my eyes slide closed and sobs shake me like the aftershocks of an earthquake, I cry and cry and cry, and I do not even know truly what I weep for.

Except,

perhaps,

everything.

FOUR

am drowning in an ocean of darkness. The sky is the sea, dark masses of roiling clouds like waves, spreading in every direction and weighing heavily on me like the titanic bulk of Homer's wine-dark seas. I lie on my back on the rooftop, leftover heat from the previous day still leaching out of the rough concrete and into my skin through the thin fabric of my dress.

I sense a presence as I wake up, but I don't open my eyes. Perhaps you found me. There are only so many places I can be. I feel you sit beside me, and your finger touches my hair, smooths it off my forehead.

But then I smell cinnamon, and cigarettes.

I crack my eyes open, and it isn't you.

"Logan." I whisper it, surprised. "How are you here?"

"Bribes, distraction, it wasn't hard." He shrugs. "You weren't in your apartment. I don't know. I just felt . . . pulled up here. Like I knew I'd find you up here."

"You shouldn't be here."

He fits a cigarette to his mouth, cups his hands around it, and I hear a scrape and a click. Flame bursts orange, briefly, and then the smell of cigarette smoke is pungent and acrid. His cheeks go concave, his chest expands, and then he blows out a white plume from his nostrils. "No, I shouldn't."

"Then why are you?" I sit up, and I'm self-conscious of the fact that my dress is dirty and wrinkled and has hiked up to nearly my hips, baring far more of me than is proper.

"I had to talk to you."

"What is there to say?"

Your eyes flick shamelessly over me. A breeze kicks up, and my nipples harden, my skin pebbles. Perhaps it isn't the wind so much as Logan, though. His eyes, that strange and vivid blue, his proximity, his sudden and unexpected and inexplicable presence on this rooftop, in my life.

"There's a lot I could say, actually." His eyes, certainly speak volumes.

"Then say it," I say, and it is a challenge.

Smoke curls up from the cigarette between his fingers. "Caleb, he's not who you think he is."

"This is not the first time you've said that," I say. "And you know, do you? Who he really is?"

"Certain things, yes." He takes a long drag on the cigarette, holds it in, blows it out through his nose again.

"You sneaked in here to tell me Caleb's secrets?"

He shakes his head, almost angrily, blond hair waving around his shoulders. "No, I didn't," he confesses. "You made the wrong choice. You should have stayed with me. We could have had something amazing."

"There was never a choice, Logan." It feels a little like a lie.

"Yes, there was." Another long inhalation, exhaling smoke through nostrils like a dragon. "Whatever. Not gonna argue with you about that. What I came here to tell you was that I did some digging."

"What do you mean, digging?" I need something to do with my hands, somewhere to look that isn't Logan.

"I looked around for information on you." He says it quietly, flicking his thumb across the butt of the cigarette, ash dropping away and scattering in the breeze.

"Did you find anything?" I almost don't want to ask.

I pluck the lighter from his hand, and it is warm from his palm. Translucent green plastic, a centimeter or two of liquid sloshing at the bottom. Black tab, silver wheel, and a mouth for the flame. I roll my thumb over the wheel, creating sparks. Do it again while pressing down on the black tab, watch flame spurt to life. The pack of cigarettes is on the rooftop by the toe of his boot. He sits cross-legged beside me, shamelessly, openly eyeing my body, my cleavage, my thighs, the black sliver of silk over my core. I reach over, take the pack of cigarettes. He watches me, but does nothing. I withdraw one of the cylinders and fit the tan, speckled end to my lips, as I watched him do. Spark flame, touch the flame tip to the end of the cigarette. When smoke rises, I inhale.

"You're going to cough your brains out," Logan warns.

Smoke fills my lungs, too much, too hot, thick and burning. I hack and hack and hack, eyes watering.

"Why do you do this?" I ask.

He shrugs. "Habit, one I can't quite quit. Not that I've really tried, though, I guess." He takes a drag. "Try pulling it into your mouth first, and then inhaling. Or just don't inhale. It's a shitty habit, absolutely horrible for you. I feel a responsibility to tell you that you shouldn't start smoking."

He doesn't try to stop me, though, doesn't take the cigarette from me. Just watches as I do as he suggested, and though I still cough, it's not as bad as the first time. I become dizzy, faint; it is a heady feeling, and I think I understand the attraction of this habit.

"What did you find out, Logan?" I ask, after a few minutes of silence.

He doesn't answer right away. Not for more long minutes of thick, tense silence, smoke rising in a thin curl, an occasional drag for him, for me. I let the silence hang, let it weigh as heavily as the clouds.

I like smoking. It gives me something to do to fill the silence, the taut space between my words and his.

"Information is power." He stabs out his cigarette with a short, angry twist of his wrist. "I want to blackmail you with this, what I found out. Not tell you unless you come with me. But then I'd be no better than Caleb."

I digest what he's insinuating. "You think Caleb knows who I am and isn't telling me?"

"I think he knows more than he's told you, yes." He stands up, unfolding his lean frame, and strides away from me across the rooftop, stopping to put his hands on the waist-high wall separating him from the tumble into space. "Do you remember that day in my house, in the hallway? When I got back from walking Cocoa?"

I swallow hard. "Yes, Logan. I remember."

This is the second time he's brought this up. I remember it all too well. It recurs, a dream, a fantasy, memories assaulting me as I bathe, as I try to sleep, lost details of hands and mouths when I wake up.

To get away from the renewal of the memory, I look up. At the sky. Dark with clouds, hazed with smog and light pollution.

I wish I could see the stars. I wonder what they look like, how I would feel looking up and seeing sky full of scintillating diamond points of light.

His words echo in my soul, throb in my ear, and I am pulled back down by the ache of need in his voice. "You were naked. Every inch of your fucking incredible skin, bare for me. I had you in my arms. I *had* you, X. I had my hands on you, had you on my lips, on my tongue. But I let you go. I . . . made you walk away." He turns, glances at me. As if he can smell me, as if he can see what lies beneath the fabric of my dress. "I don't think you'll ever understand how much that cost me, to walk away from you. How much self-control that took."

I shake all over. "Logan, I—"

He turns away, resumes staring out at the skyline, speaks over me. "I am haunted by that. I had you, and I let you go. I'm not haunted by the fact that you're gone, though, that I let you get away. It's more the fact that I still know it was the right thing to do. As much as I hate it, as much as it hurts . . . you aren't ready for me."

"That again? What does that mean, Logan?" I stand up now, tug the hem of the dress down. Seven strides, and I'm standing a few feet behind him. "I thought you said you found something out about me."

He shakes his head. "It doesn't mean anything. Never mind."

Logan reaches into the back pocket of his jeans, pulls out a square of folded paper. Holds it, stares at it. The wind plucks at the paper, fluttering the corners, as if it wants to rip it away, keep it from me, whatever is written there. He pivots so he faces me. Steps closer. I stop breathing. I tingle all over. My skin remembers the feel of his skin, the taste of his tongue. I shouldn't. That is not the choice I made. But . . . I can't forget it. And deep down, I don't want to.

"X, when I said there's so much I could say? I don't know how to say it all. I want to take you away, again. Run off with you, make you mine. But that wouldn't be enough for me. I'm a proud man, X. I want you to *choose* me. And . . . I think you will, someday."

He presses his body against mine, and I feel every inch of him, hard, taut, warm. My breasts flatten against his chest, my hips bump against his. Something in me throbs, aches. Recognizes him, feels pulled by him. I forget everything, in these moments, except how utterly stolen away and carried off into the wild wind I feel, with him.

The paper crinkles against my bicep as he grips me, a hand on my arm, a palm to my cheek.

No . . . don't; I try to form the words.

"*Don't, Logan*," I whisper, but maybe the words are only a breath, only a sigh, only the minuscule brush of my eyelashes fluttering against my cheek, the sweep of lips against lips.

He does.

He kisses me,

and kisses me,

and kisses me.

And I don't stop him. My traitorous body wants to writhe and meld to his, wants to wrap itself around him. My hands sneak up to his hair, bury in the blond waves, and my throat utters a sigh, and maybe a moan, a feverish, desperate sound.

It is but a moment that we kiss, a single moment.

A fortieth of an hour.

But it is one in which I feel utterly changed, as if some too-loose skin draped over my skeleton is snatched away and my true form is revealed, as if his touch as if his kiss as if his very presence can make me more truly *me*.

I want to weep.

I want to sag against him and beg him to keep kissing me until I cannot bear any longer the soft and tender intensity.

He backs away, wiping his wrist across his mouth, chest heaving as if desperately battling some inner demon. "Here." He hands me the square of folded paper. "It's your real name."

I feel struck by lightning, wired, surging with too much of everything, too much heat, too much fear, too much doubt, too much need.

He puts a hand to the half wall, as if supporting himself, as if about to leap over and fly away.

"Logan . . ." I don't have anything else I can say.

"You have to decide if you want to know," he says. "Because once you know . . . you can't take it back. Once you start questioning, there's no stopping it."

"I have to know now, don't I?" I ask, almost angry at him. "You posed the question, and now I have to have the answer."

"True." He lets out a breath, moves to walk past me, but stops a breath and a touch away. His indigo eyes meet mine. "You can come with me. We can leave New York." He glances up at the cloud-shrouded sky. "I can take you somewhere far away, and show you the stars."

Could he have heard that wish? Can he see into my mind, read my thoughts? Sometimes I wonder if he can.

"But . . . you won't." He wipes a thumb across my lips. "Not yet, anyway."

He almost seems about to kiss me again, and I'm not entirely sure I would survive another stolen kiss, another breathless moment far too close to a man who seems to see far too much of me.

"If you ask the questions, X . . . you can't shy away from the answers when you find them."

I don't watch him leave. I can't. I won't.

I don't dare.

A long, long, painful silence, stretching like a rubber band about to snap. When I'm sure I'm alone, I finally look away from the skyline, from the dark shapes of skyscrapers and apartment blocks, away from the clouds and the dim distant lights. The rooftop is empty once more, but for me and the ghost of Logan's kiss.

I unfold the square of paper.

My cigarette smolders on the white rocks beside me, forgotten.

There on the wrinkled, off-white scrap of paper is a scrawl of messy male handwriting, in all slanting capital letters.

The letters form a name.

My name.

If I could prevent myself from reading it, I almost would. But I don't.

Logan has given me my name.

I both love him for it, and hate him for it.

FIVE

sabel Maria de la Vega Navarro." I whisper, reading. "Isabel."

Is this me? Isabel?

How did Logan find this?

I trace the letters, imagining that I am able to feel the impressions of the pen on the paper, imagining the way his strong fingers gripped the pen and sliced firm concise strokes to create these letters. Twenty-six letters, simple strokes of ink on pulped and flattened wood. All to create a name. An identity.

Isabel.

I stare at the paper, for how long I do not know.

And then I discover something else written in the bottom right-hand corner, printed small.

Ten numbers.

212-555-3233. Beside it, two more letters: *LR*.

His phone number?

I repeat the numbers in my mind until they are meaningless, shapes in my mind, sounds subvocalized, semantic satiation. Those ten numerals are burned into my brain. I cannot forget them, no more than I could forget the four names that belong to me.

Isabel Maria de la Vega Navarro.

I turn on my heel, folding the paper into tiny squares, and stuff it into my bra. Stride to the doorway, down the stairs. Three flights, and out into the building. The hallways are dark and empty, corridors of shadow and moonlight and city light streaming from office windows in rhombuses and trapezoids across thin carpet. I find the elevator, take it to the third floor. I do not have my key, cannot go back to my apartment or to the penthouse. I do not want to go to either place.

I tap hesitantly on Rachel's door.

"Madame X?" A quizzical, sleepy stare. "It's four in the morning."

"I know. I'm sorry. I just—I didn't know where else to go."

"Come in." Fingers rub corners of eyes, feet shuffle across hardwood. "What's up?"

"Do you have a computer?" I ask.

"Sure, of course. Why?"

"Can I use it?" I ask.

"Yeah. What's going on?"

I don't know how to answer. There are too many layers to be able to explain any of them. "I just . . ." I shake my head. "I can't explain."

A shrug. "Okay." A gesture at the corner of the living room, a desk, with a thin silver thing on it. "Go for it. You want some coffee?"

I retrieve the computer, a thin laptop, a logo of an apple with a bite missing adorning the top, which lights up when I lift it open. The icons are the same as on the computer in my apartment, so I have no trouble finding the icon that will take me to the Internet. Rachel watches from the other end of the couch, curious.

I type "Isabel name meaning" into the search bar.

Why? What do I hope to find by searching for meanings in a name?

Isabel means "God is my oath."

Meaningless to me.

Maria, obviously, is a reference to the Virgin Mary, a common enough name in Latin cultures.

De la Vega. It means "of the meadow" and is a name whose bearers historically were among the Spanish nobility.

Navarro holds even less meaning for me, as it merely refers to someone from Navarre, a region in Spain.

There is a cauldron of emotions within me. Boiling, overflowing, weltering. Violent, virulent. But they are all hidden under a layer of ice created by shock.

I have a name.

A real name.

Isabel Maria de la Vega Navarro?

"Isabel?" Rachel asks. "Is that your name?"

"I suppose so. I don't know."

Logan could have just made this up. Picked the names at random. How do I know this is me?

Do I feel like Isabel? I don't know.

I look at Rachel. "You had a name, before . . . this. Before you became an apprentice."

A nod. Eyes downcast. "Yeah. Nicole." A breath, a sigh, eyes glancing out the window, seeing not the city but the past. "Nicole Martin."

"And now you're Rachel?"

Another nod. "Yeah. When I was fifteen, I got picked up by a pimp. He called me Dixie, like Dixie sugar. Because I was sweet, because he always wanted more sugar." A fake, low, gruff voice, an impression of a male. "'C'mere, Dixie. Gimme some sugar.'"

"What does that mean? Give me some sugar?"

A smile, quick, amused. "Oh, um . . . like, well, usually it means to kiss someone, like your grandma would tell you to give her some sugar, and it'd mean give her a kiss." The smile vanishes. "But for Deon, it meant get on my knees and suck his dick."

"Oh." I don't know what to say.

"So I was Nicole, and then I was Dixie until Caleb found me, and then I was Three." She brightens. "And now I'm Rachel."

"How . . ." I trail off, and try again to formulate my question. "Do you . . . *feel* like Rachel? When you think of yourself, who are you?"

A long, long silence. A shrug. "I dunno. I'm still Nicole, in my mind, I guess. There's no one in the world but you and Caleb that know that name, though."

"You don't have a family?"

"Naw. Never had a dad, mom was a druggie, which is how I got hooked myself, watching her use. She OD'd when I was just . . . shit, twelve? Never had no one else, and I ran off when the city tried to place me." Rachel is silent, staring at the past via middle distance. "I guess I'm Rachel now. I feel like that name is me. It's a new me. I can be Rachel, and pretend I never was Nicole or Dixie."

"I see."

A sharp, knowing glance at me. "You trying to figure out who you are, ain'tcha? Madame X, or Isabel?"

"I suppose you're right. That's exactly what I'm trying to do."

"In my experience, you have to kind of . . . convince yourself that you're someone else. That you really are your new name. You want to be Isabel, you have to think about *being* Isabel. Learning to answer to a new name means owning it for yourself, first."

I don't know what I want. Who I want to be.

Do I want to be Isabel?

Do I want to be Madame X?

I think of Logan, how he insists that I deserve the right to choose.

But I don't know *what* to choose.

I drift away, out of apartment number three, to the elevator, to the lobby. I don't think I even said good-bye to Rachel, or closed the door behind me.

I find myself on the street. It is still dark out, quiet for New York City. A few cars whoosh by, a yellow cab with its light on. A white panel van. A police car.

I wonder if you know where I am. If you're looking for me.

I do not want to be found.

Not by you.

A café, open twenty-four hours. An older woman, tired looking, bored, stares at me as I enter. "Help you?"

"Do you have a phone I can use?"

A blank stare. "You in trouble?"

"I need to call someone. It's important. Not legal trouble, no."

Another blinking moment, and then the woman digs into an apron pocket and withdraws a cell phone, hands it to me. It is one of those that flips open. I dial the number: 212-555-3233.

A sleepy, beautiful, sun-warm voice: "Hello? Who's'iss?"

"It's . . . it's me."

"X?"

"Yes."

"Where are you?"

I glance at the woman. "Where am I? What is the name of this place?"

The woman just gestures at the menu on the counter in front of me. I read the name of the café, the address.

"I'll be there in ten," Logan says. "Stay there, okay?"

He shows up in under ten minutes, wearing khaki cargo shorts and a black tank top that show off his sleeves of tattoos covering his arms from elbow to shoulder, and flip-flops. "X, you okay?"

I shake my head. "I have so many questions." I wish desperately to cling to him. I dare not, for fear that I will never let go. "I don't know . . . anything. I don't know what to do."

Logan glances around, eyes the menu, then slides into a booth. I take the bench opposite him. He glances at the woman. "Two coffees, please." He shoves a menu toward me. "Hungry?"

I nod, and peruse the items on the two-sided, laminated sheet. I decide on Belgian waffles and bacon. I've never had them, and they sound good. After the food has arrived, Logan and I spend a few minutes just eating; the waffles are so delicious that I don't want to waste a single minute talking when I could be eating.

We're done and Logan has his big hands wrapped around the small white ceramic mug of black coffee. He lets out a breath. "So what are your questions?"

"Where did you find the name?"

"The name?" He lifts an eyebrow. "Not 'my name,' but 'the name'?"

"Is it mine?"

"You don't trust me?" He sounds wounded.

I want to be logical, but it is hard. "I do. I want to, at least. But can I? Should I? That could be any name. How do I know it is mine?"

He nods. "You have a point," he says. "You told me you got hurt six years ago, that you had total amnesia. You didn't tell me which hospital, or anything like that, so I started broad. Did a search on nameless coma patients in the entire New York City area. Put some resources into the search, friends who know who to ask about things like this. Six years ago, there were thousands of accidents that resulted in the victims going into a coma. Of those however-many-thousands of coma patients from six years ago, all of them were identified. Most of them woke up within a few hours or days, and of those who woke up, most got their whole memories back, while some got only parts of their memories back."

"What are you saying?" I feel faint.

"Do you know how long you were in a coma?"

I think back. When I woke up, I was unresponsive. Awake, but not all there. It took time before I could even focus my eyes. Longer still before I could understand questions, or respond. I couldn't speak. Whether it was a cognitive problem or physical, doctors weren't sure. But as Caleb spent more time with me, I started to speak. Mimicking words, showing comprehension. I have no memory, however, of being told how long I was in a coma for. All of this that I know, I only know because Caleb told me. My actual memories of the time immediately after I woke up are extremely hazy.

I shake my head. "I—I don't know, no. I—Caleb never told me. I never thought to ask."

He just nods. "None of the coma patients I found out about fit your description, even physically speaking, symptoms or whatever else aside." A sip of coffee. "So I went back farther. Year by year, searching for coma patients who were admitted with no identification. A 'Jane Doe,' they call them. I spoke to hundreds of doctors and nurses, and no one knew anything."

"You did all this? The searching?"

He shrugs. "I told you I'd find proof. I'm still working on it, but it takes time. Maybe I should sell my businesses and become a private investigator, you know? I've got a knack for it, I think." A wave of his hand. "Point is, yes. I've spent every waking moment, and most of the hours I should have been sleeping, looking for information on you. I went back three years before I found anything."

He pauses, I don't know why. I am frustrated, curious, fearful. "And? What did you discover?"

"In 2006, there was a car accident. Three passengers. Mom, dad, a teenaged girl."

"A car accident?" It is hard to swallow. "In 2006? *Nine* years ago?"

He nods. His voice is tender, hesitant. "Details are sketchy. The mother and father were killed instantly. The young girl was in the backseat; somehow she survived. She was brought to the hospital, but again, the details on how she got there are murky at best. I spoke to a nurse who was working the ER that night, and she remembers only that the call came in, a sixteen-year-old girl with severe cranial injury, unconscious. That's all she knew. She worked on the girl. They were able to save the girl's life, but she didn't wake up, and was transferred to a different floor of the hospital. The nurse lost track after that, because shit, ER nurses in Manhattan . . . they see dozens, hundreds of patients every day. Can't keep track of 'em, you know?"

"A car accident?" I'm dizzy. "Not a mugging?"

"The nurse described you exactly, just younger. Dark skin, black hair. Beautiful. Latin, Mexican or Spanish or something. She described your injuries. Where you've got your scars." He touches his hip, where I have a scar. His head, where I have another, beneath my hair. "And that person, if it's you, was in a car accident. No question about that part."

"So . . . if the hospital couldn't identify me, how could you?"

"The city, the hospital, the police, they're swamped, you know? Like, they've got thousands of cases, thousands of missing persons and mistaken identities and unsolved deaths and Jane or John Does. So, I'm not excusing the fact that they gave up the search, just putting some perspective on it. They put some effort into it, but without a good reason they just can't keep spending the manpower on something forever. It wasn't a crime that landed you in the coma, just a car accident. Not an unsolved murder, or something like that. So they gave up. You were in a coma. Things get glossed over, forgotten about." He lifts a shoulder. "Whereas I have the resources, the time. And I have the motive to keep looking. So I did."

"You found me."

He nods. "I found you. Or rather, first, I was able to track down the car. Every car has a unique number—a vehicle identification number, what they call a VIN—and when the police show up on the scene, they record that number, and when the wreckers take a trashed vehicle to a yard, they record that number, and the salvage yard where the car ends up reports that number . . . everyone involved with disposing of a wrecked vehicle has that VIN. That car is kept track of scrupulously. It's kind of weird, actually, considering how easily people can be lost. But anyway, I was able to get access to that police record, find the VIN. This is basic shit, okay? There's no reason they couldn't have done this, but they didn't. What I found out is the car was a rental. That was part of the problem, what makes it tricky, because not all rental companies keep the best records. Like, the big-box rental places like Avis or Budget or whatever, they keep extensive records, but smaller places don't, necessarily." He waves a hand. "So I traced the car to the rental service, and convinced them to help me find the original paperwork. Took some convincing, because this rental service was kind of sketchy. They didn't take a lot of information, didn't ask a lot of questions, right? Just took a big cash deposit, and a name and driver's license. Even then, I don't think they'd object too hard if someone only had, say, a Spanish license but not an American one, you know?" The waitress comes by, refills Logan's coffee. He sips, continues. "So I offered the guy running the rental service enough cash that he was willing to dig up his old paperwork. The car was rented to Luis de la Vega. Cash deposit, rented for a week. No other info. Just the name, and a photocopy of a Spanish passport. Luis Garcia de la Vega Reyes. With that name, that passport picture, I had more to go on. Such as INS records."

"INS?"

"Immigration and Naturalization Service. They keep track of people immigrating to the States," Logan explains. "Luis de la Vega,

Camila de la Vega, and Isabel de la Vega immigrated to the United States of America from Spain in April 2004."

"Isabel de la Vega." I repeat the name, hoping some kind of epiphany will strike me. "Wouldn't it be Isabel Reyes, if my father's name was Luis Reyes?"

He shakes his head. "I did a brief search on Spanish naming customs, not sure why. One of those Google search rabbit trails, I guess. But apparently in Spain, you're given a Christian name, sometimes a middle one but not always, and then you have two surnames, your father's surname first and your mother's second, but when you introduce yourself in casual, informal settings, you use your Christian name and your father's surname, the first one. So your full name, Isabel Maria de la Vega Navarro, that comes from your father being Luis Garcia de la Vega Reyes and your mother being Camila Maria de la Vega Navarro. So according to that custom, you'd be Isabel de la Vega."

I try to formulate a relevant thought, a coherent question. "Did you find anything about my parents or me before the accident?"

"Your father was a skilled metalsmith, specializing in fine gold jewelry. He brought you guys over here because of an opportunity to work for a custom jewelry shop here in the city. He'd worked for himself up until 2004, but then somehow he got in touch with a guy here and decided to move." Logan twists the mug in circles on the Formica tabletop. "It really wasn't hard to find your father. I had his passport ID, so I was able to find him pretty easily. Talked to some people back in Barcelona where you're originally from. Your father's business was suffering, I guess, through no fault of his own. So when he got the opportunity to come here, he did. You were fourteen when you came to the States, sixteen when the accident happened."

I try to find something more to say, something intelligent, but I am numb and reeling and shocked and unable to think or process or feel. "So you were able to discover all this just . . . by making some phone calls?"

He shrugged. "Essentially. I mean, I guess I'm downplaying it all a bit. It was a lot of work. I must have made two or three hundred phone calls over the last few days, chased down hundreds of dead ends looking for someone with concrete information on you and your family. And even then, once you guys made it here, the trail sort of goes cold. Your father worked his ass off, seventy and eighty hours a week, and your mom was a maid in a hotel, worked similar hours. Quite a step down for you guys from the life you lived in Spain, is the impression I get. You went to a public high school, but I couldn't track down anyone who actually knew you personally. A couple teachers who taught you, but again this is New York, and the classes are huge and it's hard—if not impossible—for a teacher to recall any particular student, especially one from over ten years ago. You were quiet, kept to yourself, spoke fluent but accented English. Did your work, didn't really stand out in any way. Decent grades, but not great. You were adjusting, I guess. No close friends."

"Do I . . ." I have to pause to breathe and start over. "Do I have any family? In Spain, I mean."

Logan shakes his head, his eyes sad. "No, I'm sorry. Your parents were both only children, and their parents died when you were young, when you guys still lived in Spain. I even tracked down where you guys lived here in the city, but the apartment building where you lived didn't keep your stuff after your parents died. I mean, no one told them, right? So they put your stuff in storage for a while in case you came back, but your folks were dead and you were in a coma, and then you woke up not knowing who you were. So eventually they sold it or trashed it."

"So really, I'm back to where I started. No family, no real identity. No belongings of my own."

Logan sighs. "I guess so. I guess all that information doesn't really do you any good, does it?" He sounds bitter.

I realize I'm being incredibly ungrateful. "Logan, I'm sorry. I don't mean to make light of what you've given me. I have my name. I know my parents' names. That is a gift I shall never be able to repay." I place my hands over his, around the coffee mug.

He shrugs, a gesture of dismissal. "No big deal."

"It is, though, isn't it? To have my name?"

His eyes go to mine, and their fierce indigo brilliance pins me. "It's only as meaningful as you make it. It only means something if you *do* something with it. Identity is what you make of it, X, Isabel, whatever you want to call yourself. And that's really it, isn't it? What you *want* to call yourself. Who you want to be. All of us are looking for our identity, aren't we? I mean, we grow up, we spend our lives searching for meaning, for substance. To matter. That's why people drink, or do drugs, or gamble, or get tattoos all over their bodies, or make art, or play music in a band, or write books, or sleep with a different person every night. To figure out who they are. For some people, their identity is rooted in their history. I mean, where I grew up, I knew people who'd lived their entire lives in San Diego, never left it. Their parents moved there, and they were born there, and they'll never leave. Their dad was a lawyer, so they'll be a lawyer. That's easy, for them. It may not be much, but it's who they are. Others, it's harder, isn't it? I had to make my own way. I had to decide what I wanted to do with my life. Did I want to be a gangbanger, a drug dealer, a criminal? Did I want to end up dead, or in jail? Then I was a mechanic in the army. And then I was a security contractor, a soldier. And then I was nothing. I was wounded, flat on my back in a hospital with no future and a dead-end past. I had to start over. I had to decide all over again what I wanted. Who I wanted to be. I've always loved creating, using my hands, being active. So I got into house flipping." He flattens his palms on the table, and I can't help but be drawn to his hands, to the weathered lines, the roughness of them. They are such big, strong, capable hands. Hard as rock, rough as cinder blocks. "I ripped up old floors and knocked down walls and tore out cabinets. Stripped the houses down to studs, to bare bones. And I made them new, built new walls, new cabinets, new floors. I made them beautiful, and I sold them. And I turned that into a lucrative business. That's my identity. I build things. I built houses, and now I build businesses and sell them. Kind of like what I did with houses, but for entire companies."

"You rebuilt yourself."

He nods. "More than once."

"How do you do it? How do you build an identity?"

"Takes guts and determination, I guess. Like anything else in life, really. I mean, you look at your life and your skills and you decide what you like, what feels right, and you follow that where it leads."

I stare down at the tabletop. "I don't know if I can do that. The life I have, it's not perfect, but it's what I know. And it's all I have. It's all I've ever had. I mean, yes, you've told me I had parents, and that I went to school, but where does that take me from here? How does that help me know what to do about Caleb?"

I hadn't meant to ask that last question, but it just came out.

"I can't decide that for you. You have to figure it out for yourself." He won't look at me.

"I'm sorry, Logan. I don't mean to bring him up when I'm with you. But it's the reality of my life. I know you believe he's bad, and there are parts of him and his life that I don't like. Things that, the more I learn about them, just make me uncomfortable. But he's been there for me since I woke up, Logan. He gave me an identity, what little of one I have. He was with me every single day while I was learning to walk and talk again. I started from nothing. I mean, a lot of the basics came back pretty quickly, but my muscles were atrophied, and the part of my brain that controlled speech had been damaged, so I had to relearn how to walk and talk. The first two years of my life after waking up were spent in physical therapy and speech therapy. I had trouble dressing myself, feeding myself. Caleb was *there*. He gave me everything I have. I can't discount that because you have a bad feeling about him."

Logan sighs. "I'm not trying to say he's evil or anything, I just—" He cuts off, wipes his face with both hands, and starts again. "Have you ever asked yourself *why* he did that?"

"He was the one who found me."

"He says." Logan taps the table with the tip of his index finger. "But he also said there was a mugging. Isn't that what you told me? The facts say otherwise. I've seen the police reports. I've seen the photos of the car, the reports of a sixteen-year-old female, unconscious and unresponsive, with severe cranial trauma. I've seen the medical reports, saying you might never wake up."

"Why would he lie?" I ask.

"I don't know," Logan says. "I don't know. That's a question for him, and it's not one I can ask."

"I don't know if I can either." I feel faint, again.

My chest feels thick. The walls feel as if they're closing in. The back of the booth has hands, somehow, clutching at my throat. The world spins.

Lies. Truth. Distortions. Facts.

It all twists like smoke from an extinguished candle blown by a breath. Mixes, shifts, shapes contorting.

I'm up, out of the booth, tripping over my feet. I'm outside, and it's morning now. Sun streams from between the canyon walls of the buildings, casting a broad path of golden light onto the street, onto the sidewalk, washing over me. I walk, trip, stumble, run.

I can't breathe.

I can't see. This isn't a panic attack, this is . . . something worse. My heart is crashing and frantic and I am collapsing. Am I dying? Perhaps that wouldn't be so bad.

I catch up against a sign pole, the metal cold against my cheek.

I realize I'm crying and chanting, "Isabel . . . Isabel . . . Isabel . . ."

Warm strong hands pull me back against a broad chest. A voice like sunlight murmurs in my ear. "You're okay. Breathe, baby. Take a deep breath and let it out."

That's not what he's supposed to say. It won't help. Telling me to breathe won't make me breathe. He's not saying the right words.

"I'm Madame X," I whisper, hoping maybe if I say the words, it'll work the magic just the same, it'll force oxygen into my lungs and slow my frantic heartbeat. "I'm Madame X. You're Caleb Indigo. You saved me from a bad man. I am safe with you. It was just a dream. Just a dream."

I repeat this several times, and it doesn't help.

I hear a strangled breath behind me, feel lips brush my earlobe. His arms are crossed over my chest, like iron bands. "God, he's got you fucking brainwashed." The sound of Logan's voice as he says this is feral, rage-infused. Bitter.

"It—it calms me down when I have a panic attack," I manage.

"Well, let's try something new, okay? You're Isabel. You are strong. You are safe. You don't need anyone."

I can't. I can't say those words. I try, though. I try. "I—I'm . . . Isabel. I am Isabel. I am Isabel." I shake my head. "I'm not. I'm not Isabel. I'm not. That's not me anymore. I can't be her, she died. I died. On the operating table, I died. They brought me back, but I died. My heart stopped for almost a minute. I died. Isabel de la Vega died."

"Then be someone else."

"Who?" I cry; it is a sob. "Who else can I be? I am Madame X."

"Is that who you want to be?"

"I don't *know!*" I twist in his arms, press my cheek to his chest. "I don't know, Logan. No, I don't want to be Madame X anymore. I want to be someone new, but I don't know who. I don't know who, or how to decide."

"You are strong. You are safe. You don't need anyone."

"That isn't true."

"Maybe not yet. But it can be." He touches my chin with a fingertip. "Look at me, honey. Have you ever heard the phrase 'fake it till you make it'?"

I shake my head. "No, I haven't."

"Sometimes it's all you can do. Pretend you're okay. Pretend you're strong. Pretend you don't need anyone. Fake it. Fake it for yourself, for those around you. When you wake up, when you go to bed, keep faking it. And eventually, one day . . . it'll be true."

I have no answer. I'm spared from having to find one by the arrival of the Maybach. The long, low vehicle slides to a stop beside us.

You are on the far side, behind Len, the driver.

The window slides down, and your dark eyes fix on me. "Get in, X. Now."

"How about you let her decide what she wants, Caleb?" Logan asks, not relinquishing his hold on me.

"This is none of your business," you say. "And get your hands off her."

"I will if she tells me to."

"Would you like to go back to prison, Mr. Ryder?" you ask, your voice far too quiet. "I can arrange that, if you wish."

Logan tenses. Clearly that threat holds weight.

I feel like a bone being fought over by two dogs. I dislike it intensely. "Stop. Both of you. Just . . . stop." I turn to you. "How did you find me, Caleb?" I ask.

"You are mine. I will always be able to find you."

"She's not *yours*, asshole," Logan growls. "She's *hers*."

And then Len is out of the car, tall, wide, eyes soulless and roiling with death. A pistol emerges from beneath Len's blazer, black and big and frightening. The barrel touches Logan's head.

"Back away. Now." Len's voice is colder than ice, flat, emotionless.

"Fuck you. You won't shoot me in broad daylight." His hands tighten on my arms to the point of pain.

"Think again," Len says. He pulls back the top portion of the pistol, *snick-click*. "I sure as shit will. I haven't forgotten, Ryder."

I remember the penthouse, my bath, Len being bound and gagged at gunpoint. I see murder in Len's eyes, and I know Logan could die in a split second. Between one breath and the next.

"Let go, Logan," I whisper. "Don't do this. I will not see you hurt over me."

"You have a choice," he says. His eyes find mine, pleading. "You have a choice. In this, in your name. In your future."

"I *am* her future," you say. Not to me, but to Logan. "Just as I am her past, and her present. And you are none of those. You are a distraction."

"Let him shoot me. I don't fucking care, X. Make the choice for *you*."

I feel strangled. Choked by choice.

I look at Logan, and his eyes blaze with fury, melt with . . . some emotion I do not understand, soft and potent and boiling and razor sharp, all at once, all over me, for me, directed at me. His blond hair is long, so long now, wavy and curled at the ends, hanging past his shoulders, blond curls drifting over his eyes. I see his scars, two round holes in his right shoulder, white thin lines on his forearm and right bicep, and I know there's another round puckered scar low on his right side, just beneath his ribs, and I see his tattoos covering his upper arms in a jumble of images; I see all this in a tableau, a frozen vignette, his indigo eyes and blond hair and scars and tattoos and work-roughened hands and his square jaw and high cheekbones and expressive lips that have kissed me and never demanded more, never claimed more, needing more, wanting more, but waiting until I was ready to give it. Will I ever be ready? Will I ever be free to choose him? Am I capable of it?

I do not know.

I pull away from him, *for* him. I cannot allow him to be hurt because of me.

He is already hurt for me, though. That is written in his eyes, and it in turn strikes my heart like a knife.

I pull away, and this is like déjà vu. Logan before me, you behind me, waiting. The car. Len. My heartache and my sorrow and my confusion. I want him, but I don't trust myself. I don't trust my vision of the future with him. Do I trust him? I don't know.

You, behind me, in the Maybach. You haven't gotten out. Your eyes are darkness incarnate. Unknowable. Inscrutable. You are perfect, as you are always perfect, untouchable, carved out of living marble.

Len opens the door with one hand, gun held low in the other, out of sight. You do not reach for me. You aren't even looking at me. You are staring at Logan, but I do not know what you are thinking. What you are feeling.

I know what Logan is thinking and feeling, because he wears his emotions on his face, he does not care what anyone sees, what anyone thinks.

He *is*. He just is.

But I am in motion, and a body in motion stays in motion. I cannot stop this. I cannot flee to Logan, not now. Perhaps not ever. He is too good for me, too true, too much.

He is too real.

And I . . . ?

I am a ghost.

A ghost named Isabel.

SIX

You are silent for a long time, and I watch you as you sit in imperturbable stolidity, perhaps deciding what to say, what not to say. I don't know. I have never been able to read you.

"X—" Your voice is carefully even, precisely modulated.

"Logan found out my name."

"He thinks so, does he?" You sound cocksure, careless.

"The story he tells makes sense," I say.

"And? What is your new name then?" You are dismissive.

"Isabel Maria de la Vega Navarro." I glance at you as I say it. "A Spanish name."

You are silent a moment and again I do not know how to interpret your silence. "So you're Isabel now?"

"I don't know. That's the problem, isn't it? I don't know. Not anything."

"You do know, though. You know who you are." You slide across the seat, and I notice that there are dark circles under your eyes, and that your cheeks and chin are unshaven, dark with day-old stubble. "You are Madame X. I am Caleb Indigo—" You start.

"Am I? Are you?"

"Once you begin questioning things, you won't ever stop, X. That is a rabbit hole down which it is entirely too easy to fall."

"Funny," I say. "Logan said something very similar."

"Did he." This is phrased as a question, spoken as a statement.

"He did." Panic still overwhelms my mind, but I am learning somehow to push through it. To speak despite the turbulence in my soul. "He told me that I couldn't shy away from the answers, once I started asking questions."

"I don't care what Logan said. He is no one." Closer now.

I can feel the heat from your body, see the way your biceps stretch the material of your suit coat. Your eyes are red, as if you haven't gotten even the small amount of sleep you're used to.

"He isn't no one. Not to me. I care what he said."

"Why?"

"Because he tells me the truth, Caleb."

"How do you know?" Your hand floats out, comes to rest on my thigh.

I knock your hand away, with sudden violence shocking to both of us. "*No.* You don't get to touch me." I feel vehemence boiling within me. Rage. Raw, potent fury. At you. At Logan. At everything.

"How do you know he told you the truth?" you repeat. "He could have made it up."

"I know. I've thought of that," I say. "The trouble is, that same question can be applied to you. How do I know anything you've told me is the truth? What do I believe? Whom do I believe?"

You sigh. "The man who has always been there for you."

"And why have you been? What do you get out of it? If it weren't for the ready availability of perhaps dozens of other women at your disposal, I'd say it was just for the easy access to sex. A captive audience, if you will."

"That's not what you are to me, X."

"Stop calling me that," I snap. "I am not Madame *fucking* X anymore."

"Then who are you?"

"I DON'T *KNOW!*" I shout the first two words, scream the third. Even Len twists his head to glance at me.

"Shall I call you Nameless then?"

"Do not mock me, Caleb Indigo." My voice is thin, as the blade of a knife is thin.

"I'm not. Mockery is not my style."

"What is your style? Pimping? Prostitution? That's what those girls are, beneath the thin veneer of salvation. They are still prostitutes. But now they work for you, and you are their only client. Until you *sell* them to the highest bidder, and then they become brideslaves. You convince them they have a choice, but do they, really? Rachel does not have a choice. If she returns to the streets, she will once again become Dixie, the whore. Dixie, the drug addict. So for now, she is *your* whore, and you are her drug. She has no choice." I close my eyes and breathe out, letting the truth seep from my lips. "No more than I. We are your whores. We are your addicts. You are a drug, and you are in our veins."

"You do not understand what you're talking about, X, Isabel, whoever you are."

"Whoever I am. Apropos indeed, Caleb." I let a thick, tension-fat silence hang between us. "I'm going to ask you one question, and you will answer it truthfully, or I will never speak to you again."

"All right." You sound calm.

"How did you find me?"

A sigh. An outbreath of resignation. "You've been surgically microchipped. I paid the surgeon who reconstructed your face two point five million dollars to insert it."

This is a shock that goes beyond even numbness, a shock so great I am able to remain utterly still and calm. "Microchipped? Reconstructed?" I touch the left side of my face, just above my ear.

"You don't remember?" You seem puzzled.

"No." I try, and fail.

I think back, but the days immediately after waking up are a blur, a haze of therapy and Caleb, surgeries and Caleb, nurses and Caleb.

"The entire left side of your face was . . . a mess. The right side was perfect, unblemished. The left . . . was not. I imported the most skilled and renowned reconstructive plastic surgeon in the world, and paid him a rather large amount of money to restore you to your former beauty. The two and a half million dollars I mentioned was just the bribe to implant the chip, mind you. I paid him more than quadruple that to drop all of his other clients and fly to New York and fix you."

I suppose I should be impressed by how much you spent to have me fixed.

"When you say that I've been . . . microchipped—what does that mean?" I have trouble now forming words, forming breaths.

You do not answer for a moment. "The scar on your hip . . . it was always there, since the accident, I mean. When Dr. Frankel had you under to fix your face, however, he sliced into that scar, implanted a very small computer chip, and closed the incision, making it look as if it had never been disturbed. The microchip allows me to pinpoint your location, down to the nearest meter." You lift your phone.

I don't know what I am to think about your revelation. So I change topics. "Would you like to know the story Logan told me?"

"If you wish to tell me, I will listen." Impassive, unconcerned. Disbelieving.

Too much so, perhaps?

"There was a car accident," I say. "My parents were killed, and I wasn't. They were immigrants. The police couldn't identify me, but because I was in a coma I might never wake from, the investigation was closed, leaving me a Jane Doe."

"I see."

"You see?" I stare at you. "What does that mean, 'you see'?"

"It means there are problems with his story," you say. "Why could you not be identified? Were your parents illegal immigrants, that they didn't even carry basic ID? And even if we assume some bizarre sequence of events leading to your parents *and* you being unidentifiable, why would the investigation just be closed? They wouldn't just . . . *give up.* If Logan could figure out who you are, why couldn't the police?"

"I . . ." My throat is dry and my spirit numb, my mind confused.

"Six years, X. I've spent six years of my life caring for you. You think I would hold back this kind of information from you, if it were that easy to find it?" Do I think so? I don't know. You continue. "You've known me for six years, yet this man you've known for less than . . . what? I don't even know? How much time have you spent with him? A few hours, at most? And you are ready to believe whatever he says." You sound disgusted.

I have no answers for your logic.

"But my face, Caleb. You just said it was burned. How would that happen in a mugging gone wrong?"

"I didn't say it was burned, X. I said it was messed up. You'd been beaten, savagely and brutally. The doctors think your face was kicked, that you'd tried to turtle, you know? Hands over your head? The damage was so severe your face would never be the same. I didn't want you to have to live with that, so I had it fixed. I never said you were burned."

And just that fast, my nascent identity is gone.

I hate you.

"You are Madame X . . ." you say. And I want so desperately to be able to cling to that, but I cannot, and the words you speak, once so familiar and comforting, seem empty now. "And I am Caleb . . ."

"*Stop* it, Caleb," I say, barely able to manage a whisper. "Just . . . stop."

"If you wish to choose a new name—"

"Why do you get to decide what I am allowed to do?" I ask. "Why is my entire life dependent on *you*? Why is my entire *existence* dependent on you?"

You sigh. It is a long-suffering sound. "Stop the car, Len," you say.

The car slides to a halt in the left-hand lane of Fifth Avenue, a few blocks from your tower, early-morning traffic rushing past on our right.

You gesture at the car door, the window, the world beyond. "Then go. Find your own way."

"Caleb—"

You open your door, watching the traffic, and then circle around behind the vehicle. You pull open my door. Grab my wrist. Haul me out. Close the door, return to the rear driver's-side door. "You are not dependent on me because I insist on keeping you captive. It is just the way things are. You want your 'freedom' so badly"—you weight the word with sarcasm—"then so be it."

You lower yourself into the car. The door closes with a soft *thud*. A smooth purr of the engine, and the Maybach glides away, leaving me alone.

You have made your point: Where do I go? What do I do?

Who am I? If I am not Madame X, who am I?

Isabel? Is she real? Is Logan's story the truth?

If it is, then that means yours is a lie; if yours is true, Logan's is a lie.

There are holes in both stories. Reasons to doubt both. Perhaps neither are true.

I have been walking as I think, and I do not know where I am. Not far from where you kicked me out of the car, a block or two away maybe. There is a church on a corner, dark stone, Gothic architecture. Stairs, with people sitting on them, smoking cigarettes and drinking coffee and talking on cell phones. I sit on a stair, legs tucked demurely beneath me, fighting panic.

I am alone in Manhattan. I have no money. I have no identification. I have no identity. I am no one. If I go back to you, ascend your tower, I am consenting to be yours. Consenting to be Madame X.

I could call Logan, but what do I know about him? Very little. What he's told me, and what I feel. I feel like I can trust him. I feel, when I'm with him, that anything is possible. I do not doubt him, when we are together. I *know* him. He is *in* me. Everything is okay, with him. But now, away from him, I doubt it all. I doubt him. I doubt me. I doubt Caleb.

I don't even realize I'm crying until a foul-smelling old black man dressed in rags sits beside me, takes a swig from a brown paper bag–wrapped bottle, and eyes me sidelong. "Somebody done you wrong, huh?"

I sniff. "Yes. No. I don't know."

The old man nods sagely, as if what I said made some kind of sense. "Worst kinda pain, right there. The not knowing."

"I don't know who I am." Why am I admitting this to a homeless drunk? But I am, and it is cathartic.

"Yeah, me neither. But then I never was no one much. I ain't drunk 'cause I'm homeless, you know, I'm homeless 'cause I'm drunk." A swing, an eye cast toward the sky, as if seeking something in the clear, cloudless blue. "Or maybe it is the other way around. I can't 'member no more."

"I can't remember either. I can't remember who I used to be, and I've lost confidence in who I am now." I don't bother wiping away the tears.

"Don't need to know who you was, or who you is. Only need to know who you wanna be."

That is a surprisingly helpful statement. I stare at the man, absorbing that last sentence. I only need to know who I want to be. Rachel said much the same, and so did Logan.

The question remains, however: who do I want to be?

I don't know.

I don't know.

At some point, the old man totters off, swigging endlessly from the bottle.

I see you approaching, a god striding the earth among mortals. Navy blue suit, bespoke, of course. White button-down. No tie, top two buttons undone, baring a V of flesh. Dark hair swept back, effortless, artful. Eyes like black holes, absorbing all light and matter, absorbing, drawing, seeking, sucking everything in. Sucking me in. Dragging me in. You sit beside me, lean back, elbows on the stair behind you.

"Come home, X."

"Home?" I speak the word as a question, spit it like the bitterest gall. "Where is that?"

"Oh for fuck's sake, X—"

"I sit in your monstrosity of an apartment, waiting. You know what I wait for? You. I sit there waiting for *you*. Waiting for you to show up, so you can fuck me and then ignore me." Eyes around me seek me. I ignore them. You, however, do not look at me. You scan the crowds, watch the passersby, watch the river of cars, yellow and black and white and blue and red, watch anything but me. "I am discontent, Caleb. The status quo has been called into question. Who I am, who I was, who I will be, it's all up for grabs. Do you even know what that's like?"

"More than you know."

"I don't want to be that person anymore, Caleb."

"Then who—"

I speak over you. "I don't know yet. I don't know anything anymore. I'm not sure I believe Logan, but no more do I believe you. I don't know what to believe." I stare at you, and finally you meet my gaze. "You can't keep me in thrall with your mantra anymore either. Everything has changed."

"What changed you?"

I shrug. "Logan." It is the simple truth.

A few hours with him, and everything changed. I am not sure if I am grateful for this or not.

"He's an ex-con," you say.

I nod. "I know. He told me." I lick my lips. "He told me it had something to do with you. Or, that was the implication, at least. He wouldn't say what. It doesn't matter. I don't care."

"So what are you going to do?"

"I don't know."

"Just come back with me. I'll help you figure things out. I'll give you space."

"I don't know if I can be alone with you anymore. Not after what happened with you and Rachel."

A sigh. A long silence. Another sigh. "Come back." Your eyes meet mine. I see a glimmer of emotion in them, a tiny, infinitesimal spark. "Please."

Where else do I go? I have nowhere. No one. Rachel is tainted for me now. I cannot see Rachel without seeing you, fucking, pounding, spanking, staring at me.

I want to go to Logan. I want to bury my head in the sand. I want his arms around me. I want his eyes on mine, his hands on me, his lips. I want that, so badly. I want his truth. The ease of everything that is him. But what if he's lying, too? What if I become addicted to him the way I'm addicted to you?

You are a drug. I am hooked on you.

I read a book about drug addicts, about addiction. How even when addicts know the drug is killing them, they cannot stop. They return to it time and again, despite knowing the toll.

I return with you, despite knowing that I cannot trust you. That you are lying, that you are keeping the truth from me. That you are manipulating me into staying. I go with you, because I am addicted.

SEVEN

You pin me up against the door of the elevator, hips hard against mine, and your hands roam my body, one sliding up to grip my hair and the other stripping me of my clothes. Your mouth crushes mine, but this is not a kiss, this is a demonstration of ownership. Your mouth steals my breath. Your hands steal my will.

Your body erases my thoughts. You are hard against me, giving me no chance of arguing, of hesitating, of pulling away. I am imprisoned by your mastery over my body. You know the buttons to push, and you push them. I am rendered helpless.

You are an incubus.

Somehow, you become naked. I do not remember seeing or feeling you remove your clothes, but I feel your skin against mine. You are not gentle, or slow. You ravage my mouth with yours until I must rip my face away and gasp for breath.

And that is when your hands press down on my shoulders and I am forced to my knees. Your hand is tangled in my hair, and you force my head back. My heart hammers, and I stare up at you, lips parted in shock. This is not the Caleb I know, the man who has possessed my body every night, every day for . . . for as long as I can remember.

Your penis is an erect shaft in front of my face, thick and veined and plump-headed and as perfect as the rest of you, although I suppose I have no frame of reference, only the knowledge of your body, thus.

"Open your mouth," you command.

I open my mouth. My body obeys, although my mind is numb.

You thrust yourself into my mouth, roughly. I gag. You pull back. Thrust again.

"Is this what you want?" you demand. "The way I treat them?"

Ah. We return to this.

You thrust into my mouth, and I taste flesh, gag as you reach the back of my throat, choke as you push deeper. My eyes water, and my nose touches your belly. I cannot breathe, and my jaw aches, my eyes leak involuntary tears, and I am paralyzed by this, by you, by the ache, the choking of your erection down my throat, and I suck in a breath through my nose.

I do not like this.

I shake my head and try to pull away, but the door is behind my head and I have no escape.

"Is this how you wanted it?" you ask.

I shake my head.

This is starting to feel like violation.

Betrayal.

And then you slide your erection out of my mouth and your fist closes around it and you begin pumping your fist up and down, up and down. One hand in my hair, knotting my locks in your fist.

"You want to take it on the face, don't you? Like Rachel?"

Why are you doing this?

I could cry, but don't.

I watch your hand move in a blur on your shaft, and then your face tightens, your jaw clenches. You point the tip of your penis at my face. You release in silence, lip curled in a sneer.

You come on my face.

It drips hot down my forehead, trickles into my hair. Down my cheek. Splashes hot onto my lips, and I taste salt. Down my chin.

You step back, and I shoot to my feet, fighting sobs. I stand, chest heaving, disgusted, aching in my soul.

And . . . oh, I hate myself. I loathe myself.

Because I cannot deny the truth: If you had done that without forcing me, I might have liked it. Watching you. If it had been my hand on you instead of your own, if it had been done with any kind of mutuality . . .

But it wasn't, and I am enraged.

I spit your own semen into your face. "Fuck you, Caleb. You are a pig."

"It's what you wanted." You make no move to wipe away the spittle-tinged semen from your cheek.

"Not to be forced to it!" I shout.

I am seized, spun around, pressed flat against the door, and then you are up against me, and you bend at the knees and slide up and into me. Slowly, gently. Your lips touch my shoulder. The back of my neck, just beneath my hairline. You hold my hair up in a pile on top of my head and kiss my neck, down the curve to my shoulder again. Thrust.

You've already come, but you are either still hard or impossibly hard again already.

"Like this?" Slow, gentle, gliding thrusts, kisses to my neck.

Yes, part of me says.

"No," I growl. Push back, elbow you as hard as I can.

I let you put your penis in my mouth, but then you took more than I was willing to give.

I never said no, did I?

I question everything now. Myself most of all.

I still have your come on my face.

"Tell me to stop, X."

"Stop, Caleb." My voice is calm. I am proud of this, because I am not at all calm.

You release me, back away. Empty, I sag. Brace against the cold silver metal of the elevator door. Chest heaving. Gasping. Tears prickling my eyes. I turn around. Take a step toward you.

I slap you, openhanded, as hard as I can. My palm cracks against your face. I slap you again. And again. You make no move to defend yourself.

"That is how I treat them. I do not ask them what they want. I fuck them. I do what I want. I am not gentle. They take it, or they leave. *You* . . . I don't do that with you because *you* are not like them." Your cheek is red from my slaps.

My spit, your seed, it is smeared on your face, on my hand. We are both of us a mess.

"That's not what I saw with Rachel." I want badly to wipe my face, but I won't give you the satisfaction. "And is that supposed to make what you just did any better?"

"You could have stopped me. You had my cock in your mouth. You could have bitten me. You had both hands free. You could have hit me, punched me, grabbed my balls. Any number of things. You didn't. You just knelt there and took it." You pause for effect. "You *liked* it."

"Don't you dare turn this back on me, Caleb Indigo."

"Why not . . . Madame X? Is it not true? Couldn't you have stopped me?"

He's right. I could have. I didn't fight hard enough.

I slam into him, shoving him backward. "Goddamn you, Caleb! Why are you doing this?"

You catch your balance easily, and turn away. Wipe your face with your hand. Dress with your customary precision. "You want me to be the bad guy. So, I'll be the bad guy." When you are clothed, and I, again, am naked, you stare down at me. "And you know deep down you liked it. Maybe you didn't like that I was rougher with you than you would have initially preferred, but you liked it. Same way you *liked* watching me fuck Rachel. You hate me for that, but I think you hate yourself more for liking it."

I shake my head but cannot find the words to deny it.

You do not quite smile, but there is a ghost of amusement on your icy features. "You don't deny it."

I open my mouth to speak, but I have no words.

And then . . .

You kiss me.

It is gentle.

There is sweetness to it.

You pull away, reach into an inside pocket of your suit coat, withdraw a slippery, silky, maroon necktie. You wipe my face with it, and then you kiss me again.

Do you notice that I do not kiss you back?

I am reeling. Your emotional manipulation has left me exhausted, empty.

You reach into the hip pocket of your slacks, withdraw a slim white rectangle. A cell phone. You hand it to me. "It's yours. I programmed my number into it. Len's, if you need a driver or anything." You glance down at the pile of fabric that is my clothing, my dress, my underwear. There is a small square of folded paper. You bend, retrieve it, unfold it, read it. You toss it, let it flutter back down.

Take the phone back, tap at it for a moment. "There. Now you've got *his* number, too. This is me giving you choices."

You hand the phone back, and I take it, still and silent. I am so tired now that I can barely stand upright. You just stare at me, your expression characteristically inscrutable.

"You want to be her?" You point at the square of paper. The name written thereon. "Then be her. Be the immigrant girl."

You turn, open the elevator, step on, insert your key. I am within reach. You palm my hip, tug me to you. Kiss my mouth again, the way you never have before. And then you release me, and I stumble backward.

"You are Isabel, and I am Caleb." You leave off the rest, and somehow that is worse than if you'd said the rest.

As if by leaving off the rest, you are acknowledging the lie. That there was no bad man. That you did not save me. I suddenly want the lie.

I want the lie.

But you only repeat the new truth: "You are Isabel, and I am Caleb."

You twist the key, and the doors close, and I see your frame in a narrowing perspective, until there is just a sliver of you, and then you are gone.

And I am alone with your words.

You are Isabel, and I am Caleb.

Oh, you are cruel. Even if I am her, I am still yours.

I take a shower, a long, scalding shower, and I scrub myself until I am pink and raw, and the water runs cold. I brush my teeth until my gums bleed.

None of that scours away the scrim of ugliness on my skin, or purges the mire from within me.

I fall onto the bed, wrapped in a towel, mind spinning in dizzying circles.

I am Isabel.

You are Caleb.

I am Isabel.

He is Logan.

I am Isabel.

I think of a line from a Bible I once read, in my library, long ago, back before everything changed: "I want to do what is right, but I can't. I want to do what is good, but I don't. I don't want to do what is wrong, but I do it anyway."

I didn't understand those words then, but I do now.

I am an addict, and you are my drug.

I am Isabel.

If I want to be anyone other than the addict, the Caleb-junkie, the no one, the girl on her knees, taking what you give as if it's all I'm worth, then I have to choose someone else to be.

I choose Isabel, a dead immigrant girl I may or may not have once been.

I am Isabel.

Sleep is a long time coming, and when it does claim me, it is with tear tracks drying on my cheeks; the walls echo with the ghosts of my sobs, the specter of X writhes in my soul, and the memory of choking on you is a livid scar across my mind.

EIGHT

There are no blackout curtains in your bedroom; there is no noise machine. Those are the weapons with which I fight the demons plaguing my sleep. I haven't slept well in the months since moving up here; the nightmares wake me up, and you are always gone.

I cannot wake up, this time. I am trapped in the dream, trapped in the darkness, with sirens howling like wolves in the shadows, rain slicing my face like icy knives. Lights flash, blue and red, white lights piercing the black. Searching. Eyes, searching. Pain stabs me, grips me. I am confused, disoriented. I do not know what happened. All I know is pain. Agony. I burn. My skull throbs, my face aches. My bones shake and my muscles tremble and it hurts to breathe, hurts to sob, hurts, hurts, hurts. I crawl across cold wet hard ground, fingernails scrabbling and ripping away. I do not know where I am trying to go, just away. Away. Away from the pain, but the pain is me and I cannot escape it. I cannot escape myself. The pain is all.

I wake abruptly, sobbing, sweaty. Alone. The penthouse is dark, and silent. I know the various sounds of silence, the silence of someone waiting, the silence of emptiness.

This is the silence of absence.

You are gone.

I am not upset by this. I do not know if I can ever face you again.

I am assaulted by a wave of memory: your fingers in my hair, my jaw cracking wide and your essence on my tongue.

I barely make it to the bathroom in time to empty the contents of my stomach into the toilet. Acid burns my throat, bitter and hot. Coats my tongue, my lips. Drips down my chin. I rinse my mouth with tepid water from the tap, then brush my teeth again and wash my face with hand soap.

I am exhausted, seeing as what little sleep I did get was wracked by the nightmare and provided no rest. I am slow, sluggish, lethargic. Empty. Numb. As if by vomiting, I purged myself of any capacity to think or feel.

On autopilot, I dress myself. Black lingerie, because I do not own anything except lingerie. A simple dove-gray dress, A-line, knee-length, with a wide crimson belt and matching red pumps. I brush through my hair and leave it loose in glossy raven-wing waves. I do not know why I am getting dressed. I do not know where I intend to go, only that I cannot stay here any longer.

As I near the elevator, I trip in the darkness over a pile of cloth, and my toe kicks something hard, which skitters across the hardwood floor. I retrieve it.

The cell phone.

I lift it, press the circular button at the bottom. The screen lights up, showing the time—8:48 P.M.—and the date—September 18, 2015. Beneath that, there is a green icon. Next to the icon is a name: Caleb.

And beside that is a line of text: the code to access the phone is 0309, the date you left the hospital.

I touch the icon and swipe it to the right, and a keypad appears, prompting me to either touch ID or enter passcode; I enter the numbers, and the screen appears to fly at me as it shifts to show the message. I see the message from you in a gray bubble on the left side of the screen. I touch the thing that looks like an Internet search bar, and a keyboard appears.

I type a message in return: Thank you.

Three gray dots appear in a bubble, and then a message pops up. Youre welcome. The lack of an apostrophe to denote the contraction irks me.

I'm leaving, I type.

Where

No question mark, just the single word. I didn't expect such poor grammar from you.

I do not know. Anywhere but here. Anywhere that is not where you are.

I'm sorry, X. I went too far.

Yes, you did. Much too far.

Do you need money?

You are letting me go? I don't know what to think about this, what to feel. It is odd to be using a cell phone, to be doing something so mundane as texting. I've seen you do it, I've seen clients do it. I never thought I would do it.

> I do not want anything from you, Caleb.

> Everything you have comes from me, X.

> My name is Isabel. And yes, I know that. If I could walk out of here naked, with nothing but my skin, I would.

> You wouldnt make it far in that state

No apostrophe, no period. Why? Is it hard to take the extra time to add them? I don't understand. I notice, as well, that you do not address my statement of my name.

> No, I would not.

> Have fun with Logan. It won't last.

I don't know what that means, and I'm not sure what I can respond with, so I don't respond at all. I have seen you use your phone—which is the same as this one except yours is black—so I know that the button on the right side near the top turns the screen off. I clutch the phone in my hand and notice that the elevator key is in the slot. I twist it, remove it when the doors open, and take the elevator down to the lobby. I debate whether to take the key.

If I take it, it would be a concession. It would mean I plan to return.

I don't.

I see a security guard I recognize standing beside the reception-ist desk. Frank? I think that's the right name. I cross the lobby, my heels cracking loudly on the marble.

The guard eyes me suspiciously. "Ma'am."

"Frank, isn't it?"

"Yes, ma'am." Tall, round-shouldered, heavy brows, square jaw, shaved head.

I extend the key. "Give this to Mr. Indigo, if you would."

"Won't you need it, ma'am?"

"Not anymore." I don't wait for a response, I spin on my heel and pretend to have confidence I don't feel as I stride out through the revolving door.

Turn right, up Fifth. Try to breathe. Try to ignore the noise, ignore the panic.

Try to ignore the fact that I am alone in the world. I have nothing but my name. Even the clothes I wear are yours, the phone, the shoes. Even my face belongs to you, since you paid to have it fixed.

I am reminded, then, of the chip in my hip. Is that real? Is that possible? I make it two blocks up and three blocks over before my nerves overcome me. I huddle against the side of a building, clutch-ing the phone so hard my hand hurts.

Swipe right; 0-3-0-9; contacts; Logan.

It rings once. Twice. Three times.

"Logan Ryder." His voice alone soothes me.

"Logan? It's me. It's"—I have to suck in a breath—"it's Isabel."

There are voices in the background, a phone ringing. "Sorry, it's crazy at the office right now. Hold on, let me go somewhere quiet." I hear a door click closed, and the background noise fades. "Are you okay?"

"No. I—I left."

"Left?" You suck in a breath. "You mean you *left*, left?"

"Yes, Logan. I walked out." My voice quavers. "I . . . Caleb, he . . . we—he did something. To me." I'm not sure I'm ready to talk about that, yet.

"And he let you leave?"

"He gave me a cell phone, and even programmed your number into it."

"So he can track you, probably."

"He told me he had a microchip surgically implanted in my hip. So I don't think he needs a cell phone to track me."

"Are you joking?"

"Humor is not one of my strong suits, Logan."

"Goddamn. That's fucked up. Like really, *really* fucked up."

"I know." I fall silent as a man sidles past me on the sidewalk, eyeing me with something like greed in his gaze. I give him my best glare, and he continues past me. "Caleb, when I told him I was leaving, all he said was to have fun with you, and that it wouldn't last."

"I wonder what game he's playing," he muses.

"I wish I knew." A phone rings in the background. "Do you have to answer that?"

"No. That's why I have employees," he says. "Where are you?"

"I don't know. A few blocks from the tower. I don't have anywhere to go. I don't know what to do. I didn't want to just go running straight to you, but I don't know what to do."

"Of course you should go straight to me. I'm here for you, Isabel."

I like that. Oh, I like it very much. Hearing my name on his lips. A normal name. A beautiful name.

"Can you come get me?" I ask.

"I—shit. Fuck. I can't. God, honey, I'm so sorry. I'm at the tail end of a fifteen-million-dollar acquisition." He curses again, fluently. "My office is on Ninth and Forty-fifth. Can you make it here?"

"Yes. I'll call you again when I'm at the intersection?"

"All right. I'm sorry, normally I'd drop whatever I'm doing, but I have to be physically present for this one."

"No, it's all right."

"It's not. I don't even have a car to send for you. I keep things simple, you know?"

"Simple is good. I'll make it."

"But your panic attacks—"

I try to infuse strength into my voice. "I'll have to work through it."

"One breath at a time. One step at a time. Baby steps to Logan."

"Is that another reference to that movie?"

"Yes."

"I still haven't seen it, you know. I've never seen any movies."

"Make it to my office, and we'll set about rectifying that."

"Okay." I take a breath. "I can do this."

"You can do this." I hear a voice in the background call Logan's name urgently. "I have to go. Call me if you need me. I swear I'll answer, no matter what."

"Okay. Now go do your acquisitioning."

He laughs. "See? You do have a sense of humor. I'll see you soon, okay?"

I end the call, to save him having to. I look up at the nearest intersection, at the signs. Seventh and Forty-fourth. Two blocks up, one block over. I can do it.

I push away from the wall. Straighten my spine. Lift my chin. Breathe deeply. One foot in front of the other. Ahead, a siren blares, and I flinch, and my breath lodges in my throat, but I force my feet to move. One foot forward. Follow it with the other. One step after another. Keep breathing. Ignore the people. Wait at the intersection for the light to change, a crowd around me. No one is looking at me. I am just another face in the crowd. Anonymous. It feels good.

I make it to Forty-fifth, but then I can't figure out whether to turn right or left. I choose left, and discover that I've chosen incorrectly when I reach Sixth Avenue. I turn around and retrace my steps, wading through the ever-present crowds, wincing and flinching as my shoulder is jostled, ignoring the hammer of my heart in my chest, trying desperately to pretend I'm okay. Fake it till you make it, Logan told me. I'm trying to fake it, but it's hard. The city is loud, horns always blaring, lights blinding. The people are myriad.

I'm crossing Eighth when a young man runs across the street, arms flailing, glancing behind, running frantically. He slams into me, sends me flying, twisting. I hear a shout, and a mammoth horse gallops across the intersection, a policeman on its back. I am in its path. I am still off balance, arms windmilling, stumbling. My shoe has come loose on my foot, and my ankle twists.

A hand grabs me, jerks me out of the way at the last second.

I am pulled against a hard chest smelling sharply of cologne. I look up into the cold gray eyes of Len. Big, broad, craggy features, a man like a stone golem made flesh, but barely.

"You're here?" I ask.

"He had me follow you. Make sure nothing happened to you." Len gestures at the horse and rider in pursuit of the criminal. "Like that."

"I don't need your help," I say.

"You were almost trampled."

I will not resort to petulance. "Thank you for your assistance, Len."

"No problem. Those fuckers will run you down and not even blink twice."

"I suppose you're reporting my whereabouts?" I say, noticing the wire looped around an ear, the cord vanishing under the suit.

"Don't need to. He knows where you are."

"Of course he does. He always does."

Len just shrugs. "How he is, I guess." A gesture in the direction I was going. "Might as well walk with you now."

There isn't much to say. Len is a man of few words, and I am lost in my own mind, focusing on keeping down the panic.

When I reach Ninth and Forty-fifth, I stop. Dial Logan. "I'm here," I say, when he answers.

"Be right down."

He emerges from a doorway between shops, across the street from me, on Forty-fifth. His eyes narrow when he sees who's with me. He glances both ways, then jogs across to me, eyeing Len warily.

"You didn't say anything about Len being with you," he points out.

"I didn't know he was. I was almost run over by a police horse, and Len saved me."

"Orders from the boss," Len says.

"Well, she's safe now." Logan reaches for me, and I take his hand.

Len just nods. "I'll be seeing you." Turns, walks away.

Logan watches as Len vanishes into the crowds. "'I'll be seeing you?'" he repeats. "That's not ominous or anything."

"Len is an ominous sort of man," I say.

"No kidding." Logan's eyes find me, compassion fills his gaze. "You're about done in, aren't you?"

I can only nod. I am holding it together by a string.

Logan leads me across the street, his arm around my waist. I lean into him, inhale his scent. He is chewing cinnamon gum, but I notice the outline of a pack of cigarettes in the right hip pocket of his tight blue jeans. I notice odd details, as he leads me to his office. His shoes, old, worn Adidas sneakers, faded, scuffed, the fabric worn nearly through near the toe of one shoe. Why would a wealthy man like Logan wear such old shoes? I notice a watch on his wrist, a huge black rubber thing that looks like it could take a bullet and not suffer any harm—the only watch I've ever seen him wear. His hair, pulled back in a ponytail, low on his nape. With his hair pulled back, his looks change. Sleeker, a little older. I notice wrinkles at the corners of his eyes, from smiling, and from squinting in the sun.

I remember that he spent time fighting in the desert overseas.

I notice graffiti on the wall, on a mailbox. A homeless man huddled in a doorway, watching everything but somehow seeing nothing.

I notice Logan's T-shirt, black and tight-fitting, with a white skull painted on the front, the jaw depicted as four vertical lines extending down to the hem, the eye holes made into angry slits.

Looking at him, it isn't readily obvious that Logan is a multimillionaire. Which, I suppose, is the point. He keeps things simple.

He leads me up three flights of narrow stairs and through a door. On the other side is mayhem. It was once a large apartment, but the interior walls have all been removed, leaving the room open. The desks are tall, and none of the employees are sitting, because there are no chairs at any of the desks, so everyone at a desk is doing his or her work standing up. Instead, there are beanbags scattered here and there, thickly padded leather couches filling spaces between desks along the walls. The apartment is a large rectangle with desks lining the walls on the two longest sides. One of the short sides is composed of bathrooms, a break room, a printer/copier/office supplies room, and a conference room, and the opposite end is a giant bank of televisions, each playing something different. One TV shows music videos, with the sound on low, something driving and heavy, the band members flailing long hair and hunched over guitars. Others show sports highlights, news clips, and stock tickers, an old sitcom on mute. There is a white game console on the floor, wires trailing up to one of the TVs, with handheld controllers in the hands of two young men intently focused on their game, which involves shooting some kind of dead creatures.

This is not what I imagined when I thought of Logan's office.

The office is in chaos. Four people speak loudly into phones, six more are sitting in a circle on some beanbags and a couch, passing documents back and forth and conducting at least three different conversations at once. The young men playing the video game are shouting at each other, cursing and laughing.

A young woman approaches Logan. Short, curvy, wearing a sleeveless V-neck dress, baring skin completely covered in tattoos, so there is virtually no blank space visible anywhere, not even on generously visible cleavage. "Logan, Ahmed is on the phone. He's got an addition to paragraph two of clause four-A."

A young man shouts from across the room: "Logan! The intellectual property rider is totally fucked, man. We'd be allowing them almost total control over future projects if we leave it as is."

Logan addresses the young woman. "Tell Ahmed I'll take a look and call him back. Get me a printout, and your thoughts on his additions." He points at the man across the room. "So fucking fix it, Chris! What the fuck am I paying you for?" He then glances at me, and for the first time I see a hint of stress in his eyes. "Sorry, X—I mean Isabel. Things are whacked out right now. This acquisition landed in our laps on Monday morning, and I'm trying to get it ironed out before the weekend."

"It *is* the weekend, Logan," I point out. "It's after nine on a Friday night."

"Exactly. But the company we're acquiring is in California, so it's only six there."

"Don't acquisitions usually take months?"

"Usually. But they're desperate, and these kids kick ass." He points at the conference room. "Let's go in there. It's quieter. They can handle shit on their own for a few minutes."

I am numb.

I feel nothing; I am not panicked. I am not scared. I am not tired. I do not know what I am. I should be upset, I should be . . . I don't even know what I should be.

I don't know what's happening.

Logan leads me into the conference room, shuts the door, and twists a rod to close blinds. It is dark, suddenly, and quiet. There are no lights on in the conference room, so the only light is the ambient glow streaming in from the windows. The room is cool, air blowing on my skin from overhead. Most of the room is dominated by a long rectangular table and chairs, but there is a sectional couch in one corner. He takes a seat on the couch, and I sit beside him. I want to curl into him, nuzzle against him and forget everything.

He really must be telepathic, because he wraps a long arm around my shoulders and pulls me against him. At first, I only allow myself to lean against him. But I cannot sustain the façade for long, and I slump. Slide lower and lower, until I'm lying on his lap. There is nothing sexual about this. His hands sweep my hair aside, and then his fingers dig into my shoulder muscles and knead them with a firm but gentle touch. I moan involuntarily, melting under the massage.

"Just let go, Isabel. Relax. Let it all go."

"Caleb, he—"

"Hush, babe. Not now. There's plenty of time to tell me everything. For right now, you just need to relax."

"I don't know how," I admit.

"Don't think. Don't feel. Just focus on the feel of my hands."

I try it. I push aside the whirlwind of thoughts and shove down the maelstrom of emotions, and focus on Logan's hands on my shoulders, between my shoulder blades, down my spine, thumbs pressing into my lower lumbar, working back up. It isn't until he begins massaging me that I am even aware how tensed I am, that my muscles are all knotted up into painful boulders of stress. Moment by moment, however, I feel myself relaxing.

I smell him, faint cologne, deodorant, cinnamon and cigarettes. I feel his breathing, his chest expanding and retracting.

My breathing matches his.

I fade.

I feel a sense of spatial distortion as my eyes close, as if I'm tipping forward, as if my consciousness is leaving my body. I am heavy, limp. I spin, twist, tilt.

Logan's fingertip trails over my cheekbone, slides around my ear. I feel it distantly.

I am moments from succumbing to sleep when I hear him speak.

"You're safe now, Isabel," he murmurs. "I won't let you go. Not again."

I believe him.

He shifts, and my cheek touches leather warm from his body. Moments later, something warm and weighty is draped over me.

I have never been more comfortable in my life.

I let go.

wake sobbing.

Nightmares of sirens and flashing lights and a pair of cold cruel dark eyes staring haughty and inscrutable down at me as I am used like a receptacle. Nightmares of a perfect body pinning me to an elevator door. Sorcery, stealing my will, manipulating my desires, cool silk of a tie wiping my face. Rain cold and wet and windblown, shifting shadows and blood and pain.

My dream is pervaded by a voice: "Isabel, you're okay. It was just a dream."

Who is Isabel?

The voice is in my ear, soft and tender and warm. "I'm here, Isabel."

Oh, it's me. I'm Isabel.

I am Isabel; I have to remind myself that it is true.

I am lifted, cradled. I hear a heartbeat under my ear, feel soft cotton under my cheek. I am lying on top of him, as if he is my bed. His hands smooth in caressing circles on my back.

I cannot stop sobbing.

My eyes burn with hot tears, and I try to stop them, but I can't. "L-Logan—"

"Ssshhh. It's okay. I'm here."

"I'm sorry, I'm sorry—I can't—can't stop—"

"Don't apologize, sweetheart. Cry if you need to. I've got you. I won't let go."

I can only cling to him and cry. My whole body shakes with shuddering, wracking sobs, as if a lifetime of pent-up tears are being ripped out of me wholesale.

I don't know how long it lasts. Minutes? Hours? A measureless time of weeping. I think I have cried more in the last twelve hours than in all my life.

Eventually, I am able to breathe normally and the sobs and shudders fade.

I remain still, barely breathing now.

On top of Logan.

Aware of him, suddenly.

Completely attuned to every inch of him, stretched out beneath me. His arms around me, his chin tucked against the top of my head. His denim-sheathed thighs beneath mine, thick and hard. His breath on my hair. His hips nudging mine. My hands on his pectoral muscles, my breasts crushed against his sternum.

There is a shift then. A charge to the air. Electricity crackling.

And now, between one breath and the next, it *is* sexual, the way I'm lying on him.

I can't breathe again, but for a different reason.

I can't breathe for wanting him.

Needing him.

"Isabel . . ." he breathes.

"Logan—"

"I need you to get up," he says, and it isn't what I expected. "There are still some people working out there, and in a few more seconds I'm going to forget that."

"What would happen if you did, Logan?" I ask. I don't recognize the daring, the boldness, the raw hunger in my voice.

His fingers twine gently into my hair and pull, tipping my face up to his.

It's me, this time,

kissing him,

and kissing him,

and kissing him.

My fingers wrap around the back of his head, clinging to the nape of his neck, pulling him closer, pulling myself higher on his body, needing needing needing to be closer to him, to press my lips more completely against his, to taste him, to feel him. I breathe him. His hand, resting on my back, slides lower. I arch against him, press my body against his. There is no part of me that isn't touching him. I pause to breathe, gasping against his lips. I want more of me to touch more of him. I want all of him, all of me, all of us.

I crave completion, of a kind only Logan can provide.

He feathers his mouth against mine, a teasing brush of lips against lips, heat of breath on tasting tongue.

"That will happen," he whispers.

"Oh," I murmur.

"Yeah, oh." His fingers are tangled in my hair, applying gentle delicious pressure to my scalp, keeping my face tilted to his. "And now I can't stop."

"I don't want you to."

"I have to," he says. "Or there won't be any stopping at all."

"Logan . . ."

"I want you. I need you. But Isabel, you deserve better—*we* deserve better—than on a couch in my conference room, with a dozen people on the other side of the wall."

I ache. "You're right."

His erection is a thick presence between us, pressing into my belly.

I can't help but to writhe against him, to clutch his strong neck and seek more of him, to touch my lips to the edge of his jaw, inhale his scent and revel in the rough sandpaper of his stubble against my lips and sensitive skin.

He groans, a low rumble in his chest. I feel his palm cup my back, fingers dimpling across my spine, and now his touch slides lower. Lower. I don't dare breathe for the anticipation, waiting with aching lungs and thighs pressed tight together in a vain attempt to curb the pressure in my core. I wait, and exhale in delight as his palm ascends to follow the curve of my bottom. He murmurs wordlessly as his palm moves over the mounded taut muscle and squeezes.

"Jesus, Isabel." His voice sounds broken. "Your ass is amazing."

That compliment, those four words from this man, it means everything to me. I want to be the crux of his desire.

His other hand leaves my hair and steals down my spine to caress the other side of my bottom, so now both of his powerful hands are cupping my backside.

I have no coherent response to his statement, so I only writhe against him, kiss his cheekbone, clutch the back of his head with both hands and seek his mouth.

We kiss, and I know the taste and texture and glory of heaven.

Somehow, in my writhing, the hem of my dress rises. Rides higher. And then Logan's fingers tug the material up and his touch is against the bare skin of my bottom where it is revealed in the cut of my underwear, which is little more than a strap of lace across the upper swell of my backside and a triangle of silk over my core.

I press my knee into the couch, lifting my leg higher. Opening for him. Encouraging his touch to explore.

"How am I supposed to resist you when you do shit like that, Isabel?" The way he says my name feels like a verbal caress, as if his saying my name, those three chosen syllables, is a validation, an act of love.

His cupping hands carve lower, so his fingers tease the edges of my thighs, drifting lower and closer to my center. I can't breathe, oh god, I can't breathe, my lungs are seized and the only breath I can find is his. Mouth-to-mouth resuscitation, because I am dying from the ache within, the need burning like the seed of a star, the desire igniting like a nascent supernova.

"Don't resist, Logan," I whisper, belatedly.

He does not resist.

He exhales, the heat of his sigh bathing my lips. Fingers dare, traipse, delve. I bury my face into his throat and cling madly tightly fiercely to the column of his neck and the hard curve of his head, and push my knee higher. Fingertips, three of them I feel, dancing over the thin strip of silk, tugging it aside.

One finger, sliding into my cleft. I whimper against his skin. Quietly, desperately. That finger, thick and wonderfully rough, glides deep through wetness and through heat. Draws my essence across tender pink flesh and smears it over the throbbing bud of my clitoris. Pleasure jolts through me with such sudden ferocity that I involuntarily bite him, and he grunts.

"Sorry," I whisper, kiss the flesh where my teeth left indents. "I didn't mean to."

"Kitten's got teeth," Logan murmurs.

"I'm a lioness, Logan, isn't that what you told me?"

He rumbles a laugh. "I did say that, didn't I?" His finger delves into me once more, and I gasp. "Can you keep quiet?"

"I can try," I whisper. "But I might bite you again."

"Fine with me. I'll just bite you back." He places his teeth on the delicate skin on the side of my neck and bites down with exquisite gentility.

"That wasn't even a bite," I say.

"Of course not. I would never do anything to actually hurt you."

And then he withdraws his finger and smears it over my clitoris again, and I can't help but moan, muffling it against his throat. Again, finger sliding in, pulling out, rubbing over me. Again and again and again, until I'm aching with need for him to do more, touch me more.

"Logan," I whimper, "please . . ."

"I know, baby. Soon." Two fingers now, and I am breathing heavily against his throat, clutching his hair, his head, his shoulders.

My hips drive, seeking more.

Despite his promise of "soon," it is not soon. He draws it out. Explores me, scissors his fingers, thrusts them in, exploring my depth. Drawing out, testing the sensitivity of my clitoris, slipping it between his fingers, rubbing it, flicking it, pressing against it, touching me and touching me and touching me, but not enough that I can find release.

The more he touches me, the wilder my hips become. I bury my face in his flesh and moan ceaselessly, muffling the sound in him. At some point, the aimless thrash of my hips becomes a grinding, and god, finally, he fills me with three fingers and I grind against them, ride them.

Wantonly, I seek my release on his hand.

"Oh god, Logan . . ." I moan, and it is not a quiet sound.

"Sssshhhhh, baby. Hush. Bite me if you need to."

My teeth find the round part of his shoulder and sink in, and I taste salt flesh and flick my tongue across it, and the taste of him, the feel of his flesh and muscle under my mouth drives me even more wild. My entire body is rocking downward, pushing my core onto his fingers, driving the building tsunami of my orgasm to manic threshold.

I whimper, teeth locked onto Logan, and grind hard and fast around his fingers, which he thrusts into me.

And then, as I am close to losing it, he pulls them out and smashes them against my clit and I involuntarily arch my back, biting down on my scream so hard my molars ache. Logan's mouth finds mine, his tongue parts my lips, and he swallows my moans as I come apart. Heat blasts though me, lightning strikes my core and sizzles up throughout my body, curling my toes and causing my stomach to tense and my thighs to quiver, and I can only ride his touch with everything I possess, screaming into his breath, trying to quiet myself and failing.

"God, Isabel, baby, you come so beautifully," Logan murmurs. "I can't wait to watch you writhe like this naked for me, I can't wait to make you scream out loud."

His voice is catalytic, and I don't know if I come again, or if it's another wave of the first, but I am seized anew and his fingers are whirling faster than thought around my clitoris.

Finally, I am seeing stars, the orgasm fades, and I am left limp and wrung out, gasping. "Logan, my god Logan." The way I say that, it is ambiguous. It could mean that Logan is my god, that he has consumed my world and my belief, or it could just be a rushed-together colloquialism.

I am fully clothed, and so is he, and I've just come harder than ever before, harder than I thought possible.

Logan grabs the back of my knees and tugs them tight against his body, pulls me closer, and then rocks up and forward so I am flipped to land on my back. His eyes are hot, blazing, fierce, wild. His chest heaves, as if his control is hanging by the thinnest thread. He leans over me, his hair coming loose from the ponytail, blond curls and waves hanging over his shoulder. He dips down, kisses me. Deeply, thoroughly, so I am left utterly breathless and in no doubt as to his intentions.

Leaning back on his knees, he lifts his fingers to his mouth. I can only stare in amazement and confusion and crazed heated desire as he fits his index finger—the one that was just inside me—into his mouth and sucks my juices off. He repeats this with each finger that was inside me, his eyes never leaving mine.

"Really, Logan?"

He grins. "Really, Isabel. You taste amazing. I can't wait to have my mouth all over you."

I exhale shakily. "What do I taste like?" I hear myself ask, and it's a question I've long wondered but never had the courage to ask.

In previous encounters, questions and talking in general were . . . discouraged. My voice was heard only when I was commanded to raise it.

Logan doesn't answer, at least not in words. He pulls aside my underwear, slides a finger into me, smears my essence, and then brings that digit to my mouth. I smell musk, a sharp smell with a tang to it. And his finger moves between my lips, mirroring the way he just touched me down below. I taste his skin faintly and myself strongly.

"That's what you taste like," he says, then rises to his feet. His hands grasp mine and he hauls me upright. "Time to go."

"Where are we going?" I ask, even though I know.

"My place."

I can't help but glance down at the front of his jeans, which are visibly tented. I move toward him, wrap my arms around his neck, and then let a palm trail down his chest to the waist of his jeans. "Let me help you, first."

He grabs my wrist, gently but firmly, and pulls my hand away. "I don't think so, Isabel." He tugs me sharply so I land flush against his chest. "All I care about is making you feel good. I could, and nearly did, come in my pants just watching you. When I've got you naked in my bed, I'll get mine, trust me."

"Doesn't that ache? To stay hard like that?"

He shrugs. "A little. It'll fade, and I'll be none the worse for wear."

"I want you to feel good too, Logan."

His lips touch my throat, under my jaw, the corner of my mouth. "I will." He puts his mouth to my ear and whispers. "I want you so bad, Isabel, so bad it hurts. But I also value our privacy enough that I'll wait until I've got you alone at my house to let this go any further. If you touch me, any remaining vestige of control I might have will be gone."

I'm frustrated, because my need for him is spiraling out of control. I want his flesh, I want to touch his hardness, taste him, feel him. I want him more than I've ever wanted anything. Nothing matters but him.

Nothing matters but *us.*

This is about us, too. Not just him, not just me, but the both of us as a single entity, and that fact in itself is drunk-making.

He takes my hand, threads his fingers through mine. Leads me out of the conference room. It's night, but what time I don't know. The lights are dimmed low so the TVs provide most of the light in the office space. Pretty much everyone is still present, although all of them except three people are asleep on couches and curled up in beanbags. The three left awake glance at us as we exit the conference room hand in hand, and all three keep their expressions carefully blank and return a bit too studiously to the documents they're poring over.

I lean closer to Logan. "I think they heard us," I whisper.

He chuckles and squeezes my hand. "Actually, honey, I think they heard *you*."

I blush furiously. "I'm sorry, Logan. I tried to be quiet."

"No worries," he says as we exit the building and he leads me down Forty-fifth to his vehicle. "They'll be adults about it or they'll find another job."

"I don't want to cost anyone their jobs," I say. "It's my fault I was loud."

"It's my company, my conference room. And also, I'm pretty sure I heard Beth and Isaac in there yesterday. Either that, or they were watching porn together instead of working."

"You let your employees have sex and watch porn while working?"

"Hell no." His truck, a big silver box on wheels I've been in once before, is parallel parked half a block away. It's a Mercedes-Benz G63 AMG, I note. I wonder how much it cost; a lot, is my guess. "The computers and other devices provided by the company are for work use only, and I carefully monitor that. Porn is how you get wicked viruses, for one thing, and I don't mean of the STD variety. As for sex, as long as they're discreet and it doesn't affect their working relationship, I don't give a flying fuck what they do, or where they do it."

"You're a good boss," I say, buckling in.

"I try. Basically, I remember how shit ran in the army, and I try to be exactly the opposite." He laughs, although I don't quite get the joke. "That's only partially true. I learned lots of valuable skills in the army, including how to run a tight-knit group of people. You give them a small number of hard-and-fast rules that cannot be broken, and leave everything else up to them. In the atmosphere I've created up there, I can use a small space and a relatively small group of employees to get a ridiculously massive amount of work done. I pay them a fuckload of money, keep the mood loose and relaxed, let them work on their own time and at their own pace, sitting, standing, lying down, buzzed, whatever, as long as the quality of their work remains consistent."

"Must be nice for them."

"I hope so," he says, checking oncoming traffic and pulling out into the street. "That's the point. I want them to *want* to come to work. I require long, crazy hours, which usually entails sleeping at the office during sixty-hour marathon sessions like this one, but I pay triple overtime and huge bonuses at the end of projects like this. What you saw is my entire company, the core of it. I've got a couple other subsidiary offices in the city, and some others in L.A. and London, but those are all totally self-sufficient and don't require any input from me. Those kids up there, they're my business. All the subsidiaries, all the offshoots and spin-off branches, they run it all."

"They must work nonstop." I don't even try to follow the series of turns Logan takes to get home. I just enjoy the fact that as soon as he finishes a turn, his hand takes mine again and threads our fingers together.

His hand feels natural in mine, and that makes my heart hammer.

"They do. Sixty hours a week is standard fare, eighty or more common. And when we have a huge project like this acquisition, we basically live at the office until it's done, but then we take a few days off. Or rather, I give them a few days off."

"You don't take days off?"

He shrugs. "Not really. I'm not really a workaholic, but I like what I do, so I do it a lot. I stay home Sundays, for the most part."

"What do you do for fun?"

He eyes me. "Work out, Krav Maga, run, watch movies."

"You don't have a girlfriend?"

A shrug, eyes returning to the road. "No. I did, for a while, but it wasn't really serious. When she made it clear she needed to either get serious or move on, we broke up. It was amicable, and I was honest. I wasn't going to string her along or lie about not wanting anything super serious."

"Why didn't you want anything serious?" I ask.

We're on his street, which I recognize. It's a long, quiet, tree-lined avenue of walk-up town houses, lovely, expensive, and serene, an insular little world away from the bustle of midtown Manhattan.

He sighs. "I just didn't. She was a great girl, sweet, smart, beautiful, easy to hang out with. But it just wasn't there with her, for me, long-term speaking. I don't know. I don't really have any emotional hang-ups, you know? I'm just not going to tie myself down long-term unless I'm really sure about it. It's not fair to me, or to her, or the idea of an 'us.' A long-term relationship is only as valuable as the effort both people are willing to put in. You both have to be totally invested or it doesn't work. I was in a relationship for a while, right after I got out of the hospital, and I was all in, right? Like, gone for the girl. She was fucking *it* for me, but I was needy, I guess. Too needy for her. She wasn't feeling it. So after like, a year and a half, she broke up with me via the super awesome tactic of sleeping with my business-partner-slash-house-flipping-mentor, and then telling me about it. I was still pretty fucked up about how I got injured, you know, the guilt and confusion and everything. I'm not gonna toss out PTSD, because it's not that. I know guys who have that, and it's not pretty. I was normal fucked up. Real-deal clinical PTSD is ugly fucked up."

"And now?"

"Now I'm okay. You never completely get away from the bad dreams and occasional flashbacks, but you gotta expect that, seeing and doing the kind of shit we did over there." He pulls the big SUV into a parking spot outside his door, exits, and circles around to open my door for me. "When I said I don't have any emotional hang-ups, that was a little bit of a lie. I do, sort of, because of how Leanne ended things. I don't trust easily. But that wasn't the reason why I didn't want anything long-term with Billie. I trusted her all right, I just didn't feel strongly enough to move in together or propose, I guess, and that's exactly what she wanted. I was cool with just dating, having fun, spending the night together here and there."

He unlocks the front door of his house, disables his alarm, and closes the door behind us. At this point his dog, Cocoa, a massive chocolate lab, is going crazy, barking fit to burst.

"I'm gonna let Cocoa out now, okay? You ready?"

I nod and take a breath, grinning in anticipation. "As ready as I'll ever be, I think."

He goes down a short hallway and opens a bedroom door, and the sound of claws scrabbling on hardwood echoes loudly, accompanied by overjoyed barking, and then finally a bear-sized brown blur hurtles toward me. I'm braced for impact, though, and Cocoa's saucer-sized paws land on my shoulders and her tongue is slapping me in the face and digging up my nose and trying to do an examination of my uvula. I duck my face to escape her tongue, but she follows me, leaning down to lick and lick and lick, until finally I have to shove her off. She leaps back up and actually hugs me, her paws going over my shoulder, her nose wet in my ear. I can't help but laugh and feel happy about such an exuberant welcome.

The affectionate joy of a happy dog is balm for a troubled soul, I decide.

Logan slaps his thigh. "Cocoa! Wanna go outside?"

The dog's attention is snatched by that, and she barks once, a short sharp yip, and hauls across the house for the back door. He lets her out, watches her do her business, and then lets her back in, and she lies down on the floor in the middle of the kitchen near the stove, watching us with her big brown eyes.

He glances at me. "You hungry? I've got some leftover shawarma, and half a pizza." He opens a drawer in the island at the center of the kitchen and withdraws a stack of carryout menus. "Or I could get some takeout. Up to you."

"What's shawarma?" I ask.

"Middle Eastern food. Garlic sauce, chicken, rice. It's amazing."

I hate to admit that my diet has always been somewhat . . . limited. "Either is fine." Mostly because I've never had either, and I don't want Logan to leave, and I don't want to have to leave this house again any time soon.

He lifts an eyebrow. "How about I heat up both, and you can try them and pick. I'll take whichever you don't want."

He rummages in the refrigerator and comes out with a plastic container and a big white square cardboard box. Dumping the contents of the container onto a paper plate, he puts it in the microwave and warms it up, and then transfers the contents of the larger box onto another plate. As the shawarma heats up, the smell begins to permeate the kitchen, and my stomach rumbles. I don't remember the last time I ate, and suddenly I'm ravenous. The microwave beeps, and he slides the plate to me across the island, setting a fork on it as he does so.

"Give that a try," he says, and sets the pizza to heating.

The shawarma is possibly the most delicious thing I've ever eaten. Spicy, flavorful, tangy, garlicky. I moan as I take the first bite, and then the second. And then the third.

"So you like shawarma," Logan says, grinning. He pulls a piece of the pizza off the plate and carefully hands it to me, a string of cheese stretching between us.

The pizza is also delicious.

"I'm not sure I can choose," I admit. "They're both so good."

There's a stool under an overhanging part of the island, and I pull it out and sit down. Logan takes the stool beside me, setting down two sweating green glass bottles with white labels near the top.

"So we'll share," he says, and steals the fork out of my hands to take a bite of the shawarma. I watch him eat, because he's gorgeous even doing that.

"What's in the bottles?" I ask, eager to try something else new.

"Beer. Stella Artois, to be exact. Try it." He hands me one of the bottles, and I gingerly try the first sip.

I'm not convinced at first. It's bitter, and a little sour. But there's an aftertaste that hits my taste buds in a pleasant way, and I try a second, longer sip, which goes down easier. Before I know it, I've drunk almost half of the bottle, and my head is feeling a little loose and a little fuzzy.

Logan laughs. "Whoa, okay. I guess you like Stella. But then, how can you not?" He gestures at the pizza. "Try the pizza, and wash it down with the beer. You'll never look at cuisine the same way, I promise."

"I already don't," I say. "I've always been on an all-organic, super healthy diet."

"Vegan?"

"What's that?"

"No meat, no animal products of any kind. Like eggs, milk, cheese, if it came from an animal, vegans don't consume it."

"Why?" I ask. "That's kind of weird."

"Protesting animal cruelty in the food industry. I don't know. Good for them if that's what they believe, but I like meat."

"Me too. So no, I eat meat, just usually salmon and free-range chicken and turkey, along with salads and fruit. Mostly vegetarian, I suppose. Not a lot of red meat."

"I'd go easy on the pizza then. If your body is used to cleaner foods, the grease in that might sit heavy in your stomach."

This is so weird. Bizarre. Surreal. Just sitting in Logan's kitchen, drinking beer and eating normal food.

I have a normal name.

I'm not Madame X anymore.

I'm not with Caleb anymore.

My heart twists at that last thought, and I shut that line of thought down. I will *not* go there, not now.

Except Logan speaks up, casually, not looking at me, through a bite of shawarma. "What happened, Isabel? With Caleb? What made you leave, finally?"

I sigh. "He—we . . ."

Logan interrupts before I can work out what I'm going to say. "I don't want to pry, and I'll respect your privacy if you don't want to talk about it. But it seemed to have messed you up."

I finish a slice of pizza and wash it down with a swallow of the beer. And Logan is right, I don't think I'll ever be able to eat my normal fare again without thinking of this meal. Indulgent, unhealthy in the extreme, but so, *so* good. I take a bite of shawarma, trying to formulate what to say.

"He brought me back to his place. The penthouse? It's the entire upper floor of the building. Anyway, he brought me up there, and at first it was . . . fine. But not normal. He kissed me, which he doesn't usually do. That was a little strange. And then . . ." I sigh again, closing my eyes. Just say it. Just put it into words. "But then he pushed me down to my knees. He put . . . himself—into my mouth." It's so hard to say it out loud. Why? It feels as if saying it makes it more real. More than real. "At the end, he finished on—on my face. And then cleaned me up with his tie, kissed me as if nothing had happened, and just . . . left."

"That's rape, Isabel."

I have to shake my head. "It wasn't. Not entirely." I tremble. "But then, it also was. I don't know. It's all so confusing with him. He gets in my head, and makes all my thoughts somehow . . . not make sense. Not . . . my own. I don't know. He's all I've ever known, from the moment I first woke up. It's always been him."

"So before, in my conference room—"

"I *wanted* that, Logan. Please believe me. I wanted it so badly. I loved every single second of it. The way you touch me, the way you kiss me, I've never known anything like it and I'm crazy for it." I spin on the stool so I'm facing him, grab his knees as he twists to face me.

He eyes me carefully, his blueblueblue eyes seeing into my soul. "Don't ever lie to me, or tell me what you think I want to hear. Okay? Please? I'd rather hear the unpleasant truth than an easy lie."

"I promise I will always be truthful with you."

We've somehow finished all the food and both beers, and Logan slaps the countertop rather suddenly. "Movie time."

"What?" I'm baffled by the sudden change in topic.

"I swore to you that I'd bring you home, feed you beer and pizza, and binge-watch movies with you." He nudges an empty bottle. "We've had the beer and pizza, so now it's time for a movie."

"Okay." I don't know how to say that as much as I want to watch movies with him, I want to finish what we started in the conference room even more.

He takes my hand and leads me to his bedroom, which I haven't seen yet. It's simple but beautiful, and comfortable, like the rest of the home. Muted green paint on the walls, thick dark carpeting on the floor, exposed beams on the ceiling, a wide bed on a high, dark wood frame, a flatscreen TV mounted on the wall opposite.

He gestures to the bed. "Only place to watch TV, so get comfy."

I smooth my dress over my hips with my palms, a nervous gesture. "Okay."

The bed is high, and my dress isn't really made for climbing. At least not gracefully or modestly. I try to slide up onto the bed backward, keeping my knees pressed together. I'm not sure why I'm trying to be modest, considering what we did not that long ago, where his fingers were, but it feels necessary. I don't quite make it, and only end up pressing my backside against the edge of the mattress and wiggling gracelessly. I try to catch a foot on the edge of the frame, but I can't quite manage that either, not without flashing Logan. Especially not wearing heels.

He laughs, and I can't help but laugh too, because my efforts to get on the bed were rather comical. "Isabel, honey. That dress is gorgeous, don't get me wrong. But . . . would you like something else to wear? A shirt of mine, maybe?"

"Wouldn't your shirt be rather large on me?" I ask.

He nods. "That's kind of the point. It'd be like a nightgown."

"Sure. I'll try that." I manage to sound casual, but the idea of wearing one of Logan's shirts has my stomach in twisting knots.

He pulls open a drawer of the bureau underneath the TV, pulls out a neatly folded black T-shirt, hands it to me. "That's one of my favorite shirts. I've had it since I was in high school. It's really soft and comfy, so . . . yeah." He turns away. "I'll give you a second to change."

I kick off my shoes, and my feet immediately thank me. Logan is at the bedroom door, rubbing the back of his neck, and I realize that by giving me a moment to change he meant he'd leave me alone.

"You . . . um . . ." I pause to rally my nerves. "You don't have to leave, Logan."

He stops, his hand on the doorknob. "I'm not making any assumptions, Isabel. This whole thing happens on your time, okay?"

"You've already seen me naked, Logan."

"Doesn't mean I'm going to just assume you're okay with me watching you change. That's kind of intimate."

"So is what we did in your conference room."

A smile crosses his face. "True." He puts his back to the bedroom door. "I'll stay, if you want me to."

"I don't mind," I say, reaching up behind my back to tug down the zipper of my dress. "I don't really want you to leave, if I'm being honest."

I can't quite reach the tab of the zipper, though, without contorting. Logan crosses the room in three long strides and stands behind me. "Let me."

His fingers touch the back of my neck, brush my hair over my shoulder, and I feel my dress loosen as he pulls the zipper down.

I expect more, but I feel him step back. "There."

I pivot to face him. His eyes rake over me, and I cannot mistake the hunger for me that I see there. "Logan," I start, not quite sure what I was going to say.

There's nothing *to* say, I decide. I keep my eyes locked on his as I shrug my shoulders, letting the garment droop forward to hang from my arms, which are bent at the elbow, clutching my belly. I'm nervous, but I'm not going to let that get in the way. I palm my thighs, and my dress pools on the floor around my feet.

Logan's eyes immediately devour my body, and he draws in a ragged breath. "You are *so* beautiful, Isabel."

"I'm not even naked," I say, uncomfortable with compliments.

"You don't have to be naked to be beautiful, you know." He takes a step toward me, and his fingers touch my waist. "You're so sexy, just like this, in your underwear."

My cheeks flame, and I duck my head, unable to sustain the eye contact. "Thank you." It's all I can summon.

I latch onto his wrist with my fingers, so he can't escape. He doesn't try, just flattens his palm against my spine, directly at the center of my back. He's not touching me sexually, I notice. Avoiding any erogenous zones. For me, or for himself?

The next step, other than throwing myself at him, is to finish undressing. I swallow my fear. I know he's not rejecting me, I know that he's being respectful and giving me time, which I should need, considering what happened not that long ago. But all I can think of is his kiss, his mouth on mine; all I want is his touch, to come again, for him. To feel him. To make *him* come. I want to know what he looks like when he loses control.

I reach up behind my back and unhook the first eyelet, and then the second, and then the third. I don't give myself time to think, I just slide my arms out of the straps and toss the bra to the floor. His nearly iridescent indigo eyes rake down from my face to my breasts, and my nipples harden under his gaze. They harden so fast they ache. I can feel my heartbeat in my chest like thundering drums, hear nothing but my pulse in my ears. Sliding my thumbs into the elastic waistband of my underwear, I shimmy them down over my hips, and it's hard to breathe, and I don't dare look anywhere but at the floor.

The silk and lace fall to my ankles, and I'm naked.

I've been naked in front of Logan once before, but that was accidental. Sort of. Whatever that was, it's different than intentionally, purposefully removing all my clothes so Logan can look at my nude body. This is making a statement.

"Fuck . . . Isabel . . . you're so insanely sexy it's hard to breathe when I look at you." His voice is a silken murmur.

I summon every ounce of courage I have. I reach for him. My index finger hooks in his belt loop and I pull him closer. His eyes narrow and his nostrils flare and his Adam's apple bobs. I feel need, such blazing, furious, undeniable need. I am on fire with need. The tips of my breasts brush his chest, and I drag my fingernails upward between us, catching the hem of his T-shirt and lifting it up. His arms go up, and I carefully work the shirt off, tossing it aside. Shirtless now, Logan is breathtaking. As in, looking at him, I can't breathe.

My hands are moving of their own accord. They find the loop-and-button of his jeans, slip the button free. He is motionless, staring at me, breathing heavily. My fingers clasp the tab pull of his zipper and lower it, and now his bulge spills out of the opening. My throat clogs. My breathing stops.

He just blinks at me and remains still.

I push the denim down, and Logan steps out of his pants. His underwear is gray, tight stretchy cotton molded to his body. I cannot look away from his groin, from the outline of his penis bulging and thickening as I stare at him. He inhales deeply, and his brows furrow as I reach for him one last time, slipping my index and middle fingers of each hand between the elastic and his flesh, running them around the circumference of his torso, and my fingertip brushes the crest of his erection. He flinches at this contact, and sucks his belly in. I tug down, and his shaft sways free as the fabric releases him. A lift of each foot, and Logan is naked with me.

We are naked together.

I feel giddy, and terrified.

I have to touch him. My palms roam across his chest, down his sides, and carve around to clutch his buttocks. Pull him closer. He lets out a breath, palms my hip, and then his lips touch my shoulder.

"Logan," I breathe. It is a plea, and he knows it.

His mouth descends, crossing my breastbone, and he bends, kissing the slope of my right breast. Strong fingers trail up from my hip, and he cups my breast from beneath and lifts it to his mouth. His touch is gentle, his mouth warm and wet. I moan at the feel of my nipple being flattened in his mouth, the feel of his tongue flicking over it, striking a chord of desire within me. Stoking the flames.

Just as I'm about to reach for his erection, he backs away. His gaze glints, gleams.

"Lie down on the bed, Isabel." His voice is soft, as warm as it always is, yet now insistent as well.

I back up. My bottom bumps up against the mattress, and I lift myself up onto it. Lie back. Shimmy backward so my head is on the pillow. Breathe hard, my breasts rising and falling, swaying, shaking with each breath. My nipples hurt. My core aches. I am drenched. I do not mean to, but I find myself posing for Logan. One hand threaded through my thick black hair, one foot planted, knee up, thighs touching to block his view of my privates, my other arm barred across my chest.

He, naked, hard, just stands and stares at me for a moment, and I stare back.

He is glorious.

Tattoos, a jumble of images, sleeve his arms from shoulder to elbow. His hair is loose and wavy, curling at the ends, hanging down his shoulders. His body is a warrior's body, whipcord lean, hard as diamonds and sharp as a blade, every muscle defined as if etched by a razor into marble. His manhood is . . . I bite my lower lip as I stare at it. Longer than it has any right to be, thicker than I'd expected, a very subtle inward curve to it. I want to touch him, wrap my fingers around him and put my mouth on him and feel him against my tongue, taste his skin; I want to guide him to me and feel him penetrate me.

I want him. I *want* him.

I let my knees spread apart, and he growls.

Climbs onto the bed. Kneels between my thighs, leans over me, one palm in the mattress beside my face, the other burying in my hair. His lips brush mine, a tease.

Not a kiss, yet, but a tease.

A lick of his tongue, flicking against my lower lip, where I'd bitten it.

I remember putting a glass of whisky to my lips, putting my mouth where his had been. I remember the taste of the whisky against my tongue, the burn on my throat, the way I wanted it to be his mouth on mine.

His fingers spear through my hair and scrape downward to cup the back of my head, and he lifts me up, brings my mouth to his,

and kisses me,

and kisses me,

and does not stop for an eternity.

Not until we are both breathless and his tongue has tasted every corner of my mouth, has licked across both of my lips, has slashed against my tongue, not until I cannot help but pull away just so I can breathe.

That is when he leans back, slides his palms over my shoulders, down to the slopes of my breasts. Cups their weight. Thumbs both of my nipples at once. Bends, kisses the skin between my breasts.

"You deserve to be worshipped, Isabel," he says. "You deserve to be shown how perfect you are."

NINE

have to blink back a surprised wash of intense emotion: wonder, embarrassment, need, tenderness, raw lust.

I find my voice, and my own words surprise me. "Then worship me, Logan. Show me."

He licks my nipple and plunges a middle finger into my cleft. "I'm going to." A curl, a come-here motion with his finger, and I cannot stop a moan. "Be loud for me, Isabel. I want to hear every sound you make."

Mouth latched onto my nipple, one hand between my thighs, he cups my breast with his other. Sucks, swirls his tongue around my nipple. And then pulls away. His finger slides out of my opening and brings my essence with it, smearing it onto my clitoris. I ache, oh I ache. I'm going to come again. Soon, and hard.

As he finds a circling rhythm, slow and soft touches of two fingers against my throbbing clit, he alternates kissing and suckling both of my breasts, one and the other, one and the other. Tension coils inside me, centered low in my belly. I tighten. Curl up, knees rising, and he does not speed up his rhythmic touching of my most sensitive flesh. I am moaning, I realize. Nonstop. Aching. Needing. Feeling his touch and needing more.

"Can I taste you, Isabel?" Logan asks.

"Please, Logan."

"Please what? Tell me what you want, sweetheart, and I'll give it to you."

"Taste me. Make me come. Touch me. Let me touch you."

He kisses his way down my body. Sternum. Belly. Hip. Thigh. Over and over, he kisses my body, not missing anywhere. He lifts my left leg and kisses the back of my knee, and I whimper at the soft warm touch of lips there, and then he's flicking his tongue and sliding his mouth over my thigh, and I moan. A single flick of his tongue over my nether lips, and I'm writhing, gasping. But he doesn't give me what I need, not yet. He transfers his kisses to my other thigh, kissing downward now, to my calf, lips feathering over my ankle.

"Logan . . ." I gasp.

"I know, honey. But I told you that you deserve to be worshipped. Let me worship you." And he kisses the top of my foot.

Now his mouth travels back toward my core, over the top of my thigh, lips landing on the crease where hip meets leg, such an erogenous spot. Inward. To the mound just above my privates. To the very top of my core, and his tongue laps out, licks the very crest of my core, where my labia meet.

"Oh god. Logan, yes. Please. *Please.*" I am breathless, gasping each word. Begging. He makes me beg, just by the way he touches me, kisses me.

He fits two fingers into my opening, slides them deep. Curls them, withdraws, inserts. Starts a thrusting rhythm. His tongue lashes against my clit, and I writhe into his tongue, into his tongue, into his fingers. Move against him shamelessly. Bury my fingers in my hair, grip it, lift my hips.

"Can you come?" he murmurs.

"So close."

"How close?"

I can only whimper wordlessly and arch off the bed and grind against his mouth and fingers. His mouth covers my core now, and he sucks my clitoris between his lips and creates a suction, flicking it with his tongue, sliding his fingers in and out, in and out, and his free hand reaches up to pinch my nipple.

"Now, Isabel. Come for me, right now. Let me feel you squeeze around my fingers, baby. Let me feel you come so hard you can't breathe." His words are the catalyst I need. "Ride my fingers, ride my mouth. Take it from me."

I gasp, and lights flash behind my squeezed-shut eyes. The tension in my belly breaks apart, and I'm crying out loud. I bear down, clenching around his fingers with all the force I can muster, and then all control is gone as he matches my desperate rhythm with his mouth, with his tongue, with his fingers, taking me to the upper reaches of my climax and pushing me past it, to a place I didn't know existed.

"Yeah, that's right, just like that. Scream for me. Come for me." He whispers against my flesh. "You are so fucking beautiful, Isabel, so sexy, so fucking sexy."

I come down, and he's kneeling upright. Watching me. I'm sweaty, gasping. My breasts sway with my heaving breaths, and he watches their motion openly.

I'm still shaking, trembling from the force of my orgasm.

"I want to touch you now, Logan." I sit up. Reach for him.

He moves closer to me, kneels astride me. Gazes down at me. His erection is in front of my face, his hands on my shoulders. "Touch me then."

I tear my eyes from his and allow my gaze to roam his body, tracing the wild profusion of his tattooed arms. There are pinup girls, playing cards, crossed assault rifles, Old English–style lettering, sparrows, spiders, skulls, handguns, characters that must be from movies, masks, all woven together and growing out of a tree trunk whose roots spread around his biceps and the crease of his elbow.

I look down then, down to his erection.

I wrap one hand around it, slide my palm down the soft flesh to the base, and then circle my other hand around him, spanning most of his length, although a bit of the head protrudes above my upper hand. I lick him there, flatten my tongue over the tip of him. He groans, and his grip tightens on my shoulders. I glide my palms up, and then down. Let go with one hand and stroke his length from tip to base, over and over, learning the feel of him, the way he fills my fist, the way his skin slides and stretches. How he moans, what makes him grunt. I squeeze gently, and he gasps. I have nothing within me but desire. Need. I want all of him.

I wrap my lips around him, fit my lips to the groove under the bulbous head. He moans, a long, sustained growl. "Isabel. Don't."

"I want to."

He pulls back, sinks to sit on his heels. "Let me taste you again."

I shake my head. "I want you, Logan. I want to touch you. I want to make you feel good. I want this."

"But what happened—"

"Had nothing to do with you. Has nothing to do with how much I want you." I lean into him, kiss his mouth. "Lie down and let me worship you too, Logan."

He moves to his back, pillowing one hand beneath his head, reaching for me with the other. "I want this to be about you, Isabel."

"It is. This is what I want."

I take my time then. I start at his sharp, high cheekbones, kissing each one, and then kiss his mouth, lick his lower lip, the upper. Take his tongue into my mouth and suckle it. Kiss his throat. His chest. Flick my tongue over each of his nipples, run it along the grooves under his pectoral muscles, through the ridges of his rippling abs. Down, down. To his hips. Palm his hips, flatten my hands on his belly. Run them up, smooth them back down to his thighs. Kiss down one, as he did mine. Proving to him that his body is as beautiful to me as mine is to him. I memorize him. The taste of him. The sight of him, stretched out beneath me, his lean body hard and radiating lust, oozing masculine sex appeal. I take him in my hand, caress his shaft. Take my time with that too, enjoying the feel of him in my hand more than I have ever enjoyed anything in my life. More than junk food, more than freedom, more than antique books, just touching him and kissing him is better than anything I've ever known.

I am overwhelmed, so full of joy and exuberance and gratitude and raw fierce lust that I cannot contain it. I sink my mouth around him, sudden and fast. Take him deep into my mouth, opening my throat and tasting him on my tongue. He groans, shudders. I back away and replace mouth with fist, smearing my saliva on him. Stroke him. Faster and faster.

Feel him tremble under me, feel his moans in his chest, hear them echo in the bedroom.

I know he's close. I can feel it, taste it in the leak of clear fluid from the tip as I lick him, suckle him, feather kisses to the side, lick up the length. He throbs at my touch, thickens between my lips.

"You taste so good, Logan," I hear myself say. "Let go, let me taste you on my tongue. Give it all to me."

Who is this, speaking this way? I have never said such words. I have never even thought such words. Yet they pour from my mouth, and they sound sexy. *I* sound sexy. I sound worldly. Womanly. Sensual.

"Is—Isabel." He is out of breath, his voice tense. "Jesus, what are you doing to me?"

"Making you feel good, I hope."

"This isn't feeling good, Is, this is heaven."

Is. Like, a diminutive? A nickname? "Is?"

"You don't want me to call you that?"

"No, I do. I like it."

"Is. Izzy?"

"Is. I like that."

Abruptly, Logan rolls us so I'm beneath him. Kneels between my thighs, staring at me, chest heaving. The tip of his penis leaks fluid, evidence of his nearness to climax. "Will you do something for me?"

"Anything." I mean it, too. I will do anything he asks of me. It's crazy to feel so strongly so quickly, but I do.

"Touch yourself."

I've touched myself before, of course. In the dead of night, awake, unable to sleep, wrestling with old nightmares and new needs, I have touched myself. But I've always been vaguely ashamed of it, for some reason.

To touch myself in front of him? While he watches? My chest contracts and my skin feels too tight on my bones, and my heart hammers. I tingle. Blink at him. Press my thighs together.

"Logan, I don't know . . ." I whisper, not able to look at him. "I don't know if I can."

"I want to watch you make yourself feel good. It'll be so sexy, watching you." He sinks to sit on his shins, and his erection juts high and hard and proud. It is huge, and begs for my fingers, my lips. My core. "Like this, Is. Watch me."

He wraps one hand around his thick shaft, and his fist looks so hard and so big like that, so rough. It should be my hand there, not his. But it *is* hot, watching him. He strokes himself slowly, one pump of his fist. The head protrudes, and the skin stretches backward, and then he brings his hand back up. He thumbs the tip, and then plunges his fist down again.

Oh.

Oh, god. His face, as he does this. The way his eyes narrow. His jaw clenches. His chest expands and contracts heavily. His testicles hang and sway beneath his fist.

It is almost involuntary then, how my fingers steal across my belly and between my thighs. My core aches, watching him pleasure himself. I throb, tingle, burn. I have to touch myself, if only to alleviate the pressure. A bolt of lightning strikes me as I touch three fingers to my clitoris.

Swipe, circle, press.

My breath hitches, and I stare into his eyes, force myself to remain open, to splay my thighs wide and tuck my heels against my buttocks, to let him watch. And oh, oh, god, yes, it *is* erotic, *so* sexy. Touching my privates and knowing he's watching. Seeing him do the same. The intimacy binds us. I cannot look away, cannot stop. I'm rising toward climax, a mountain of heat washing over me, a tidal wave of intensity crashing through me. And I'm watching his fist pump harder and harder, and his touch is so rough, so harsh, so vigorous. I would be gentler, softer. I would caress him with such gentility, such exquisite tenderness.

I keep one hand between my thighs, stroking myself in ever-quickening circles, but I *have* to touch him. I knock his hand away and replace it with mine. I stroke us both, and he watches.

My hand is a plunging blur around his thickness, pumping up and down and up and down, faster and faster. He's groaning, and I'm whimpering, and he's thrusting into my hand, rutting hard into my fist. I'm grinding against my fingers, and I feel my climax approaching, feel it like not just mountains about to collide, but continents moments away from smashing into each other. I cannot breathe and cannot stop, and all I see is his face, his incredible blue eyes and his heaving chest and his tattoos and his erection in my hand, and my own fingers circling desperately.

"Oh fuck, Isabel. I'm so close," he grunts between clenched teeth. "I love watching your hand on my cock."

Cock. His cock. A new word. I've heard it, of course, but I've never said it. "I love touching your cock. I can't wait to watch you come, Logan."

"You talk dirty like that, I'm gonna come even sooner."

"You like it when I say those things?"

"Fuck yeah," he rumbles. "It's hot. Everything you do is hot. But this? Hottest fucking thing ever."

I'm stroking him hard and fast, plunging my fist down his length as fast as I can. When he starts to grunt and I watch his jaw clench and feel his cock throb in my fist, I slow.

"Fuck, Isabel, I'm right there, please don't stop."

"I'm not stopping," I whisper. "I promise."

I want to watch this. Feel it. Experience every moment of his orgasm, and the delirious joy of knowing I'm giving it to him. Nothing matters now but bringing Logan to orgasm.

I feel it begin.

I'm feathering slow, soft, gentle strokes, shallow ones, and he's going mad, thrusting, and I know he wants it hard and fast, but I know he'll feel it all the more intensely if I give it to him slow and gentle. And I want to make it last. For me. This is selfish, what I'm doing. Dragging it out. Memorizing it.

So good.

I'm still touching myself too, and I'm reaching climax as well, but that's subsumed beneath the tsunami of ecstasy I feel watching him.

Sweat dots his upper lip, his forehead. Shines on his chest. His hands are on my thighs for balance as he thrusts up into my fist, seeking more.

"Oh . . . Oh fuck. Isabel . . ." His voice is ragged, guttural.

I pull him closer, and he rises up, plants a knee on either side of my body, and now I can taste him and touch him at the same time. I take him into my mouth and stroke him at the root and finger my clit and groan, and he gasps. I feel him tense, feel his body tighten.

"I'm coming, Is . . ." he groans.

"Mmmmmmm." It's all I can manage, because I'm writhing with my own climax and because I'm too carried away with his to form words, and because I've got his cock filling my mouth.

He thrusts, and I like it.

I taste him.

But I want to watch.

I back away and he's kneeling upright, grasping the headboard of the bed while I'm lying down. I stare up at him, and his eyes fly open to meet mine. I finger myself and feel climax rip through me, and it's a hot knife slicing me apart.

I'm bucking and writhing, coming, coming, coming, moaning, whimpering.

And then Logan comes.

He grunts, and his seed gushes out of him. I watch it spurt between my fingers and slide over my knuckles and splash onto my breasts. He watches this as well, and groans, thrusts hard into my hand, and I lean up and take him into my mouth and suckle as he grunts a curse, thrusting into my mouth.

Orgasming still, now shooting his come onto my tongue.

I taste his essence, smoky and thick and salty, and I like it.

He's got more, and I want to watch him come some more.

So I let him fall out of my mouth and caress his length, plunge my fist to his base and pump him hard, and another jet of semen shoots out of him and onto my breasts in a white-hot sticky line on my skin.

So much come, and looking up at him, watching him thrust, I see that he's not yet done.

I mouth his cock and taste skin and semen, take him deep and suck and stroke his root and cup his testicles and touch him and suck him and take the come that lands on my tongue and swallow it and suckle him yet more.

I let him fall free one last time and he sags, and a droplet leaks out of him; with his eyes on mine, I lean forward, extend my tongue, and lick it away.

"Jesus, Isabel," he growls.

"You taste amazing, Logan."

I have my hand around him, still, and don't want to let go.

He's lowering himself to lie down, though, so I have to let go. A moment of silence then, wild and fraught, as we lie side by side.

He gets up, leaves without explanation. I hear water running, and he returns with a washcloth. I reach for it, but he just shakes his head, takes my hand in his, and gently, tenderly washes his sticky, drying come off my fingers. And then he folds the washcloth and wipes, cleaning me in gentle strokes of the warm cloth, perhaps with a little extra attention for my breasts, holding each one in turn and making sure they are both wiped clean. He leaves once more, tosses the washcloth into the bathtub, and returns to the bed, sliding under the blankets beside me.

I remain where I am, lying next to him, a couple of inches of space between us.

I have no clue what comes next. I want more. I want him. I want us. But I don't know what he wants and I don't know how to ask, and I don't know what normal people do in circumstances like these.

He looks at me. "What are you still doing way over there?"

I frown, puzzled. "Way over where? I'm right beside you."

"Exactly. Too far away."

His arm scoops under me, and I'm rolled into him, my face pressed against his chest. I'm on his left side, and I can hear his heart beating: *thrumthrum-thrumthrum-thrumthrum*; a timpani, hammering under my ear. His arm tightens, pulls me closer yet. Lifts me, settles me bodily on top of him so I'm half on him, half on the bed. He cradles me, his arm a taut band over my shoulder, across my back, his big wide rough palm cupping a globe of my bottom. My thigh lies over his. My hand nestles on his chest.

"Better," he says.

I can't breathe.

This is too much. This is too right.

I don't deserve this. This is too much happiness, too much perfectness, too much wonderment, too too too much. Ecstasy has me seized in crushing talons, making it hard to breathe. I'm near tears.

He's *holding* me.

Just holding me.

I listen to his heartbeat and try to settle myself, try to calm my frantic heart.

And of course, Logan is tuned in to my plight. "Isabel, honey. You're shaking like a leaf. What's wrong?"

I shake my head. "I don't know."

"*Bzzzzzt,*" he says, a sound like a buzzer. "Wrong answer. Try again."

"It's too much."

"What is?"

"This." I pat his chest. "Us. You holding me. I don't know how to—it's too good. I like it too much. I want it too much."

"How can something be *too* good?"

"It just is. I don't know." I am so emotional, suddenly. Gripped by something so intense I cannot fathom its scope. I am near tears and can't seem to stop them, even though the last thing I want is to cry after such a sensual, sexual, incredible experience.

But I sniffle, and I hate myself for it.

"Hey, hey." He touches my chin, tilts my face up to look at him. "Is this good tears or bad tears?"

I can only shrug. "I don't know. Not bad. That was so incredible, and now this."

"Just let me hold you. It's okay," he breathes. "You can cry. It's okay. Whatever you need, it's okay. Just let me hold you."

"I don't know how."

"You don't know how to what?" His lips brush mine, not a kiss, but a reminder of a kiss, a promise of a kiss to come.

"To let you hold me. This is all so new for me."

He knows exactly what I mean, and he doesn't like it. But he doesn't say anything. Just tightens his arm around me, kneads his fingers into the muscle of my buttock, caresses it, reaches down to clutch one of the globes, smooths his hand over both, as if he just can't get enough of touching my bottom.

And then he reaches out to the drawer of the nightstand beside the bed, opens it, pulls out a long black remote, and turns on the TV. Searches through something called Netflix and finds a movie. The one he's told me about, *What About Bob?*

Naked, emotional, being held like I've never experienced before, the taste of his essence still in my mouth, his hands on my backside, his chest under my ear, we watch a movie together.

It's silly, funny, ridiculous, cheesy, and wonderful.

When it's over, he scoots off the bed. "Stay here."

He doesn't explain what he's doing, so I remain where I am. He returns with four bottles of beer in one hand and a bag of potato chips in the other. He arranges the pillows behind our backs, and we sit up together, a thin sheet across our laps. He hands me a bottle of beer, sets the bag of chips in the space between my thigh and his, and brings up another movie.

P.S. I Love You, it's called.

We drink our beer, and eat the greasy, unhealthy, and incredibly delicious chips.

And I cry.

Sob, actually.

So sweet, so sad, so romantic. I swoon, and push the bag of chips away and snuggle closer to Logan, and he wraps his arm around me again. This time, his palm finds my thigh, clutching it possessively, stroking now and then lower or higher, making me wonder in the back of my mind if he plans to touch me again, if he'll steal his touch inward. I don't quite tense, but I want to.

I've lost track of time, and I don't care. I'm not tired at all. The sky is dark outside, and the world is quiet.

That's not true, though; the world isn't quiet, because there is no world. There is only this bubble of purity and perfectness and wonder, this bed, this man. Our skin, my scent on him, his smell on me. His taste in my mouth, a lingering memory of kisses shared. There is only this, and this is all I ever want. I beg the universe to let this last forever.

He fetches us each one more beer, and a carton of strawberries, which we eat by pinching the green leaves and biting beneath them.

I'm dizzy, a little drunk, and wildly happy.

He turns on *The Day After Tomorrow*, an apocalypse-scenario movie, and I like this one, too. It's easy to watch, easy to relax into and not think about anything.

Except the man cradling me in his strong arms.

I've slunk lower in the bed, so my head is on his chest, my beer finished, and I don't want any more. I just want to be here, watching movies with Logan, holding him and being held. My arm is across his hips. His fingers trace circles on my back, dare to my hip, dance over my bottom, slide up my spine, and steal lower again.

I find my hand skating over his stomach, under the flat sheet covering us. Seeking skin.

And then, with a glance up at him, I dare to touch him first. He smiles down at me, grips my backside, kneads it, teases a touch almost-but-not-quite between the cheeks, making me squirm and gasp. I have one hand around the hardening thickness of his cock, and I watch as it straightens, thickens, burgeons fully erect in my hand.

I don't know what I want to do to him first. Everything. I want it all, and I want it now. I want to just hold him like this in my hand, to stroke him with my fingers until he comes over my knuckles and into my palm. I want to wrap my mouth around him and suck him until he's exploding onto my tongue again. I want to lie beneath him and beg him to masturbate onto my breasts and onto my face. I want to climb astride him and put him into my core and ride him until we're both spent and gasping.

I want all of that, and I don't know where to start.

I just know I ache for needing him, for wanting his touch, that I'm desperate to watch and feel him explode because I can make him feel better than he's ever felt.

"Logan," I breathe. "I want everything with you."

"I know," he says. "I want it all with you, too. I want to fuck you and love you and taste you and come on your tits. I want to lick your pussy until you're begging me for more. I want to feel you shiver beneath me as we come together."

I'm stroking him, long slow slides of my fingers around his cock. Watching the way my fingers splay around his flesh. Watching his skin move. Watching his hardness grow harder. I want him inside me.

He slides a finger into me, an unexpected but gentle touch,

exploring my wet warmth. He strokes inside me, adds a second finger. Thrusts gently. Adds a third, the three fingers bunched together to fill me. His fingers slide in and out of me, and I have to close my eyes, because I'm focused on the feeling, utterly swept away by the feel of his touch within me. He drags my wetness over my clitoris and smears it in circles, and I moan, and he delves his fingers back into me.

I lose track of what I'm doing, and he rolls me to my back. I let him, and my thighs splay apart. He pushes my legs wider open, cups both hands under my bottom and lifts my entire lower half off the bed, bringing my slit to his mouth, and now he devours me as if he's starving; he feasts on me, licks, slurps, sucks my throbbing clit between his teeth and I come within seconds, but he doesn't stop. He keeps me aloft with one hand, effortlessly holding me up with one arm under my bottom, and now his other hand finds me. My heels rest on his shoulders, my knees dangle draped apart. I'm spread open for him, and he feasts.

I come, spasming, arching my spine to crush my core against his mouth.

And then he slides his essence-slick fingers out of my slit and drags them down. His eyes meet mine. "Has anyone ever touched you here?" he asks, and touches me somewhere sensitive and forbidden.

I shake my head. "No," I breathe.

He doesn't ask permission. He feathers a gentle touch over me, back there. I moan low in my throat and swallow hard. His tongue flicks my clit, and I spasm, and then he's lapping at me until I'm writhing again, and I feel his fingertip touching me, pressing in gentle circles and I feel the pressure of that touch all throughout my body, feel it tightening my muscles and gathering heat in my core, and I don't stop him. I want his touch. I want him. I want every orgasm he will give me; I'm greedy for them. Desperate. Willing.

I press my heels into the hard muscle of his shoulders and push down with my hips, opening yet farther. His touch at my backside is still so gentle, so careful. Yet insistent. Matching the pace of his tongue, the suction of his lips around my clitoris. I feel yet another orgasm welling up within me hard and fast, rising like the tide, inevitable, powerful. This one, perhaps, more potent than anything I've ever felt in my life. His fingertip touches, presses, circles, and I'm writhing. Gasping. Whimpering.

"Tell me how you feel, Isabel," Logan says.

"So good," I answer. "I like this. I'm going to come soon."

"Hard?"

"Yes, Logan."

"How hard?"

"Harder than I've ever come before in my life."

"You like how I'm touching you?"

I nod. "Yes."

He presses a little harder, and my instinct is to bear down and clench up, but I don't. I feel myself stretched, just the tiniest bit. I flex my hips and open my knees and breathe hard, and allow his touch.

"No one's ever touched you like this?" he asks.

"No. Never."

"Does it feel good?"

I whine in my throat as climax roars in my ears, my blood thundering, my core tightening. "Yes."

"Curse, Isabel. Say all the dirty words you know." He licks at my clitoris, and I shake, aching, trembling. "Scream my name when you come."

"Logan . . ." He wants bad words. He wants me to be dirty. "This feels so *fucking* good, Logan. I'm going to come so hard."

"I can taste it. I can feel it. Come on my tongue."

"Give me more," I whisper, speaking my darkest desire. "Your finger . . . give me more."

He wiggles his finger, and I groan loudly. "This? You like this? My dirty girl likes it when I touch her asshole."

I moan in equal parts mortification and desire. I *do*. Oh god, I do. I like it so much. It feels so good. "Yes, Logan. I like it. I'm your dirty girl, and I like it." Did that sound stupid? It did, to me. It sounded idiotic. Cheesy.

But Logan moans against my core and his finger throbs in and out of me in shallow pulsing thrusts and I'm whimpering and grinding against his mouth and taking more of his finger and I feel fire blossoming now. Perhaps it only sounded stupid to me, because I feel so self-conscious, despite how incredible this is.

Whatever I'd felt before, any other time in my life, any orgasm I've ever experienced, it was but a shadow of what is about to occur.

I shatter.

I scream. My scream deafens even me.

There are no words to capture the intensity of my orgasm. It is fire. Wildfire, sunfire, angelfire. All the stars in the galaxy going nova in my core all at once. Volcanoes erupting, earthquakes wracking the tectonic plates of my being.

"Logan!" I scream.

I am left breathless, shaking, trembling, shivering, and I can't help crying. I am so limp, so utterly wrecked that I can only reach for Logan and cling to him and shake, and try to breathe. After I don't even know how long, the shivers and shakes subside, and I can breathe. And Logan is still painfully erect, prodding into my belly.

I shift, and I'm on top of him. The tip of his cock presses against my opening, and his eyes are hot and wild, yet tainted by some stain of conflict.

"What, Logan?" I ask, and settle onto his stomach, rather than pushing him into me. "What's wrong? I see it in your eyes."

He shifts me off him, and we lie on our sides, facing each other. "Not yet, Isabel."

I blink. "Not yet?" My throat is tight. "Why not?"

"I want to, so bad. I know you do, too. But I don't think we should, yet."

"Why not?" I feel desperate.

And angry. Unreasonably angry, feral with unsated need. I feel rejected, denied. Spurned. Confused. My chest tightens and my eyes sting, hot.

His thumb wipes at my eyes. "Don't cry, Isabel. Please." His voice is low, quiet, careful. "It's all so hard to explain."

"You can put your mouth on me, and let me suck you, and you can put your finger in—in my . . ." It's hard to say out loud, but I force myself to speak my mind, bluntly and without filter. "You can put your finger in my asshole. You can come on my breasts. You can lick my pussy. But you can't have sex with me?" I feel proud of myself for saying those words, for speaking so daringly.

It's not my way. Or rather, it wasn't Madame X's way, but perhaps it is how Isabel talks.

He closes his eyes, squeezes them tight, breathes out a harsh sigh. "Isabel—"

"I don't understand, Logan. I'm trying, but I don't."

"Everything up until now, it's been amazing. *You* are amazing. You're a dream. You're so much—so much *more*, in every way, than anyone I've ever known. You overwhelm me." He touches my cheekbone with his thumb. "I feel like I'm drowning, sometimes, like you're an ocean and I'm just trying to stay afloat. And . . . the thing is . . . I *want* to drown in you. I like the way it feels. To lose myself in you. I feel like—god, it's hard to put in words. Like there's nothing else, no one else, like the world doesn't exist. I feel like in this moment I could just be with you and make love to you and touch you and make you feel good, and there would be nothing but us forever. I could sink into you, and we'd disappear into each other. It'd just be us."

"Me too, Logan. I *am* drowning. I've drowned. I can't breathe without you. I've tried. I don't know anything else. I just want this. I want you. I want *us*. Please, Logan." My voice shakes on the last two words.

His eyes waver, flick from my eyes to my mouth, back to my eyes. "There's more than just us, Isabel. I can't ignore that. I want to, but I can't. There's so much that's gone before this moment, and we both know it. There's just . . . *so* much." He breathes, long deep breaths, as if girding himself to speak unpleasant truth. "I want you, Isabel."

"You *have* me, Logan."

"Let me say this, okay? First, you have to understand that I'm not rejecting you. I *want* you. I want this. I want *us*. And this is honestly the hardest thing I've ever done. Saying no, it's harder than anything I've ever had to do, and I mean that. I see that it hurts you, and I hate it more than anything."

I draw a breath. "You told me you'd rather have an unpleasant truth than a good-sounding lie. Well, so would I, Logan." I sit up, bringing the sheet over my chest and facing him. "So give me the truth."

He sits up, too. Drapes the sheet over his lap. His brows furrow. His hair is tangled, and his mouth flattens in a hard line. "If Caleb showed up right now, what would you say to him?"

I sag, my breath leaving me. I burn, and I want to weep. "I don't know. He's not here."

He lets silence hang for a moment. "You've walked away from me for him twice now, Isabel. I don't hold it against you. I understand your position as well as anyone can, I think. But . . . until I'm sure you won't walk away from me for him a third time, or a fourth, I just . . . I can't commit all the way. I want you. But I don't want to share you."

"You're not sharing me, Logan. And—" I break off, summon strength from anger. "But you can do all those other things with me, touch me in a way no one ever has, do things with me that I've never done before. But you can't have sex with me?"

He just looks at me. There is sadness in his blue eyes. "Yes, Isabel. I can make you come with my fingers and my mouth. I can touch you, and kiss you . . . I can do all those things. And if you walk away from me, I'll survive it. I'll have those memories, for good or ill; I'll never forget this time with you, whatever happens next." He pauses to think. "If you were just some girl I was passing time with, we wouldn't be having this conversation. But you . . . you *mean* something to me, Isabel. If it were just about sexual attraction, I'd be inside you right now. I want that so bad I can fucking taste it. I can feel us, Isabel. But I just—I know beyond a shadow of a doubt that if we have sex, it won't just be having sex. When we do that, it will mean . . . *everything*. For both of us. And when we do that, I know I won't be able to quit you, and I won't be able to let you walk away, and I won't survive it if you walk away from me."

"I won't walk away."

His eyes blaze. "You can't say that. You and Caleb have unfinished business. You know it, I know it, and he knows it. And you can't promise me that if you come face-to-face with him again, you'll choose me instead of him."

"Logan—" I say, but I stop because I'm choking. "Damn it, Logan."

"Say I'm wrong, Isabel." He touches my chin and I have to look at him. His indigo gaze is the most tortured thing I've ever seen. I believe him when he says this is the hardest thing he's ever done. I see the pain in his eyes. "Sex *means* something, honey. It does. People pretend like it doesn't. People pretend like they can just fuck a thousand different people and none of it ever means anything, that it's just doing what feels good. But if you find that one person who resonates with the music of your soul, when you find that one person whose very presence takes up all the spaces in your heart and makes your soul sing, makes your body feel more alive and beautiful and loved than you've ever felt, you realize that sex *does* mean something. I'm guilty of cheapening it just like everybody else. But I know better. If sex were meaningless, if it were just hormones and fluids and pheromones and a few minutes of pleasure, it wouldn't hurt when we get cheated on. But it does hurt, because it does mean something. When Leanne cheated on me, it broke something inside me. I tried with Billie, but the longer things went, the more I realized that I was shut off, and that I'd never invested in her, or in any idea of an *us* between her and me. It was casual sex, just with one person over a long period of time. But it was still empty and meaningless and didn't fill anything inside me, didn't resonate. I thought Leanne and I resonated, and she proved me wrong."

"*We* resonate, Logan." My voice cracks at the end.

"I know we do. So powerfully that it makes a joke out of what I thought I felt with Leanne. But I know the power of that now. I know how badly it can wreck me when it—*if* it goes wrong."

"So you don't trust me."

"Isabel, it's not that simple. This isn't a normal situation."

"I don't even know what to say." I'm hurt. I'm angry. And I'm also all too aware how right he is. And that makes me all the more angry. "I need a minute."

I slide out of the bed, achingly aware that I'm naked, and he's naked, and I feel the ghosts of his touch on my skin. I can't help glancing at him as I find the shirt he left for me. He's still hard, thick, rigid, painfully erect, the outline of his shaft visible against the sheet. Instead of reaching for him like so much of me wants to do,

I tug the shirt on. I almost moan at the slide of the downy fabric over my skin, at the smell of Logan on the cotton.

"I'm not leaving," I tell him. "I'm going in your backyard. I just . . . I need time."

"Whatever you need."

"I need *you*, Logan," I say, before I have a chance to think better of it.

He leans his head back against the headboard. "Jesus, Isabel." A smile. "You look good in my shirt."

"What?"

He shakes his head. "Nothing. It's just a line from a country song."

His eyes rake over me. My nipples are hard, poking at the fabric. The hem comes to midthigh, and when I reach up to brush my hair back out of my eyes and pull it into a ponytail, the edge rides up and bares my core.

"You are the most beautiful woman I've ever seen in my life, Isabel."

I'm caught by his gaze. Reeled in. Drawn closer. I find myself on the bed with him again, somehow, and the shirt is gone, abandoned. Pulling the sheet away. Reaching for him. "Let me help you, Logan. I want to make you feel good."

He resists, grabbing my wrist to stop me. "It'll subside eventually, Isabel."

I'm dizzy with need. "Logan . . . you've made me feel so good. Let me touch you."

"I'm weak, Isabel. I want you, and I'm trying to do what's right for both of us."

"Then we shouldn't have started this. Because now I've felt you, and I want more." I rub him with my thumb, and his grip on my wrist tightens.

He sighs harshly. "Fuck, Isabel. Fuck! I want you so goddamn bad."

"I want you just as badly, Logan. More. I can't breathe because of it." I lean closer to him, touch his jaw with my lips.

I know what he said, and some distant part of me knows he's right, but like this, kissing his skin, his erection in my hand, all I know is desire.

His grip on my wrist loosens, and I stroke him. Slow caresses of his length.

And then, faster than a serpent strike, I'm on my back and he's levered above me, and his breath on my lips is warm. His body is hard and heavy. His erection is insistent, and my heart hammers like a drum.

I touch him, reaching between us to grip his thickness and feather soft quick strokes of my fingers around him, root to tip. Lift my hips. His remain hard, immovable.

His forehead touches mine. "No, Isabel. Not until you're mine, and only mine."

I go limp then, sucking in a breath and fighting tears. "I *am* yours, Logan. That's all I want to be, is yours."

"But you *aren't*. Not yet. Not totally."

I'm still touching him. And he's thrusting into the circle of my fingers, his abs tensing and his buttocks flexing. I cup the hard round bubble of his buttock and revel in the feel of it, even as my soul aches and my heart cracks.

But I can't stop touching him.

And he can't stop either. His mouth descends and his lips touch my nipple, and I pull at his buttocks.

"Isabel—"

I bring his face to mine and touch my lips to his. "Ssshhh. Just this, Logan. Give me this, at least."

His breathing is ragged, and the motion of his hips faltering. I help by thrusting my fist down to his root and then back up, and then we begin to move in sync, him thrusting into my hand as I stroke down. His forehead touches my shoulder, his lips my breast-bone. He moans.

Time fades, ceases to exist, and I know I can't push him for more than this. It would be taking something he isn't ready to give. And there's a doubt deep inside me, a tiny seed that wonders if he's right. That I'm still weak and vulnerable and addicted to something toxic.

Some*one* toxic.

But I need this, at least. This pretense, this imitation. This game of pretend, where he's above me and moving as I want him to move, and I can feel him, I can caress his spine and bury my fingers in his hair and grip the flexing mound of muscle that is his ass. I can feel him move, hear his breathing shift to become even more desperate and I can feel him thicken between the ring of my fingers.

"Isabel . . . shit . . ."

"Logan, let it go. Let me have it. Let me feel it. Let me feel *you*. I want as much of you as I can get. Even this much."

He groans and goes still, tensed and taut as a piano wire. I take over, plunging my fist around him hard and slow, root to tip, and his hips flex. I watch between our bodies for the moment when he lets go.

He splashes hot seed onto my belly, groaning, and I watch it happen, watch him unleash and watch the semen leave his cock and watch it slash white across my dusky skin. I stroke him fast now and he comes and comes, and I watch him, not missing a single second. His forehead is pressing hard against my shoulder, and his arms are hard bars beside my face, and I twist to kiss one of his biceps. The other. And then I nuzzle his cheekbone with my lips, and he presses his mouth to mine, and kisses me,

and kisses me,

and kisses me.

I am lost to this. I weep. His come is a tacky pool on my belly, and his cock is still hard in my hand. I wouldn't give up this memory for anything, even if it was a pale imitation of what I really want.

"Isabel—"

I shake my head. "Mmm-mmm. No." I kiss his lips. Taste his breath, and feel his emotions like a wave. "You're right. I hate it, but you're right. I *don't* know what I would say. I want to say—I want to promise that I'd choose you. I *do* choose you. I want you. Only you. Only always you. But he messes me up and I know there is more between Caleb and me that I can't back away from. I need answers from him. And I—I want so much more than this, but you're right."

He rolls off me, lies on his back, gasping, chest heaving, a forearm across his eyes, one knee bent, foot planted in the mattress. I stare at him, devouring his beauty. Tracing the contours of his muscles with my gaze, picking out individual designs from the jumble of his tattoos, the fall of his hair, the tension and conflict in his features.

"I wanted so much better for you than this," he says, not looking at me. "You deserve . . . everything. Better than . . . this."

"No, Logan. This was perfect."

"I shouldn't have let this get started."

"If you tell me you regret this, Logan, I shall be very angry." I don't bother covering, don't bother with the shirt, don't bother sitting up or even wiping away the sticky pool of his come on my belly. I want it there. I like the feel of it there, the evidence of his desire for me visible as it dries on my skin.

He eyes me, and even now his eyes roam my body, my breasts, the shadow between my thighs. Then his gaze goes to mine. "I don't regret it. I just wanted more for us."

"So did I," I say. "So *do* I."

"Then why does this feel like good-bye?" He finally sits up, fore-arms resting on his upright knees, fingers hooked together.

It does, doesn't it? The realization makes my chest ache. "Why do we never get more than a few hours together, Logan?"

"I don't know. I wish I did. I wish I knew how to—how to fix this. You. Me. Us. Everything. But I can't." He swivels, and his knees brush my hip and my thigh. I remain as I am, staring at him, drinking him in. Memorizing his features, this moment, this feeling. "You have come so far from the broken, mysterious woman I met at that stupid auction. But you have a long ways to go yet. I can't make the journey for you. I can't make the choices for you. I can't face Caleb for you. I can't free you from him. He let you go, Isabel. But he didn't set you free. He won't do that. He's not that type of man. He's just not. You have to free yourself, and I can't help you with that. I want you, but I also know anything that could be between us can only work if you're strong and independent and fully your own person."

"And I'm not, am I?" I rip my gaze away from his. "Not yet."

A silence hangs. It is a strange, fraught quiet, filled with a thousand unspoken things. Words, sighs. Moans. Ghosts of the love we should be making right now, but aren't. Because Caleb still has claws in my mind.

"Logan?"

He glances at me. "Hmm?"

"Tell me what you know about Caleb. Tell me what happened between you."

He looks away, out the window. Gray tinges the sky. Exhaustion creeps at the edges of my mind.

Moments pass, and I begin to wonder if he's not going to answer me. But then he speaks. "I was flipping houses, still. Making a kill-ing on it, too. I had good taste, and an eye for the houses that would flip well and the ones that wouldn't. I was getting to the point that I'd started hiring guys to do the actual construction work, and I was just picking the houses, buying them, and selling the flipped ones. And then I took a gamble on a huge mansion that had been foreclosed. It was outside Chicago a ways, in this gated community. On like six or seven acres. It was a fucking mess. It had been bank owned for several years; no one wanted it. It was old, some pipes had burst, and it was just ugly, you know? That sort of overly gaudy decor rich people think they need to show how rich they are. Plush burgundy rugs, gold-plated door handles, thick dark walnut everywhere, too much furniture and not enough floor space. Ugly as fuck, but it had beautiful bones. It was a huge project, which was why no one wanted it, you know? It really was a complete gut job; all the grass would have to be ripped out because it was all overrun with crab grass, all the beds were overgrown. Most flippers have a sweet spot of around two or three hundred thousand as a max purchase price. Once you get higher than that, you're entering a whole new tier of things. You buy at four or five hundred, to get a good return you have to start seeing a sale price of nearing a million, and that level comes with its own complications. Well, this property was a huge risk. I got it for four hundred, because they were fucking desperate to unload it at any price. That was a huge chunk for me, and I knew I was in for at least half that much in reno costs. It was worth easily double what I paid for it, just going based on previous sale prices of that property and area comps.

"So I went for it. I gutted the place, ripped every stick of flooring out, knocked down every single non-load-bearing wall, the stairs, the ceilings. Ripped out all the landscaping. I mean I took that fucker down to bones. This was six months after I found out about Leanne cheating on me with Marcus, the man who'd been a sort of flipper-mentor for me, as well as my business partner. I walked away with nothing but what I'd saved and the return on the house I was in the middle of finishing. And this huge risk, it was the first job I was doing without Marcus. I was in a bad place. Fucked up emotionally, having flashbacks from the war, not sleeping. I got myself in over my head, really. Looking back, I should have gone smaller. Done a couple properties of the type I was familiar with. A tenthousand-square-foot mansion on six acres, one that needed a complete gut and rebuild? It was idiotic of me."

He rubs his face, crosses his legs, and covers his lap with the sheet.

"To this day I'm still not sure how I pulled it off. I was drinking all the time, like, the whole project is kind of a haze, because I was half wasted the whole time. I was a goddamned mess. But somehow, I scraped together the money to finish it, pulled a lot of all-nighters. Point is, I finished the flip in like three months, which considering the size of the job is pretty incredible. I finished over budget, though. By a lot. Bought it for four, spent another three hundred thousand on reno costs, most of which went to rewiring and redoing the kitchen. Get the kitchen right, and you can sell just about any house. So I had an overhead of seven fifty. Highest comp in the area was a flat million, but that place was fifteen hundred square feet less than my property, and was on half the acreage, and wasn't updated." He glances at me. "Shit, I'm boring you, aren't I? You don't give a shit about the flip. Short version for real now. I sold the house for one point eight. Made a killing. But I was burned out, by then. That job just . . . fried me. I didn't want to touch another flip. So instead of sinking that money back into another flip, I went a different direction. One of the guys I'd hired for the flip had an uncle who was selling his computer parts manufacturing business. I bought it. Streamlined the business, fired a bunch of people and rehired better ones, put in a manager I trusted, got the place running like a top.

Started churning out a profit in no time. One of the people I'd hired was the main sales account manager, and she got us six new accounts that were insanely lucrative. That process landed me a lead on a computer supply company that was going under, so I bought that and, essentially, flipped it. Made cuts, hired new people, got new accounts. Used my parts supply facility to get the computers built more cheaply, so I turned a higher profit on each sale. And then a real stroke of luck for me. I met a guy who owned a whole chain of used-car lots, a couple restaurants, and a gas station. Dude had terminal cancer and was selling everything at a bargain basement price. Bought him out lock, stock, and barrel. He was a hell of a businessman, so his stuff was all in good shape. Saw a return on that investment in a matter of months."

He glances at me. "Seriously, babe, just bear with me. I'm almost to the interesting stuff. Once the companies I bought were all turning a profit, I sold them. I wasn't interested in the actual running of the business, just the buy, improve, and sell. I kept that one guy's chain of business, though. Sort of out of posterity or something. He died a few months after I bought him out, but I still own all those businesses. Well, anyway, I kept making bigger and bigger investments. Buying larger companies for larger payouts when I ended up selling them. Finally, the business took me to New York. A research and development company working on future tech for cell phones and such. Better touch screens, holograph displays, all sorts of stuff we won't actually see for years yet, even now. The owner of that company, right after we signed the deal, pulled me aside. Said he had a good lead for me. Couldn't tell me much, but it was a chance to buy into a company with real earnout potential. Millions, he said. Hundreds of millions.

"Well, of course I was skeptical. Someone says shit like that, you gotta throw some side-eye, you know? Like, what's your angle? He put me in touch with Caleb. The investment opportunity was a partner stake in a futures trading company. Stocks. Hard to explain if you're not into business. Point is, there is a fuckload of money in futures, if you do it right. Caleb, it seems, does it right. This was new, for me. I was still a builder, essentially. I just built businesses instead of buildings. Stocks, futures, market indexes? It was all new."

A long pause now. A sigh. "I was in it deep with Caleb before I figured out that he was rigging things, insider trading, corporate espionage. All sorts of dirty shit. Pissed me off. I confronted him."

He is quiet for a long couple of minutes, staring into space.

"He's a sly, manipulative bastard. Talked me around. Wasn't hard, I guess. I mean, I was making serious bank. More than I'd ever made in my life by a factor of at least ten. I wasn't stupid, I was scattering the accounts all over the place. Hiding some in tax shelters, offshore accounts, all that jazz. Nothing illegal, just spreading the money around so it wasn't all in one account. But he had me by the balls, you know? Had me dead to rights. I was in it, I was on the hook as much as him if anything happened. Just go with it, he said. It's only temporary. He was building up capital for a big buyout, a merger that would make both of us billions, billions with a big fat *B*. So I went with it. Obviously, hindsight is twenty-twenty. A basic life principle for you, Isabel: If something seems too good to be true, it probably is. In this case, the big buyout was all a setup. He was working twice as hard as me behind the scenes, doing an end run on me. This is a complex world we live in, and the high-dollar, big-business scene here in Manhattan? It's a small world. You don't run the kind of game Caleb was running without attracting attention. He was getting too big too fast, making too much money too easily. People were suspicious. But it was his world, his game, and I was new to it all. What you have to understand here is that I'm glossing over the details because the real nitty-gritty of how Caleb set me up is boring business bullshit. It's not an exciting narrative. He was running a scheme that ran the entire gamut of white-collar crime: embezzlement, money laundering, insider trading, corporate espionage. He's smart, and he's careful. Very little, if anything at all, can be directly traced back to him. I wasn't innocent, mind you. I knew I was part of something dirty. I won't bullshit you about that. But I wasn't part of the grand scope of things either; I was just a piece, a minor player. I was good at the organizational stuff, getting the right people hired for the right job, keeping track of what went where and who did what. Caleb was the one running the big numbers, you know? But he had it all set up so that there were layers and layers between the actual dirty work and him. The SEC got a tip-off, probably. I don't know. They came sniffing, and it all went to shit. Lots of people went down. His setup was elaborate, lots of people involved, and all of them knew to one degree or another what was going on, that it was a dirty operation. I think there were something like a dozen people who were arrested for a wide variety of white-collar crimes, including yours truly."

A silence, and then a wave of his hand. "I was an idiot, and paid the price. No one to blame but myself. So I sang like a canary about everything I knew, except Caleb. I wasn't protecting him, mind you. But telling stories about a ghost is how you get turned into one yourself. I told them everything I knew in exchange for a reduced sentence and a transfer to a more white-collar prison. Got ten years, did five."

"And the only reason you did any prison time is that Caleb didn't warn you?"

"It wasn't that he didn't warn me so much as that he made sure I was left out in the open for them to find. That was always the plan.

There's always someone as bait. He set me up, and I spent five years in a federal pen for it."

"What I don't understand is why you got involved with it in the first place. I mean, if you knew it was illegal, why do it?"

Logan doesn't answer for a few moments. "You didn't grow up the way I did."

I quirk an eyebrow at him. "I don't know how I grew up."

A sharp exhale. "Shit, I'm sorry. You're right. But my point is, I grew up poor as dirt. Skipping school, smoking pot, running in a gang. I watched guys OD, watched my best friend die in front of me because of drugs. So, those kinds of crime, they have victims, to me. I see the effects. They're immediate. You sell coke, that means someone is hooked on coke. And if you've ever seen a real-deal cokehead, it's not pretty. So I'd never do that shit. I'd never sell drugs. But flipping houses, that was good hard honest work. I was making decent money, and no one was shooting at me, I wasn't gonna step on or drive over an IED, or have a rocket shot at my helo. But it wasn't, like, lucrative. I was making good money, but it all went back into the next flip. So when I made that big sale and was actually flush with real cash, I wanted out. I had that tip on a parts facility, and I smelled money, you know? There's always money in technology. Always. You just have to suss it out and figure out how to sell it. Well, I went into the deal with Caleb skeptical, but at first it seemed legit. And it was big money. The idea of a big payout, like two or three commas and a lot of zeroes in your account? For a hood rat and ex-grunt like me, that was an opportunity I couldn't pass up. And he worked me into things gradually, kind of like how you cook frogs, you know? Start 'em out in the water, keep it warm, and gradually turn up the heat until they're cooked, and they never even realize it. Caleb did that with me. Hooked me in, bit by bit."

"How well did you actually know him?" I ask.

A shrug. "Not well. He was always a mysterious sort of cat. You rarely saw him in person, usually just talked to him on the phone, or got an e-mail from him. So did I know him, personally? No. I met him maybe three times, and each of those times was for maybe twenty minutes, max. He was just . . . cool and aloof." He pauses, takes a breath, and continues. "So that's how I got involved in a crooked business, and went to jail for it."

"And you blame Caleb for that."

He bobbles his head. "Yes and no. I knew what I was doing was wrong after a certain point, but by then I was making so much money that I couldn't make myself back out. Once you're clearing a million here, a million there, it's hard to stop. So in that sense, no, I don't blame Caleb. I can't. It was all me. But I do blame him for setting me up, letting me and the other twelve people who went to jail take the fall for him. But then again, we were the dumbasses who let ourselves be taken, so can we blame anyone but ourselves for that, in the end?"

"I see your point. It's a very mature way to look at it, I would say."

A snort of laughter. "I had five years to think about it. At first, yeah, obviously I placed all the blame squarely on Caleb's shoulders. I spent hours just dreaming up ways I'd get even with him when I got out. But as time went on and I started to really think about it, I came to the conclusions I just shared with you. Yeah, he's culpable, and I do hold him accountable for me doing jail time. But the real blame falls on my shoulders. Both for doing dirty business and for being an idiot about it. Don't get me wrong, I'm still pissed off at him, and I was even more so when I first got out. I went looking for him, planning on exacting some kind of revenge, I guess."

"How did you find him?"

"It wasn't easy. He's not exactly listed in the phone book. Nor are any of the companies he's legally associated with in his name. Also, I couldn't just sit around and hunt for him. I had to start over. See, when I started working for him, I made sure I had money stashed all over the place that couldn't be easily tracked back to me. So when I got out, I had seed money. Started over. Started small. Made sure my record was buried as deep as it could go, made sure I kept myself out of the light, bought up companies via dummy corporations and turned them over, one by one, small ones, building up capital. And the whole time I was looking for Caleb, on the side, sort of. Eventually I started hearing little rumors. Mostly about a kind of escort service for the super rich. Not really an escort service though, I discovered, as much as a kind of matchmaking program. Nothing illegal about it, on the surface. You weren't buying a match, you were paying for a service. And that service could be a date for an event, a long-term companion, or if you were serious, a potential bride. It was wildly, prohibitively expensive, super secret, super exclusive. 'The first rule of Fight Club is you don't talk about Fight Club' sort of thing." He glances at me. "That's another movie reference that went straight over your head. Whatever. The undertone of the whole thing is that you were for all intents and purposes buying the girls. Not outright, and they weren't sex workers. You couldn't initiate sex during contracted events, that sort of thing. It was the kind of thing you didn't talk about, so it was hard to find out much because no one would talk about it." He eyes me speculatively. "And then as I got closer to the actual service, to the real Indigo Ring, I started hearing about another layer, an even more exclusive service that was even more hush-hush. You."

"Indigo Ring?"

"That's what it's called. The Indigo Ring, capital *I*, capital *R*. That's not what he calls it, I don't think, but that's the name for it

among the people I could actually get to talk about it. I tracked down
a guy who'd married one of Caleb's girls. He was a forty-five-year-old
multimillionaire, not really sure how he made his fortune. He was
awkward and lonely and difficult, one of those work-all-night-and-
all-day-for-a-week-straight sorts. His wife was twenty-nine, beautiful,
voluptuous, smart, a real knockout. But apparently she was also an
ex-drug addict and former sex worker; this is what she told me herself. She ended up in Caleb's program somehow, got clean, worked
her way through the program. I don't know how she met Caleb, and
she was squirrelly about what she meant by 'program,' wouldn't
answer me directly." He shrugs. "She seemed grateful for Caleb, and
also seemed to really love Brian, her husband. He helped her get a
college degree of some kind. Apparently she was actually pretty
intelligent, but the way she'd grown up had precluded her from really
pursuing any academic interests. Once she went through Caleb's
mysterious program and got off the drugs, she was able to get a GED
and explore what interested her. And Brian is a computer geek, devel-
oped a software program or something, I really don't remember. But
he sent her to school, and she got a degree. I don't remember what,
economics or politics, or social work, maybe? Something along those
lines. It was kind of cool, to be honest. I mean, they were two totally
different people from wildly different backgrounds. He was white-
bread, from a well-to-do upper-middle-class suburban family, grew
up in Connecticut, and she was a Latina girl from Queens who'd
spent most of her youth hooked on drugs and turning tricks. But
they met through Caleb and for all that I could see legitimately fell
in love. It was weird."

I think back to Rachel. "I know one of the girls in the program
right now. When I ran away from Caleb the first time, I hid in
her apartment. The girls in the program live in the tower, sequestered

in these apartments. They're all like that girl, the Latina who married the rich computer guy. Drug addicts and prostitutes living dead-end lives, and Caleb finds them and puts them through his program. It's basically just getting off drugs, getting educated, learning how to function in normal society, how to be a good escort, basically. A companion, a Bride."

"So they're really not prostitutes?"

I shake my head. "According to Rachel, no. If there is sex, it's always their choice. Of course that's expected if they become a Bride, or a long-term companion, but it's not part of the contract, explicitly. The client is not allowed to proposition the girls, and no money directly exchanges hands between the client and the girls. The client pays Indigo Services, who takes their cut, and then pays the girls."

"So they're basically contractors."

"I suppose so." There's so much more to this, so many layers, and I don't know how to put it all into words.

"What aren't you saying?" he asks.

I shrug. Try to breathe. "The girls. The sex thing. There's more to it. Caleb . . . trains them. Sexually. So when they become long-term companions and Brides, they know how to please. How to be good at the kind of sex men like."

Logan blinks at me. "Jesus. By 'train,' I assume you mean he fucks them all and calls it training?"

"There are actual lessons. Weekly reports and assessments. Techniques."

"So the clients aren't allowed to fuck the girls, because they belong to Caleb." This is phrased as a question, but spoken as the bitterest of statements.

"I hid under Rachel's bed during an assessment," I whisper.

"Meaning . . . you discovered all this by accident? Overheard Caleb having sex with some other girl?" he asks.

I nod. "Right." I swallow hard. "Then one time I was visiting Rachel, because we were kind of friends, and I needed someone who wasn't Caleb to talk to. He showed up, and caught me watching. Listening. So he . . . he forced me to watch while he—finished. With Rachel."

"Isabel. God." Logan wipes his face with both hands. "This is fucked up on so many levels."

"I admitted to him later that I was confused by the difference in the way he treated Rachel versus the way he treated me. He did things both to and with Rachel that he never did with me. And I wasn't—I wasn't saying I wanted those things, just that I was confused. He'd say things to her, do things with her sexually that—" I cut myself off, start over. "So then the next time I saw him, he did . . . what I told you. Which was the kind of thing I heard and saw him do with Rachel."

I cannot put into words the confusion. The anger. The fact that part of me liked what was done to me. That part of me craves those moments of helpless weakness, those moments of *belonging*, of being owned, dominated, subjugated. I hate that part of me, and cannot speak it into truth.

But Logan, oh . . . he sees. His eyes, crystalline and indigo and piercing me like scalpels slicing through tissue. Cutting me open and baring my secrets for his perusal.

"Isabel." His voice has that note of warmth. That layer of understanding. "There is nothing you could say, nothing you could do, no truth that could change my feelings for you. Do you know that?"

I cannot move, breathe, or feel, much less speak. I try to nod, try to seem like I am giving him an affirmation. But it ends up a sniffle and a wobble of my head. My eyes are squeezed shut and my head is ducked, and I am clutching myself, arms wrapped around my middle.

"You watched, and you were curious." His voice is a murmur in my ear. "You saw him do things to that other girl that he didn't do with you, and you were curious."

I nod. I owe him truth, even embarrassing, disgusting, mortifying truth.

Logan continues baring the secrets I cannot say. "You didn't . . . *want* those things. But you were curious. And Caleb is a perceptive motherfucker. He can read people as easily as you read books. So he saw that. Saw your curiosity. And he's a manipulative bastard, so he used it against you. Used your curiosity as an excuse to force those things on you and make you feel like maybe you asked for it. That maybe you did want it, and just didn't know how to say it. Like maybe it was you all along, and not him."

I am choking. Oxygen is not reaching my brain. Thoughts are like moths fluttering in kamikaze circles around a burning-hot lightbulb. How does he know? How do these men see so clearly into me? Do my thoughts and desires and emotions appear on my forehead in visible form?

I roll away. Logan is at my back, hand on my shoulder, mouth at my ear. "Hey. Talk to me, Is."

"And say what?" I speak to empty air in front of me rather than facing Logan. "That you're right? Fine. You're right. And so was he. I . . . *was* curious. And part of me *did* want it. Just . . . not the way he did it. I didn't want the humiliation. With her, it seemed like it was mutual. Maybe he was teaching her, but there was a two-directionality to the way they interacted, sexually. And . . . god, this is so hard to say out loud, especially to you. But with Caleb and me, it has always seemed . . . one way. Him doing what he wanted *to* me, and me allowing it. I wanted that—I don't know how to put it. I wanted that feeling of being an active participant and not just a . . .

a receptacle for his needs. And all I got for my curiosity was to be used yet another way."

"What did you feel with us? You and me, just now?"

"There is an *us*. There always has been. I've always felt like with you, that you see me. You . . . you both *see* me, and see *me*. The emphasis on both words is important. You care about what I want. You care about who I am."

"Caleb doesn't."

I have to let a silence hang until I can force the words out. "I don't know if that's true. I think he just cares about me being the version of me he wants me to be. The version he created, rather than the version I am becoming."

Lips touch my spine between my shoulder blades. "And I care about you, who you were and who you are and who you're becoming. All of you."

"I know."

His hand tugs at my arm, and I roll to my back. He's levered over me, staring down at me with too-bright eyes. Knowing eyes. A gaze full of understanding and compassion and hurt and love. Yes, love. I see it there, though neither of us will speak of it outright. "But for all that, there's still something there between you and Caleb, something you can't deny and can't ignore. And I can't have you until you've seen that through."

"I hate how right you are, so much of the time," I say.

"Me too," he says.

"I don't know what it is, between Caleb and me. I wish I did, so I could be done with it."

"Me too," he says again. "But until there's an end between you and Caleb, there can't be a beginning between you and me."

The silence quavering between us then is rife with pain. This hurts. Worse than anything I've ever felt, this hurts. My throat closes, and my eyes sting. It's hard to breathe for the weight of pain in my chest. For the weight of the good-bye swinging like a thousand-pound pendulum between us.

I have nothing else to say. No more words. I leave Logan's bed and his room, and I take a shower. I take my time, scrubbing every inch of my body carefully. I don't want to. Even now, I want his scent on me. I want to be marked by him on the outside the way he's marked me on the inside.

My dress has been laid neatly on the bed, along with my under-garments, and my shoes are on the floor near them. Logan is nowhere to be seen. I dress carefully, smoothing the worst of the wrinkles out of the dress as best I can. My hair is still wet, because Logan doesn't own a hair dryer, and my hair is thick. I braid it and tie off the end. Slip on my shoes.

And yet, when I look in the floor-to-ceiling mirror in Logan's closet, I see only Isabel. Despite the familiar clothes, I do not see Madame X. I see me. I see a person. A woman becoming her own individual. I inhale deeply, run my hands over the bell curve of my hips, exhale, and then go in search of Logan.

I find him in his backyard, pacing in troubled circles, smoking a cigarette, drinking a beer. Cocoa lies on the ground near the door, chin on her paws, watching him, thick brown tail thumping the flagstones.

He halts, and his eyes rake over me. "You are so beautiful, Isabel."

"You've already seen me in this dress, Logan," I point out.

He shrugs. "Doesn't make you any less gorgeous than the first time I saw you in it."

I try another breath, but my lungs don't seem to want to inflate all the way. "I should go."

A long inhalation of the cigarette, causing the orange tip to flare bright. "I know." Smoke trickles out of his nostrils. "I'll take you."

The drive back through the pink-to-gold light of dawn is silent. The radio is off. Logan does not speak and neither do I.

He pulls up directly in front of Caleb's tower. Finally, he looks at me. "You know how to find me. I will wait, Isabel."

"For how long?" I ask, wanting to look away from his indigo gaze and finding myself unable to do so.

"Until you tell me to stop waiting."

TEN

stand alone in the middle of the lobby of your tower. The reception desk is fully staffed: two older white men, a striking young black woman with a shaved scalp, and a Hispanic man of indeterminate age, which means probably about thirty. They all glance at me, notice me, and then return to their work, but the black woman makes a very brief phone call. Which means they know who I am and have alerted Len, most likely.

Indeed, it is Len who appears from the bank of elevators, expression inscrutable, aged, weathered, hardened features cast in stone. He does not greet me, doesn't say a single word. Merely gestures at the elevators. I nod and accompany him onto the elevator marked *Private*.

The ride up is long.

"Len," I say, curiosity getting the better of me. "How old are you?"

"Forty-nine, ma'am."

"What is the worst thing you've ever done?"

A very thick silence as Len stares down at me. "I would say it's probably impossible to pinpoint one single thing. I'm not a good person, and I never have been."

"Indulge me."

An outbreath, blown between pursed lips, eyes cast to the roof of the elevator car. A moment of thought, in which Len looks nearly human. "I fought in the first Desert Storm. Marine Recon. We caught this insurgent, me and two guys from my unit. We holed up in a little hut near the Kuwaiti border and tortured the unholy fuck out of the poor bastard. He knew where some high-ranking Iraqi military generals were hiding, and we were told to get the intel by any means possible. So we did."

"What kind of torture?" I cannot help asking.

"Why would you want to know this shit, Madame X?"

"I'm not Madame X anymore, Len. My name is Isabel. And I'm learning that no one is ever as they seem."

Len nods. "Fair enough. We ripped his fingernails out with pliers. Cut strips of his skin off with a box cutter. Burned toes off with a blowtorch. Waterboarded him. Beat him half to death. Stuck pins in him until he looked like a pincushion, and then heated 'em up with a lighter."

"My god," I breathe. I am horrified. "Did he survive it?"

"Oh yeah. Point of torture is to cause pain so bad they'll tell you anything to make it stop. So yeah, he survived long enough to sing about the generals, but when we had what we needed, we put a couple rounds in the back of his head."

"Double-tap," I say, thinking of Logan.

Len nods. "Yeah, we double-tapped him, and left him for the vultures and the ants."

"Tell me one more thing," I ask.

"Sure, why not."

"What's the best thing you've ever done?"

"That's a helluva lot harder." Len is silent for a long time. "There was this girl. In Fallujah. Local girl. We were headed out on foot after a raid, and I heard screaming. Followed the sound, against orders. Discovered some local fellas running a train on the girl. Killed 'em all. I had some local currency in one of my pockets, and I gave it all to her, then pounded leather back to my unit. Whenever I could, I stopped by and helped her out. Brought her money, food, clothes. Whatever I could scrounge up. I still dunno why. I don't stand by rape, I guess. I'm an evil motherfucker, don't get me wrong. I'll beat up, torture, and murder men without thinking twice about it, but I won't touch a woman in violence, and won't stand to see it happen. I may be a bastard, but I've got my own code of honor. Such as it is, at any rate."

"What happened to her?" I ask. "The girl?"

A shrug. "Lost contact with her. Battle of Fallujah happened, and it got to where I couldn't really go looking anymore without getting my ass shot off."

"Have you ever killed anyone for Caleb?"

A stony stare. "We're not talking about Mr. Indigo."

"You have." I meet Len's glare. "Would you kill Logan if he told you to?"

Len's answer is immediate: "In a heartbeat."

"Why?"

"Because he's dangerous."

"So are you. So is Caleb. I'm surrounded by dangerous men, it would seem."

Another shrug. "You're not wrong there." The car stopped a long time ago, but Len has been holding the doors closed. Now he allows them to open. "He's not back yet, but he will be shortly." The conversation is over, apparently.

"Thank you, Len."

Len seems puzzled by my thanks. "Yeah." And then he's gone, doors closing between us.

I don't know what I'm going to say. What I'm going to do. You will be here soon and I've got a million, billion questions, and answers that I don't know the questions to, and demands I don't know how to formulate. Needs I don't know how to meet. And all of this requires that I face up to you and not flinch, speak to you and not succumb to your sorcery.

I do not have the best track record when it comes to that. I am weak.

I stand for long moments a mere three steps into the colossal space you call home, the echoing, open-plan apartment occupying the entire footprint of the tower. There, the couch. Where you fucked me. Here, where I stand, the carpet under my feet where you shoved your cock into my throat and came on my face. The haptic memory is overwhelmingly strong, a twinge in my jaw reminding me how wide I had to stretch my mouth, a ghost of heat and wetness on my face where you finished on me. There, the kitchen, the break-fast nook. You pulled me down onto your lap in that chair, the westward-facing one, with all of Fifth Avenue spread out for you. You pulled me down onto your lap, wrapped your fist into my hair, tugged my head backward so I was forced to stare up at the ceiling while you thrusted up into me and bit my neck in sharp nips. You never spoke a word, didn't touch me other than to fuck me and bite me. It was almost like a punishment. But for what?

Strange that I remember that encounter. You'd woken me up out of a dead sleep at three in the morning, hauled me into the kitchen, yanked off my underwear and tossed them onto the table, and then proceeded to fuck me until you came, and then you were done. You shoved me off you, snatched my underwear and shoved them into your pocket. Tossed back the last of your doppio macchiato, strode out without a backward glance. I went back to sleep, and the next morning it had seemed like a dream, easily forgotten.

There is a crystal bottle of something amber on a side table near a window. It is an artfully crafted little vignette: a small round table of dark wood, a cut-crystal decanter and two matching tumblers on a silver tray, the table and tray nestled against the wall between two floor-to-ceiling windows. There are two overstuffed armchairs facing the table at oblique angles, and each armchair has a tiny table near to hand, on which rests a cut-crystal ashtray, a silver cigar cutter, and a torch-style lighter. A few feet away, between the next pair of windows, is another small table, this one with two rectangular boxes, glass-topped. Cigars. I open one of the boxes, select a cigar. I bring my cigar with me and pour a measure of scotch whisky into a tumbler. I've seen you do this a thousand times. I cut the end off the cigar with the platinum cutter sitting on the table nearby, put the freshly cut end to my lips and light it, rotating the cigar and puffing as I've seen you do. When it's smoking merrily, I suck in a mouthful and taste it. Thick, acrid, almost sweet. Blow it out. Roll the smoke around in my mouth, let it trickle away. Play with it. I try a sip of the scotch. This, I've had before. I think of Logan as I roll the powerful liquid around my mouth and then swallow it.

I wait for you this way, the way you have often waited for me, a cigar coiling serpents of smoke toward the vent cleverly hidden in the ceiling, a glass of scotch in hand. Eyes dark and brooding, watching traffic and the sunset or the sunrise. Time seems to have no bearing on you. You are the same at dawn as you are midnight, always put together and perfect and silent and powerful and tensed.

The elevator whooshes open, no *ding* here. Just the door sliding open to frame you. My throat closes and my mouth goes dry. You are shirtless and sweaty, wearing a pair of tight black sweatpants with the elastic cuffs tugged up to the knee, pristine white socks peeking up over the edge of black athletic shoes. Your muscled chest is coated in a sheen of sweat, beads trickling down between your pectorals, shining on your biceps, running down from your hairline over your temple and into the day-old stubble on your jaw. Your chest heaves rapidly. Cords trail from your ears, meet beneath your chin, and extend to your cell phone, which is in your hand. You are speaking rapidly in fluent Mandarin as you enter, and your eyes find me. A gleam mars the blankness of your expression as you see me, and I think you almost smile.

Even half naked and sweating, you are a work of art, perfect even thus—perhaps even especially thus—crafted particularly to please the female eye. To rile the female libido.

I take a large swallow of whisky to fortify my nerves, letting out a breath as you approach, still talking in a low voice in Mandarin. You stand two feet away from me, and I smell the sweat on you. The person on the other end of your conversation is speaking now, judging by your focused silence, and you reach down, take my glass from me, drain the rest of my scotch.

Gesture at the bottle with the glass as if I'm your servant, sent to fetch more for the imperious master.

I do so, refilling the glass, but I remain by the table and drink it myself, staring at you. I place the cigar in my teeth, baring them, an unladylike expression in the extreme, and replace the crystal stopper in the decanter. You lift your chin and your eyes crackle, spark, spit fire. You see then. You see that I will not be cowed any longer.

You spin away, stalk to the kitchen, say a few angry-sounding words in Mandarin, then resume listening as you pull two bottles of water from the refrigerator. You down one without stopping for breath as you listen. Say a few sentences, pause and listen, say a few more, and then slowly drink the second bottle.

Ignoring me now, are you? Fine by me. I take my seat and stare out at Manhattan, swilling my second glass of scotch and feeling the first. Smoking my cigar. Studiously not rehearsing what I will say, because I know whatever I might imagine you will say, it will not be close to the truth. You are not predictable.

Finally, you say what sounds like a good-bye, touch the screen, and stand in silence for moments more, finishing your water.

You turn to me. "Good morning, Isabel." This, from the kitchen, many feet away from where I sit.

"Good morning, Caleb."

"Early for scotch, isn't it?" Your voice, so calm, so deep, so deceptively hypnotic. Like staring into a sinkhole, unplumbed depths, darkness and mystery and danger.

I shrug. "I haven't been to sleep yet, so it is late, for me."

Your expression hardens at this. "I see. And how is Logan?"

"None of your concern," I return. "What *is* your concern is that he told me how you got him put in prison."

You smirk. "Ah. He told his side of the story, did he?"

"His side?"

A nod. "There are two to every story, aren't there?" You swagger to me. Sit in the chair opposite mine, nearly empty water bottle in hand. "He went into the situation eyes open, Isabel. He knew exactly what he was getting himself into, but wasn't smart enough to not get caught."

"So what he told me is true."

"Oh yes. Very much so. He was a pawn. I used him, kept him disposable, and let him take the fall when the SEC came knocking. I was grooming him for it the entire time, keeping him isolated, keeping him flush with cash, making sure he had the requisite skills to do what I needed. And he did. So I made use of him. Lured him in, hook, line, and sinker. And then, yes, I intentionally set him up to take his share of the blame when things went bust, as I always knew they would. And really, I didn't set him up. I just made sure he was out in the open and I wasn't. I didn't accuse him of or frame him for anything he didn't do. If you're going to commit a crime, you have to plan on getting caught, and have a plan for getting away when you do. Your boyfriend was a sucker, Isabel. And if you're expecting an apology or an explanation for that, or for any of the many ways I've made my fortune . . . well, don't hold your breath. I will not apologize to anyone, not for anything."

"I would never expect an apology from you, Caleb."

"You know me better than that, obviously."

"No one knows you, Caleb."

You finish your water and crumple the bottle into a ball, twisting on the cap. "Not true. You know me. Better than anyone, I think."

"Which is saying something, because you are a complete mystery to me."

You merely breathe and stare at me for a while, and I merely breathe and stare back. I set my scotch down. I've had enough. I'll need my wits about me for this, something tells me.

The silence extends. The history between you and Logan is irrelevant, really. It doesn't concern me, or the crux of my problems. It's rather underwhelming, actually.

"What do you want, Isabel?" you ask, eventually.

"I don't know," I say, truthfully. "I wish I did."

I hand you my glass of scotch, but keep the cigar. It's something to do with my hands, something to distract myself from your beauty. You take the tumbler and swirl the amber contents, toss back a sip. I watch your Adam's apple bob as you swallow.

Your eyes pin me. "You *do* know, you're just afraid to say it to me."

Damn you for being right. "I want my freedom. I want to be . . . a real person. I want to love and be loved. I want a future." I swallow hard against the hot stone of emotion searing my throat. "I want my past back. I want . . . I want to not need you. To not be addicted to you."

"I will give you anything you ask me for, Isabel. I have never kept you prisoner. I kept you isolated, it is true. Sequestered, perhaps. But it was for your own good. And also, truthfully, because I am selfish. I do not want to share you. Not with anyone. Not any part of you. I must, however, so I do. I do not like it, but I do."

"So if I asked you to have the microchip in my hip removed, along with any other means of tracking my whereabouts, would you do it?"

"Is that what you are asking me for?"

"Are you a djinn, that I must phrase my requests with precision so as not to be tricked?"

You smirk. "Yes, Isabel. I am a djinn. I've been meaning to tell you."

Humor? Sarcasm? I really do not understand you. "It feels that way, sometimes. The more I try to extricate myself from your clutches, the more deeply entangled in you I become. I am loath to ask you for anything, because then I will only be all the more indebted to you."

"You owe me both everything and nothing." You gaze down at the scotch and do not explain that statement any further.

I wait. Finally, I must break the silence. "That does not make any sense, Caleb."

"It does, if you think about it. I created you in a sense, as we have both stated before. I was there when you woke up. I was there when you relearned how to walk and talk. I was there when you chose your name. I am woven into the fabric of your very personality. So yes, you owe me. But then again, you are a person, not a robot, not an object to be owned or made. So you owe me nothing. Some days I feel one way, some days the other." You take another sip, still not looking at me.

"I want the chip out, Caleb." I say.

You touch and swipe at the screen of your phone several times in quick succession, and then hold it to your ear. "Good morning, Dr. Frankel. I am well, and yourself? Good, good. I'm calling to see how soon you can be in New York. That facial reconstruction you did six years ago? The young woman? I would like you to reverse a certain element of that procedure. I'm sure you're aware what I mean. Correct . . . I think ten million dollars is a little high, Doctor. How about two? Eight? I think not. It's a very simple procedure, Doctor. It will take you twenty minutes at most. Fine, three, and I'll arrange a night out with one of the girls to an exclusive club I know of. Very good. Tomorrow then. I'll have Len meet you with the car at ten A.M. Eastern time, domestic arrivals at LaGuardia. Excellent. Thank you for your time, Dr. Frankel." You end the call with a touch of your index finger, set the phone on the arm of your chair, and glance at me. "There. By noon tomorrow, the chip will be gone."

Silence between us then, equal parts awkward and comfortable.

After a time I cannot measure, you stand up, drain the glass, set it on the table. "I have much yet to do today. So if there is nothing else, I need a shower. You are, of course, welcome to stay as long as you wish."

It cannot be that simple. That easy. There is so much I want to say, but I don't know how. Nothing fits. None of the puzzle pieces click properly. I feel panic at the sight of you walking away so easily.

"Wait." I stand. Take careful steps across the thick rug and halt behind you, mere inches from the rippling plateau of muscle that is your back. Watch you breathe. Watch your shoulders rise gently and fall subtly with each breath. "Tell me the story, Caleb. How you found me."

"I thought you'd be past that by now." You do not turn around. Your hands clench into fists.

Early-morning sun blazes through the eastward-facing windows, bathing us in brilliant yellow light. Dust motes dance in the gleaming spears of sunshine.

"I'll never be past that, Caleb. I need to hear it." What I do not say, a truth I do not dare utter, is that I doubt you.

I doubt the truth of the story. I wonder if, perhaps, it is just that: a story. A fiction you fabricated in order to bind me to you. But I have to hear it, one more time.

As Isabel.

You move with slow, lithe steps to a window. Rest a forearm against the frame, and your forehead against your arm. "It was late. Past midnight, I believe. It was raining, and had been for hours. The whole world was wet."

A flash of olfactory memory hits me: wetness, damp concrete, the smell of rain. I choke on the remembered scent.

"The sidewalks glistened in the streetlights," you continue, "and I have this very specific memory of the way the stoplights looked on the wet pavement of the road, red circles, yellow circles, green circles. I remember the way my shoes sounded, clicking dully on the pavement. I was alone on the sidewalk, which is rare in New York, even at midnight. But it was October, so the rain was cold, and it was windy. The kind of weather you didn't go out in unless you had to. The wind was so strong it would turn your umbrella inside out. It had done it to mine, and I'd stuffed it into a trash can. I was so wet. I'd been walking for blocks in the pouring rain. Funny thing is, I don't remember why I was out. Where I was going, where I was coming from, or why. I was absentminded. Just trying to get home as quickly as possible. I would have walked right past you. I almost did. I don't help the homeless as a rule. Not because I am too important, or because I'm too cheap, or any of that. But because I know from experience any help I give them will only go to more drugs, more alcohol, more gambling. I cannot help everyone in the city. When I first began making real money, I tried. I think everyone who first moves to New York tries to help the beggars. It's a rite of passage to becoming a New Yorker, I think. Eventually, you have to learn that you cannot spend all your money tipping the homeless. Especially when many of them aren't really even homeless, but merely too lazy to work. I know this, as well, from personal experience. I know their addictions. I know their predilection for destructive substances."

"You're wandering off topic, Caleb," I say.

You sigh. Make a fist and tap your knuckles against the glass in a rhythmic pattern: *tap-tap—taptaptap—tap-tap—taptaptap.* You are still staring out the window, head cradled against your forearm.

"Indeed I am."

You lapse into silence, into stillness.

When you speak again, your voice is slow and cadenced. "You were lying on the sidewalk, facedown. Wearing that blue dress. Curled up in a ball, in the rain. Just lying there, so still. I walked past you, and then something made me stop, I still don't know what. I turned around. Looked at you. Really saw you. I've walked past a thousand homeless men and women and not really seen them. But I saw you. I saw your hair, thick and black and so long. Wet and matted and sticky with blood. I saw that. The blood. Maybe that's what stopped me. You were bleeding. Not homeless, but hurt. Curled up, but you were trying to move. Trying to crawl. I turned back, and you reached out a hand, tried to drag yourself across the sidewalk. Your fingernails had been ripped off from dragging yourself like that for who knows how long. Your fingers were shredded. Your toes, too. Bloody from crawling across the ground, bleeding. Alone. Cold and wet. Dying."

You pause, and I see us in the reflection. Your face in profile, high cheekbones, square jaw, brownbrownbrown eyes like fragments of deepest space, black hair swept back and damp with sweat, a single strand curling on your forehead as if placed there by an artist. My profile is very similar: dark skin, olive-caramel, black eyebrows, black hair. Exotic features, wide, almond-shaped eyes darker even than yours, not truly black, which is biologically impossible, but so fiercely darkly brown as to appear so except under direct illumination. The sun is in my eyes now, so the brown is almost visible. My hair is braided, the queue hanging over my right shoulder onto the dove-gray fabric of my dress.

You breathe in, continue. "You looked at me. *'Ayudame,'* you said. *'Ayudame.'*"

A bolt of something hot and sharp and hard and excruciating hits me. "'Help me.'"

I slump forward against the window, leaning against it beside you.

You look at me in our reflection, surprise on your features. "You remember?"

I shake my head. "No. No more than ever, just faint impressions, like a memory of a dream. Some things are more . . . visceral, like the smell of rain. The smell of wet concrete. But I just . . . *know* . . . what that word means."

"*Que utilizas para hablar español, creo,*" you say.

You used to speak Spanish, I think.

"*Si lo hice,*" I respond, surprising myself. "*Aún lo hago, parece.*"

Yes, I did. I still do, it seems.

"I don't know why it never occurred to me to try speaking to you in Spanish," you say.

"Strange, indeed."

You eye me directly then, perhaps catching the sarcasm in my tone. It was faint, but present. "You looked so . . . pitiful. Helpless.

I picked you up. You were speaking, but it was too faint and too rapid for me to catch it. Something about your parents, I remember. Spanish is one of my weaker languages, and you were mumbling, and your accent was odd. Proper Spanish, I think, from Spain. Different from the Spanish spoken by Mexicans and other Latin Americans, which is the Spanish I know."

"How many languages do you speak?" I ask, curious.

"Five. I know some French, but not enough to be fluent, practically speaking. English, Czech, German, Spanish, and Mandarin. I'm strongest in German and Mandarin, my Czech is old and I don't speak it much anymore, and obviously English is my primary language now."

Now? What does that mean? I open my mouth to ask, but you speak over me, as if you realize that you've given something away, engendered more questions.

"You clung to me when I picked you up. More strongly than I'd thought you capable of. Begged me to go back, go back. I caught that much. But I couldn't figure out why. I asked you what was back there, and you became frantic. Incoherent. Screaming, thrashing. You were bleeding all over me, and I knew I had to get you to a hospital soon or you'd die. I have many skills, but dealing with injuries is not one of them. So I held on to you and carried you to the nearest hospital, which happened to be just a couple blocks away. It was where you were going, I think. Or trying to. You wouldn't have gotten there. Not in the shape you were in. As it was, the surgeons say you barely made it. You'd been bleeding profusely for a long time." You pause, and your eyes go vacant, unfocused, staring into memory. Something tells me you are telling me the truth. At least part of it. "I'll never forget it. That night. Holding you in my arms. You were so frail, so slight. So young. Only sixteen, I think. Or thereabouts. Sixteen, seventeen. A girl, still. But so beautiful already. Dying, terrified, lost, and your eyes, when I set you down on the stretcher when we got to the ER, you looked up at me with those great big black eyes of yours and I just . . . I couldn't walk away. Something in your eyes just caught me. You *needed* me. You clung to my hand and you wouldn't let go. I followed the medics as they wheeled the stretcher through the halls of the ER, to the operating room. They wouldn't let me back there with you. I think they thought I was your boyfriend or husband, which was the only reason they'd let me get that far. I remember so vividly the last moment I saw you. You were twisted on the stretcher, trying to see me. Desperate for me. It was like I knew you. Like you knew me. I'd never seen you before, never met you. But I just . . . I *did* know you. I don't know. It doesn't make any sense. But I couldn't leave. I couldn't. I walked out of the hospital, but it was like there was this . . . this *rope* tied around me, and you were pulling on it, pulling me back in. So I waited in the ER waiting room for the next six hours as they worked on you."

I believe this. I also believe you are lying about something. Not this, but something. Maybe lying by omission. I don't know. I don't dare ask. This is the most detail you've ever given me out of the thousands of times you've told me this story. I need this. *Need* it. I let you speak. Lean against the glass in silence as you talk. I feel as if I've been listening for a thousand years now. Logan, and now you. Hours of listening. I'm so tired, so exhausted, but I cannot turn away. Cannot turn a deaf ear to this, not when it contains truth you've kept so long hidden.

"They'd shaved your head." You glance behind, at your phone on the arm of the chair. Retrieve it.

I watch as you swipe across the screen, press your thumb to the circular button, and a plain black background appears. No, not black. Stars. Speckles of silver, a constellation. Which one, I don't know, can't tell. You tap on a white icon with a multicolored rosette, like a flower made of all primary colors in an overlapping wheel. Photos appear. You tap a button near the top, and the photo icons get smaller, multiply, arrange themselves by year. You scroll down so the photos move backward in time. I catch your face, a car, snow, a painting, me, me, me, in states of undress, asleep, not looking at you, clasping my bra behind my back, head turned in profile. So many photos of me. None of Rachel, none of Four or Six or anyone else. Just me. Tiny little squares of color like a mosaic, a composition of me. You scroll down, down, down through the years. To 2006— not 2009. You touch the row of photos so fast I almost doubt what I saw, and they expand, organized now by location, some from New Jersey, most from various boroughs of New York City. More scrolling through the photos from that year, until you find one. *The* one. Me, again. So young. My god, so young.

I barely recognize myself. My face is battered. Scratches. Cuts. Bruises. So thin. Delicate-looking, birdlike frailty. My head is shaved down to black stubble, highlighting the contours of my skull and the high sharpness of my cheekbones and the almond-shaped width of my eyes. There is a bright, wicked, reddish-pink scar on my scalp, on the left side, crossed by jagged black threads. I am looking at you. At the camera, the phone. Not smiling, just staring. Wide eyed and curious.

I do not remember this. But I am staring at you. I am lying in a bed. The frame of the photograph contains a bit of silver rail, pillow, some blue fabric, probably the hospital gown. How can you have taken this photograph of me, looking so fresh, so candid?

"You came out of the initial surgery just fine. Woke up after, everything seemed fine. I snapped this. You remembered me. We didn't really talk, just sat together. Then the nurses kicked me out, saying you needed to sleep. And when I came back the next day, you were gone. They said something had gone wrong during the night. Swelling in your brain. They had to do emergency surgery, put you in a medically induced coma. You didn't wake up from it for six months."

I take the phone from you and stare at myself. The younger me. As if I could find clues to my past, to my former self in this digital photograph, nothing but pixels, nothing but ones and zeroes. I cannot. I do not see myself in this. I see a girl, a sixteen-year-old girl. Lost and alone, trying to be defiant. Staring up at a camera held by the man who'd saved me, unhappy but daring. Brave, but scared. I see this. Did I know then that my parents were dead? Did I even have a chance to mourn? Or did the bleeding in my brain steal that from me as well?

I cannot get over the way I appear in the photo. My head shaved, how it highlights my eyes and cheekbones, the delicate but somehow strong shape of my head. I look a little masculine, but I am yet somehow unmistakably female. Involuntarily, I run my hand over the top of my head, almost expecting to feel stubble.

Could I?

What would it feel like? To feel nothing but scratchy stubble and scalp? No hair, no long thick black tresses.

I could do it. Perhaps I will.

Perhaps to truly become Isabel, I must shave my head and regrow my hair once more. Cut away the coiffured, styled, curled, brushed, perfect locks of Madame X and become Isabel, a new woman, rebirthed and fresh and raw.

You turn in place. Take your phone back, shut it off, toss it aside carelessly. It lands on the seat of the armchair and bounces once. You are looking down at me. You take my braid in your hand, tug my head back. You are standing close, not quite touching. Towering over me. Blocking out all the world with your muscled bulk, and I smell you. Feel your heat.

Anger flushes through me. I push you away, but you do not let go of my hair, and I must return to you or suffer the pain. "Let *go*, Caleb." I accept the pain and continue to push away.

You swell with an inbreath. "No," you growl. "I know you're angry. But you cannot deny that you feel this, Isabel."

I do. Oh, I do. And that is the true source of my rage. That I cannot help but *feel* this. Somehow your proximity eradicates all that exists beyond you, all that exists outside of you and me. Your heat and your brutal strength occlude my ability to remember why I hate you, why I do not trust you.

This feels familiar.

I know when you will move next. You will wait a beat . . . a second . . . a third, and then—yes. Now. You cup the back of my neck, my own hair crushed against my neck, soft and silky against my skin, between my neck and your hand. And you lift me up thus, force me up to my tiptoes and your lips are insistent on mine. The kiss blasts me. Shadows of confusion contort and cavort with rays of truth, dance on the walls of my twisting mind like a puzzle of chiaroscuro. You kiss me dizzy and then release me. Abruptly, violently.

"Fuck," you snarl. "*Fuck*. I taste him on you. I *smell* him."

"You knew," I say, wiping at my lips with the back of my wrist. "You knew where I was going, and who I'd be with."

"That's different than tasting it."

"And how do you think I feel, watching you fuck Rachel?" I hiss. "How do you think that feels for me, knowing you leave me, still smelling of me, and go to her. Bed *her* . . . taste *her*, fuck *her*. And then come back to me, and bed me, taste me, fuck me, and now both of us are on your skin. Or more, even? The other girls on that floor, too, maybe. Are there others? Other girls, in other buildings? Girlfriends elsewhere in the city, who know nothing of each other? Like that girl from the limo . . . what was her name, the Jewish one?"

"Isabel—" you begin.

"There is nothing you can say to me, Caleb. Nothing that will make it better. Nothing that will take away that betrayal. And then you did what you did to me, right there by that elevator. The way you *used* me." I swallow hard against the rage and the hurt. "The way you've *always* used me. It's never been about us. It's been about me belonging to you. Being your *whore*. Only you do not pay me in money, you pay me in *life*. You pay me in things, in false memories and mantras in the night, old stories and half truths. You pay me in things far less useful or tangible than mere currency, Caleb. And I will not accept those forms of payment anymore."

I turn then, and you let me go. Allow me to walk away. But then you're behind me. Standing far too close. Breathing on me. Your front touching my back. I can feel your erection against my backside, and your hands clutch my hips. Your lips touch the curve of my neck, near my shoulder.

You murmur to me.

"Can you walk away from this, Isabel? How right we feel together? Yes, I use you. But you use me just the same. You accept what I give, and you take more from me. You do not stop me. You do not say no. You beg for more. Not in words, but sex is not about words, is it? You beg for more with the way you breathe, the way you tense when I draw closer to you, the way you arch back into me. The way you lift your hips when I touch you. The way you moan when I make you come, over and over and over. You come for me, Isabel." Your large, powerful hands with your squared-off, manicured nails and rough calluses paw across my hips, one scraping up to cup my breast, the other down to my core. "Do you remember the first time I touched you?"

I cannot breathe. God, I remember. All too well, all too vividly. I remember. I'd felt it coming for so long. Weeks. Months. Years, even.

Tension building, heightening, mounting. The way you looked at me, didn't quite touch me. Almost, but not quite. We were in my condo, which was new. Still smelling of fresh paint. I'd lived in a different apartment in that building until then, a smaller one. Much like it, but not as large, not as nice. But very similar. I was standing at the kitchen counter, looking at my new home. Admiring the dark hardwood floor and the bookshelves, daydreaming of all the books I'd put on them—*you'd* put on them. And you came up behind me, just like this. An inch away at first. I smelled your cologne, and felt you there. You put your hands on the counter to either side of me. Just stood there. Inhaling my scent. I wanted you. I wanted to touch you. I remember that. Needing to know how your muscles would feel. Needing . . . something. I wasn't sure what, but something. And when you edged closer so your body was touching mine, I knew. I'd straightened, and you'd moved closer. I felt your chest against my back, and the thick ridge of your erection. I remember fighting it. Not knowing if it was right or wrong, nor understanding the potency of my desire.

But when your hands touched my waist and skated down to cup my hips, I had no choice but to let out the breath I'd been holding and melt into you.

Second by second, you seduced me with nothing but touch, and I let you. I ate it up, truth be told. Devoured every touch. Felt you remove my clothing, bit by bit, until I was naked in that kitchen and your hands were on my skin and you were tasting my flesh and I was moaning. You tasted me then. Buried your face between my thighs and made me come. And then you bent me over the counter and drove into me right there. It surprised me, but excited me. And when you were done, you carried me to the bedroom, set me in the bed. Touched my skin. My curves. And in not too many minutes, you were ready again and this time you rolled me to my hands and knees and took me once more, and you commanded me to keep quiet and told me not to come until you instructed me to do so. It lasted for a time I could not measure. You allowed me to come close to climax, and stopped. Closer, and stop. Closer and closer, stop. And when you did let me come, I was ripped apart by an orgasm so potent I cried.

My skin is hot and my breathing falters, just remembering.

"You remember." You pinch my nipple through dress and bra, and I gasp. "I waited so long to have you. Years, I waited. I wanted you every single day, but you weren't ready. So I waited, and waited, and waited. When we moved you into that condo, I was planning to wait longer yet. But you were standing there, and you were just so fucking beautiful that I had to be closer to you. And the way you reacted, I knew you wanted me. I knew you were ready. Not before or since have I ever experienced anything so beautiful and erotic and incredible as that first time with you. You were so responsive. You knew what you wanted. You weren't a virgin, Isabel. You had no more memory of yourself then than you do now, but I could tell. You knew what you were doing, and what you wanted, even if you didn't know you knew."

"Years?" Those early years are a blur. I remember your presence, always you, only you. I remember wanting you, wondering why you didn't touch me, kiss me. And then you did, and I glutted on you.

"Every single day, every moment I was near you, I wanted you. Obviously, at first, you were barely able to function. But after you regained mobility and speech, it got so much harder to resist you. I taught you, educated you, trained you. Worked out with you, ate with you. And all that while, I craved you." You drive a finger against my core, through my dress. "As I crave you now."

My next words are foolish, daring, and so very, very stupid. But I cannot stop them. "And do you still crave me, knowing another man has touched me, Caleb? Do you still crave me, knowing another man has *tasted* me, touched me, kissed me?"

You spin away with a snarl so feral I wonder if perhaps you truly are an animal in human disguise. You scrape your hands through your hair, stalk away, glance at me with unbridled rage so fierce it frightens me. A rare look into your deepest emotions. You pace with angry, leonine steps to the table containing the decanter of scotch, pour a huge measure, and toss it back in one swallow, hissing at the burn.

"Do not test me, Isabel."

"Or what?" I ask, my voice calm and quiet, filled with the venom you taught me so well. "Will you beat me? Kill me? Turn me out? What will you do if I continue to test you? You are a hypocrite and a liar, Caleb Indigo. If that's even your name." Rage suffuses me. "You crave me, but not me. Not *me*, Isabel. You crave *Madame X*, the nameless, identityless woman you created. I was your golem, Caleb. I know this. I see this. You formed me out of clay, baked me in the fires of your controlling and mysterious ways. But now—now the clay and the stone are cracking and falling away, and the true woman beneath the perfectly shaped skin of the golem is emerging, and you hate that. You *hate* it. Because I'm not the woman you thought I was. Because I am not so completely *yours* anymore."

"Such poetry, Isabel. You are very eloquent in your anger." Your voice is low, thinner and sharper than the blade of an electron splitter.

You move with the slow, precise gestures of a man in complete control of his rage. You are better than useless displays of anger, better than tantrums. You do not hurl the glass to smash on the floor or against the wall. Such a gesture would be satisfying, perhaps, but useless. Petty, and empty. No, you take a moment and merely breathe. I watch your chest swell and contract. I watch your fists clench and loosen. I watch your eyes pierce me, unblinking, staring, and you are utterly inscrutable. I do not know your thoughts. I do not know what moves beneath the surface of your carefully shuttered expression, coiling and diving and not quite breaching the surface.

You are leviathan.

And my rage is the callow fury of a young woman only now learning how to express her emotions.

You stand before me. Stare down at me. "You cannot deny me, Isabel. You walked away, and yet here you are once more. In *my* home. You tremble. With rage, yes."

A step closer, and your chest brushes against the tips of my breasts, and even through the fabric of my dress and bra, my nipples respond to your proximity.

"But also, you tremble with desire." Your lips brush my earlobe. "For *me*."

I am stronger than this.

I am stronger than this.

You cup my core with a broad, hard hand. "Your pussy is wet." You bite my earlobe, whisper dirty secret truth against the shell of my ear. "For me."

I am stronger than this.

I am stronger than this.

Your words leach my lungs of air. Your proximity snarls my will and tangles it. You are a sorcerer, and you weave magic of singular purpose: to seduce me.

You slide your hands up my front, grasp my breasts.

Clutch the V of fabric between them.

Slowly, slowly, with exquisite control, you rip my dress open from top to bottom. Unclasp my bra with a single deft flick of your hands. Tear apart my underwear at the seam over my hip, and the scrap of lace tumbles to the floor.

I am gasping for breath, my breasts heaving. My blood thrums as I hunt vainly for the will to resist you.

I sob once, and then your lips are on mine and your hands are lifting me and somehow you've shed your sweatpants and shoes and socks and you are utterly naked with me in this echoing space with dawn light battering blindingly upon us, illuminating us, leaving no shadows in which my weakness can be hidden, no darkness that can absorb the stain of my sin.

You press my spine to the coolness of the window glass. Your hands are large and rough and strong on my backside, holding me up, spreading me open for you.

I bite your shoulder as you thrust into me, taste blood as I am filled by you.

As Madame X I was owned by you.

As Isabel, I am fucked by you.

A thrust. A thrust. I sob, and you buck into me. My flesh squeals against the glass. This is agony, this is ecstasy. You move like a machine, hips driving you into me with pistonlike power.

But . . .

There is a void within me now. It was always there, perhaps, but now I feel it most keenly, as you fill me and fail to sate me.

I know your patterns. I know your needs.

You cannot stomach being face-to-face very long. I wait, but it isn't long before you lower me to the floor, spin me in place and press me to the glass. Not just my hands, but all of me. Breasts smashed flat against the cold glass, thighs, stomach, cheek. Naked, I am pressed against the glass for all the world to see.

I am exposed.

And you are behind me, pushing into me. One hand on my hip, guiding my motions, the other clutching the queue of my braid.

You fuck, and you fuck, and you fuck.

In this, there is no pleasure for me. For the first time that I can remember, you do not spare a single moment of attention for me. You only drive with single-minded madness into me again and again and again, hips slapping loudly against the taut roundness of my backside. I hear that, and only that. The *slap-slap-slap* of your body meeting mine. I glance out the window, and across the street I can almost see a face in a window, watching me.

You come, and I feel the hot rush of your seed filling me, dripping out of me.

You have claimed me, but there is a secret only I know: Your mark does not adhere to my skin, your claim does not sear into my soul.

In the last few minutes, I felt the earth shift, felt the shackles of your sorcery fall away.

You step away, and I spin in place, rest my bottom and shoulders against the glass, stare at you.

Something within me aches.

There are no words to speak.

I turn away from you, return my gaze to the world beyond the glass. After a time the silence grows profound, becomes empty, and I know you've walked away.

My cigar, at some point set in an ashtray, still smolders. I place it between my teeth, pour a measure of scotch, blow thick plumes of smoke into the rays of sunlight, and swallow burning mouthfuls of scotch in an attempt to drown the screams of self-loathing welling up within me.

I smoke, and I drink, and I listen to you shower.

I remain naked, because clothes cannot cover my shame.

You emerge dressed, hair wet and clean and slicked back, dressed in a tan suit with a pale blue shirt, no tie, baring that sliver of skin. You stare at me, a frown pinching your face, razoring a line into the bridge of your nose.

I want to yell at you. Tell you how much I hate you. Tell you how empty I feel. Tell you that everything is different now, everything is changed. I am changed. If I am addict and you are a drug, the high has soured.

I say nothing, however, because there are no words that can express the weltering chaos within me.

Neither of us speaks, and after a moment, you leave. The elevator doors close together, narrowing my view of you until there is nothing left but the doors.

And I am alone once more.

I give in to the screams, and my voice echoes off the glass in raw, ragged, jagged fragments. I scream until my voice gives out, and then I weep.

I allowed you to use me again. I feel the cancer of it like a film of grease on my soul.

No more.

Never again.

I cease weeping, and I shower you off me.

I step into a long, loose dress, wrap myself in a blanket. While away the hours with a book, bored and alone and drowning in self-loathing and disgust. Eventually, the day fades, and I fall asleep on a couch, because I do not want to be in your bed, even to sleep.

ELEVEN

Rain slices like knives forged from ice. I shiver, but not from cold; I bleed. I taste blood in my mouth, feel it spill warm and wet from my head and my hip, dribble down my cheek and drip off my chin. Darkness. All is dark. A pale rectangle of light from a window illuminates a portion of sidewalk and some of the street, the curb between them.

I hear sirens. They sound like the warbles of prehistoric birds, echoing off cliff faces.

I want only to be warm.

I want to not hurt.

My stomach shudders, and I hear a sound. A sob. A scream.

My throat aches, and I realize the sobs and screams emit from me.

I am alone.

I cannot lift my head.

I can stare sideways at the pale scrap of light and wish I could reach it, crawl to it, lie in its warmth. Anything must be warmer than here, where the rain batters me and the cold cracks open my bones, freezes my marrow.

Why am I here? I don't remember.

I have an idea of horror, dreamed remnants of terror. Smashing glass, twisting metal. Razors splitting open my skull. Hammers bashing my body. Weightlessness. Darkness.

Blood.

So much blood.

A face appears. An angel?

No, too dark, the eyes like glinting shards of night betray too many devoured dreams, speak of nightmares feasted upon.

An incubus.

I fancy I can see his wings spread to either side of his wet, muscular body, thick coiled whipping things like feathered serpents. I blink, and he is only a man.

I blink, and I know his face.

I scream, or perhaps I only try to. He is lifting me, and I see blood on his hand as he brushes my hair away from my eyes.

The world tilts and darkens, and a hole attempts to swallow me from inside out, and then I see the flames. I want to be in those flames, where it is warm. I want to be in those flames. I want to be with those in the flames.

I strain, and iron bands hold me back. I reach for the flames. I peer into them, and I can see a hand, blackening. A shirtsleeve crisping, curling. Perhaps I imagine it all. Perhaps I imagine the flames.

I don't know. I know I am cold.

So cold.

I know pain is all.

I know the iron bands strapped around me are warm and breath smelling of whisky bathes my face.

I look up, and eyes pierce mine. "Sssshhhh. You'll be okay. I'll get you help." The voice is the texture of a blacked-out room, smooth as velvet, powerful and deep.

I am falling. I fight against gravity, because that way lies darkness, and in the darkness lurks obscurity. I don't know what that thought means, but I know I must fight.

I lose.

I fall.

Through depthless dark, I fall.

wake with a start. My voice is hoarse. My throat hurts.

You brush away a flyaway strand of hair. Shush me.

I taste the dream, still.

I push you away. Your touch holds no comfort, your voice no respite from the images haunting my brain. "Get away."

"It's me, it's Caleb."

"I know." I struggle for a single deep breath. "Don't—don't touch me."

I sit up, curl the blanket tighter around my shoulders, hunch in on myself, eyes clenched shut so hard I see stars and my eyes hurt. I do not want to share this with you, but I must speak it out into the world so it doesn't die the death of dreams, lost somewhere between brain and tongue.

"I remember how wet it was," I whisper. "I remember the darkness. I remember hurting. I remember being so cold. I remember being on the sidewalk and seeing this patch of light and wishing I could just make it to the light, because maybe it would be warmer there. And then you . . . and flames. I feel like—I feel like there was more in the dream, but I can't remember it. I can't see it now."

"But you're safe now. You're okay."

I shake my head. "No. I'm not safe. Not with you. You do not tell me all of the truth. There *is* no truth. And I'm not okay. I'm a splintered ghost of a person. And I don't know how to put the pieces together. I don't even *have* all the pieces."

"Isabel—" you begin.

I chop out with my hand to silence you, and make contact with your leg. "No. Shut up. You are an incubus. You lie."

A moment of silence. And then your voice, cold and distant as you stand up. "Dr. Frankel is here. There's a clinic a few floors down. He's setting up there."

I stand up, let the blanket fall to the floor at my feet. "I'm ready. Let's go."

"Do you want anything to eat?" you ask.

"Do not suddenly begin pretending as if you care, Caleb." I breeze past you.

You seize me in a vise grip. Spun around. Fingers pinch my jaw, as if to pry the mandibles apart. "You will *never* comprehend how deeply I care." You release me.

"No, I will not." I stare up at you. Your eyes are blazing, hot, open, wild, glinting with fury and agony. "Nor do I wish to." This is a lie.

You stare down at me, jaw muscles clenching and pulsing, eyes darting, seeking something in my gaze. Not finding it, I do not think. "I do not know how—I don't know how to make you understand. I am not that man."

"You have not tried."

"I have. For so long, for—"

"How long, Caleb? How long?" My understanding of my own life's time frame doesn't make sense.

The years, the dates, how long I was in a coma, how many years of memory I have, how reliable the memories I do have are . . . all of this is in doubt. Nothing I know, nothing I *think* I know, is necessarily true.

"How old am I?" I ask.

"They weren't sure exactly how old you were when the accident happened," you say.

"And what year did the accident happen in?"

"In 2009," you say, immediately.

"And I was in a coma for how long?"

"Six months."

I push past you. "I think you are a liar."

"Isabel—"

"Take me to Dr. Frankel."

Your teeth click together, your head tilts back, your eyes narrow. "Very well, Ms. de la Vega. As you wish."

We wait for the elevator in tense silence. As the doors open, I turn to you. "Tell me the truth, Caleb."

"About what?"

"About me. About what happened. About everything."

You twist the key. "Dr. Frankel is waiting."

Not another word is spoken. We transfer elevators one floor down, and go from there to the thirty-second floor. Bare hallways, featureless, identical doors differentiated by alphanumeric designations. A sparse white room, a bed with white paper laid over hard, plasticky leather. Dr. Frankel is a short, pudgy man at the unforgiving end of middle age, a man to whom time and gravity have not been kind. Jowls hang and sway, a pendulous belly covers a belt buckle, khaki pants are tight around thighs and loose around calves. Brown eyes reflect a quick mind, with hands that are small and quick and nimble and gentle and sure.

"Ah. The patient. Very good." A pat of a hand invites me to sit on the paper, which crinkles and shifts under my weight. "Yes, yes. I remember you. A rather remarkable work I did, if I say so myself. Not a trace of your old injuries remains. Very good, very good. This will be quick and easy. A local anesthetic, a quick incision, and it'll be done. No pain, no mess."

I lie down on the bed. "Let us proceed then."

A clearing of the throat. "Well, the incision is in your hip, you see. So I'll, ah, need you to disrobe. From the waist down, at least."

Without hesitation, I hike my dress up to my waist, staring at the wall, and work my underwear off. "Better?"

"Um. Yes. I would have left the room, you know."

"I want this over with. I want the chip out."

"I didn't think you knew."

"I didn't," I say. "I do now."

A bob of a heavy head. "I see. I see. Well. I'll just spread this over you . . ." Dr. Frankel drapes a large square of blue tissue over my waist, a square in the middle left open.

The square encloses the scar on my hip, and the doctor uses medical tape to make sure the tissue remains in place. Dr. Frankel dons a pair of blue exam gloves from a packet, very carefully not touching any of the glove except the very ends near the wrists as he slides them on.

Lifting a syringe, the doctor casts a glance to me. "A little pinch now." There is a brief sharp poke, coldness against my skin, and then nothing. "Some iodine to sterilize your skin . . ." A small white carton has its lid torn off, revealing a brown liquid and a sponge.

The iodine is cold and turns my skin orange.

Another packet is opened, revealing a scalpel and a pair of forceps. Dr. Frankel lifts the scalpel and prods my scar with it. "Can you feel that?"

I shake my head. "No."

"Very good. I'll begin. Look away, perhaps? And if the anesthetic wears off, let me know right away and I'll administer some more. I don't want you to feel a thing."

"All right. Carry on then."

I watch in curiosity as Dr. Frankel presses the tip of the scalpel directly over my scar, free hand keeping my skin taut. After a glance at me to make sure I'm not experiencing any pain, the incision is lengthened, precisely to the size of the previous one. Blood wells after a moment, and a cloth smears it away, and then forceps delve into the opening of my skin. I am morbidly fascinated, watching as my skin is parted. The scar isn't actually directly on my hip, but nearer to my buttock, just behind the bone, which explains how something like a chip could be inserted subcutaneously without leaving a bump. A moment of searching with the forceps, and then Dr. Frankel withdraws them, pincering a tiny red-dripping square of plastic. The chip is so small I wouldn't have suspected anything amiss even if it had been placed where it would leave a bump. It clatters in a bowl, and then Dr. Frankel deftly sews the incision shut with a few quick loops of black thread and tapes a bandage over the area.

The entire procedure took perhaps five minutes from start to finish.

"Wonderful. That's that." Snapping the gloves off, Dr. Frankel wraps up the entire mess, sans surgical instruments and syringe, and discards it in the trash, and the instruments are deposited in a box on the wall labeled SHARPS.

"Thank you very much, Dr. Frankel," you say. "Your balance should reflect your payment by the end of business today."

"I have no doubt." A quick glance at Caleb. "And this evening?"

"A limo will be waiting for you at your hotel, with your companion for the evening already in attendance." You pause. "I must remind you of the rules regarding my employees. They are companionship for the evening *only*. And, of course, your complete discretion regarding the procedure you just performed is expected."

"Don't have to remind me on either score, Mr. Indigo. I know the rules. I signed an NDA years ago, and besides, I didn't get where I am by having loose lips."

"Of course not," you say.

A glance at me. "Take it easy on those stitches. There aren't many, and they'll come out on their own in time. But try not to get them wet for forty-eight hours at least."

"I'll keep that in mind. Thank you, Doctor."

"Pleasure. Next time, try to give me more than a couple hours' notice, will you?"

"Hopefully there won't be a next time," you say.

Dr. Frankel laughs. "Ah yes, the plight of the doctor. Happy to see us show up, happier yet to see us leave. And happiest of all to never have to see us in the first place." With that last quip, Dr. Frankel is out the door.

When the good doctor is gone, you glance at your watch, and then at me. "A rather expensive seven minutes, I'd say."

"If you hadn't put it there in the first place, you wouldn't have had to spend three million dollars to have it removed." I frown. "Why *did* you have him put a tracking chip in me, Caleb?"

A breath that isn't quite a sigh. "A last-minute quirk, you could say. A means of ensuring I could protect—"

"Your investment?"

"Are you so determined to believe the worst?"

"Yes." I step into my underwear and allow my dress to fall back into place as I stand up. I wobble, as my hip is still numb. "With reason."

"You misunderstand me, and the situation."

"Because you do not tell me the truth. Thus, I have no way of truly understanding the situation." I prop myself on the bed in an attempt to find my balance. "Or of understanding you. You, most of all."

You merely stare at me. At a loss for words, perhaps? I wait, but you say nothing.

I shake my head and walk away, or try to. I have to cling to one surface or another, have to surf from bed to door post, door post to wall, wall to elevator. I have to lean against the elevator wall and focus on breathing. The local anesthetic is beginning to wear off, and my body is now reminding me that I just had my skin sliced open and sewn shut. It isn't a pleasant sensation. At no point do I stop to wonder if you'll follow me, because you won't. This isn't new.

I had a cell phone, at one point. But I am unaccustomed to carrying any possessions with me, and I've misplaced it. At Logan's home, perhaps? I don't know. I wish I had it now. I would call him. Beg him to come get me.

I make it outside, where the world is bright and loud and chaotic. I feel panic creeping at the edges of my mind, lurking at the bottom of my lungs, stealing my breath. I focus on walking, clinging to the wall of the building. It is a laborious process, made all the harder when I run out of building and must totter to the intersection and pretend I am not about to collapse. The light turns, the crowd around me surges forward, and I am swept off balance. I nearly fall several times but rebound off those around me and manage to stay upright. Reaching the far side of the intersection feels like a miraculous accomplishment. I still cannot breathe, and the edge of my vision darkens, narrows, but each step requires such focus and determination that I cannot allow myself to falter, or I will fall.

And then I feel peace wash over me. I look around, and there he is. Tall, golden-haired, golden-skinned, eyes gleaming indigo. Striding toward me, arms swinging freely, the smile on his face a tender one, calm joy at merely seeing me. He's wearing the same tight dark blue jeans as the first time I saw him, this time with a red T-shirt, on which is written in large black letters: *VOTE "NO" ON DALEKS, STOP EXTERMINATION TODAY*, with a picture of some kind of robot covered in black knobs and armed with a gun. I do not understand many of his T-shirts. References to pop culture, I believe, things I've not seen either pre- or postamnesia.

He wraps me up in his arms, pulls me to his chest. He is warm and solid and comforting, his scent now familiar, cinnamon gum and cigarette smoke. I rest my ear over his heart and listen to his heartbeat, and I merely breathe for long moments. He doesn't speak, as if understanding without needing to be told that I am fragile right now.

His palm skates down my waist and comes to rest over my hip, over the stitches. I gasp in pain, and his hand flies away.

"Shit, are you hurt?" He holds me by the shoulder and examines me for signs of injury.

I shake my head. "No. Well, yes. I just had the microchip removed from my hip. No more tracking me. Not that way, at least."

"When did this happen?"

I shrug. "Ten minutes ago, perhaps?"

"Damn it, Isabel," he sighs. "You shouldn't be on your feet." He suits action to words, scooping me up in his arms and cradling me against his chest.

"Put me down, Logan," I murmur, hiding my face in his neck. "I'm fine. And besides, you can't carry me down the streets of Manhattan."

"The hell I will, the hell you are, and the hell I can't." He moves through the crowd with me in his arms as if I weigh nothing, and he is careful to make sure my head doesn't bump into anyone. "If a man carrying a woman down the street is the strangest thing these people see today, then they're not paying attention."

I don't want him to put me down. Not really. So I let him carry me. I enjoy his presence, his heat, his strength. Being taken care of. Cared for. Cared *about*.

"So . . . you and Caleb." It's a gentle prod, a hesitant inquisition.

My throat seizes. "I can't, Logan. Not just yet."

His lips touch my cheek. My forehead. "When you're ready. Or not at all. I'm here, okay? That's all you need to worry about. I'm here, and I've got you."

His big boxy silver SUV is parked a couple of blocks away, and he carries me all the way to it, never faltering or shifting his grip or acting for even a moment as if my not-insignificant weight is a burden. He sets me on my feet, opens the passenger-side door, and helps me in, closes the door after me.

Slides in behind the wheel, touches a button to start the engine. Immediately, loud, wild, raucous music fills the cabin. The music is chugging yet melodic, the singer a woman, her voice sweet yet full of rage, moving easily from singing to screaming—*I am the dark you created, I am your sin, I am your whore.* Logan moves to turn it off, but I stop him.

"Wait." There is something in the way she sings, the way she screams. Something in the lyrics. Something visceral in the madness of the instruments. "What is this?"

"The band is In This Moment. The song is called 'Whore.'"

"It could be about me."

We sit and listen. I am moved, deeply. The rage she so obviously feels, her ownership of the darkness within her, the demand for an answer to a question that has none . . . I empathize in some vulnerable corner of my soul.

And then the next song comes on. *Are you sick like me? . . . Am I beautiful?* There is more ire in this song, more deeply felt hatred and self-loathing and understanding of one's own filth.

It is all too close to the state of my existence, too near to who I am. I could devolve into a creature carved from fire and rage. I have been lied to and possessed and forced into molds that do not fit me; I have been brainwashed and made to be a thing I am not. My past has been hidden from me. The truth of all that is me has been kept buried. Even still, my desires are used against me. My needs made into weapons, forged into blades slicing open my own flesh.

I tremble, like a dry leaf in a long wind.

"I think that's enough," Logan says, when the song ends.

"No. One more."

He turns on a song called "Blood," and I focus in on the lyrics. *Dirty dirty girl . . . everything you ever took from me . . . dominate and you violate me . . .*

I close my eyes and fall into it. Give in to it. Scream with her. Sing with her. Lose myself to it.

He plays another one, "The Promise," and this one has a male voice added, and the promise of the title is that they will hurt each other.

I know that feeling. I feel it now. I risk a look at Logan, and I know it's true. I'll hurt him. I have hurt him. He just doesn't know it yet.

He drives, and I let him play whatever he wants. He tells me what each song and band is as they come on, one by one. He plays Halestorm, Flyleaf, Amaranthe, Skillet, Five Finger Death Punch— how do they come up with these names?

The one constant is rage.

This . . . this I understand.

We reach his house, and I've had a brief introduction to music that can reach the secrets in your soul and turn them real and give them voice. It turns out my voice is angry.

"My girl likes metal," Logan says, as he shuts off his truck.

"I'm not your girl." I hate how harsh I sound when I say this, and a look at Logan tells me I've hurt him. "That came out wrong. I'm sorry."

"No, it's true."

"But it's not what I meant. Or—it is, but not the way it sounded. I can't be your girl. I want to be, I wish I were. But . . . I can't. Logan, I just . . . *can't.*"

"Why not?"

"Because I'm broken. I'm all sharp edges and fragments. I'll just cut you to pieces if you try to keep hold of me."

"I don't mind bleeding for you."

"You shouldn't have to." I swallow bitterness in my throat. "Not for me. I'm not worth it."

"Not worth—?" He seems to choke, but I can't look at him. "Not *worth* it? God, that bastard's really done a number on you, hasn't he?"

"I did it to myself."

"I was right, wasn't I?"

"Yes." I step out of his vehicle, and he follows. He takes a seat on the bottom step of the stairs leading up to his home. "Why were you there, Logan? Just now, I mean. How are you always just . . . *there* . . . when I need you most?"

"I just . . . knew. I don't know. I can't explain it without sounding like a whacko. I just . . . knew I should be there. I knew you'd need me. I couldn't sit around and do nothing. We finished the acquisition and now we're off for a week, and I just . . . I was going crazy without you. And I knew you needed me." He digs in a pocket of his jeans and pulls out my cell phone. "Also, you left this at my place, so I was going to return it."

"Thank you."

A shrug. "What happened, Is?" He lights a cigarette and inhales deeply.

I take it from him, smoke with him. It tastes horrible, but the lightheaded dizziness is worth it, the sense of floating above it all, the momentary sensation of freedom. And it binds me to him in some way.

"More stories, more half truths, more lies." I stare at the concrete under my feet. "More of my weakness. More of all the things I've always known."

Logan is silent for a very long time, the cigarette pinched between forefinger and thumb, lazy tendrils of smoke curling up around his face. "But I was right."

"Do not mince words, Logan. Not to spare my feelings." I take the cigarette from him, inhale, watch the cherry glow brighter. Hand it back. "Or your own, for that matter."

He just blinks at me, takes one last drag, and with a violent flick of his hand sends the butt flying a dozen feet into the street, where it lands with an explosion of sparks. "Did you fuck him?"

I can barely manage a whisper. "Short answer . . . yes."

A silence, short and brutal. "Fuck. I knew it." He rises, paces away, tugs his hair free of the ponytail with a jerk, and shakes it out, spears his fingers through the wavy blond locks. Looks at me from ten feet away. "What's the long answer?"

"I hate myself for it. I knew it wouldn't change anything. It wouldn't change him. It wouldn't change me. It wouldn't bring answers. But . . . I'm weak, Logan. He mixes me up. I . . . don't even know how to explain it. But this time . . . I felt . . . empty. I realized if he does care at all, he just can't show it. Or he has a very bizarre way of showing it. I don't know. I'm no closer to knowing anything about myself or my past than when I left here, and now . . ."

"And now what, Isabel?"

"You, and me. How can you look at me?"

He touches my chin with a finger. I didn't know he was there in front of me, so absorbed in myself am I. "Why do you think I let you leave in the first place? Why do you think I wouldn't let us actually have sex?"

"I don't know."

"Well, that's bullshit, because you do." He sits beside me again. "I told you why."

I think back. "You said that there couldn't be a beginning to you and me until there was end to Caleb and me."

"Right." A pause. "And? Was that the end?"

"I don't know. I know you're hoping for a decisive answer here, but . . . I can't give it to you. It was an end to his hold on me, physically. But emotionally? I don't know. There are still so many questions I need the answers to. I—I'm tangled up, still, Logan. He *knows* things, but he's not telling me. You were also right about that. But I don't know why he's keeping things from me. What is there to be so secretive about? I just . . . I *need* to know more. And until I do, until I feel complete, I won't ever be totally free of Caleb."

"Can't fault you for that, I guess."

"And I don't know if this means anything to you, but . . . I didn't fuck him. He fucked me, and I let him. It's the way it's always been. I was complicit, I have to be honest about that. I allowed it, the way I've always allowed it. In the moment, when he's there, I just . . . I lose myself. I lose myself." I want to take his hand, but I am afraid to; I suffer a moment of bravery, slide my fingers under his. "Where does this leave us, Logan?"

He threads our fingers together. "I'm hurt. I'm upset. I mean, I knew it was going to happen, which is why I held us back. But it still sucks." He stands up, leads me inside. "I just need some time, you know? Put some space between you and him and . . . you and me."

I'm in no state to think about him and me. I can barely function. My mind is whirling like an orbital model of our galaxy, a million thoughts each spinning and all of them revolving in complicated, heliocentric patterns around the twin suns of Logan and Caleb. They are both supermassive entities, each possessing their own gravitational pulls on me.

Or maybe Caleb is a black hole, sucking in light and matter and all things in inexorable destruction, and Logan is a sun, giving life, giving heat, permitting growth.

Logan leads me to his living room, nudges me toward the couch. I sit. He lets out Cocoa, who welcomes me with exuberant puppy kisses and then lies on the floor and watches us. Logan vanishes into the kitchen and returns with two open bottles of beer and a half-empty bottle of Jameson. "A caveat, before we start drinking: This doesn't fix anything. But sometimes you need to just get hammered and not worry about the fucked-up mess that is your life. It gives you some space from everything. And I've discovered that I do my clearest thinking about problems when I've got a wicked hangover. Something about the pounding headache and roiling stomach just makes me more brutally honest with myself."

He hands me the bottle of whisky and one of the beers.

I just stare at him. "Where are the glasses?"

A laugh. "No glasses for this kind of drinking, sweetheart. Just pull right off the bottle."

"How much?"

"Two good swallows is about one decent-sized shot. But under the circumstances, I'd say just keep drinking until you can't handle any more."

This strikes me as very bad advice. But then, maybe that is the point: to get me very drunk very quickly.

I lift the bottle of whisky to my lips and take a tentative sip. It burns, but not the same way exactly as scotch. It's easier to drink, actually. I let the burn slide down my throat and breathe past it. And then I do as he suggested: I tilt the bottle up and take one swallow, a second, a third, and then it burns too badly and I'm gasping for oxygen and my throat is on fire. I drain half my beer in an attempt to assuage my protesting throat, after which my head is spinning.

Logan takes the bottle and does the same, drinking the same

amount as me and chasing it with beer. And then he does something truly strange. He lowers himself to the couch, sets the whisky and his beer on a side table, and drapes my feet onto his lap, tossing my shoes to the floor. Lifting one of my feet and cupping it in his palms, he digs his thumbs into the arch of my foot, immediately eliciting a moan from me.

"What are you doing, Logan?" I ask.

"Giving you one of life's greatest pleasures: a foot rub."

It is incredible. I don't want it to ever stop. It is intimate, so pleasurable it is nearly sexual. His thumbs press firmly in sliding circles over my arch, into my heel, the ball of my foot, and then his fingers crease between each of my toes and I giggle at the tickling touch. After a brief pause to sip beer, he gives my other foot the same treatment.

And then his fingers dimple into the muscle of my calf, kneading it in circles and from one side of my leg to the other. Higher, higher, near to my knee, and the massage becomes all the more intimate with every upward inch. The stretchy cotton of my dress is draped over his hands, one of which is holding my leg at the ankle, the other massaging my calf.

I've forgotten my beer; I take a pull, then peer at him. "This feels amazing."

"Good. You need some amazing things in your life."

"There's you." I didn't mean to say that; whisky loosens my tongue, it would seem.

Logan doesn't laugh at my faux pas. "One might say I'm a bad influence on you." He hands me the whisky, and I take it, down two swallows, and immediately chase it. "Case in point: I've got you chasing whisky with beer."

"That is true," I say. "Very true, indeed. But I don't mind. Mainly because your brand of bad is always so good."

This earns me a laugh. "I'm glad you think so."

His touch shifts from right leg to left, and it's impossible to think of anything but his hands on my leg, the way his fingers dig into the muscle and the smooth skin just beneath the back of my knee. The intimacy of it, the way I wish and want, in the dirty places in my mind, for his touch to slide upward, even though I know that's the worst thing that could happen right now.

"Hungry?" he asks.

I nod sloppily. "Yes. Very. Veryvery."

"You're drunk," he says, laughing.

"I am. Yes indeed, I am drunk. *Aaaaaand* I like it."

I also like this spot on the couch. It's comfortable, cozy. The couch has swallowed me, sucked me in.

"Good. That was the point. Didn't take much, though, did it?"

"I don't really drink very much, or very frequently. Caleb kept me . . . *healthy.*"

"Well I've got something unhealthy and delicious for you. Just hang tight." I hear plastic crinkling, silence, and then the microwave door open and close, the gentle hum of the microwave heating something. I'm curious, but far too pleasantly and comfortably drunk to make the effort of looking to see what he made. I smell it after a moment, but can't identify it.

He plops himself down on the couch beside me, a ceramic plate in one hand, two more beers in the other. He takes the bottle out of my hand—I hadn't realized it was empty, nor do I remember finishing it—and replaces it with the full one. I take a sip, and it is, like every sip before it, delicious. But then I smell the food. I don't remember the last time I ate. The plate holds chips, yellow corn chips with cheese melted on them, liberal glops and strings and pools of orange cheese piled high on triangular white-yellow chips.

I try one; oh. Oh my. OH MY GOD.

"Wha-is-this?" I ask, my mouth full of chip and cheese.

He laughs. "It's like feeding an alien. I swear you've never had any good food. It's nachos, man. Cheesy chips. Best drunk or stoned food there is."

"Except pizza," I add, "and chicken shawarma."

"And potato chips."

"And beer."

"Beer is very, very important," Logan agrees. He reaches for a chip, but then stops and laughs. Apparently I've eaten them all. "You are hungry, aren't you?"

I stare at him, embarrassed. "Sorry. I didn't mean to pig out."

Logan just shook his head, laughing. "Don't be ridiculous, and don't apologize." He reaches up and tugs a lock of my hair. "You want something else?"

I just nod. I can't believe I ate all that already. It was a big plate full of chips. "Yes, please."

He heads toward the kitchen but then stops and leans over the back of the couch, resting his chin on my shoulder. I want very badly to kiss him, his cheek, his mouth, his temple, his anything. I don't dare.

"You ever have a P-B-and-J?" he asks.

"A what?"

"I'm guessing that's a no. Peanut butter and jelly sandwich."

I shrug. "Not that I remember."

"Comin' up then. You'll love it. Another staple food. I lived on P-B-and-J growing up. Still a go-to when I don't know what else to have."

He returns in a few minutes with four sandwiches, two for me, two for him. The first bite is . . . delectable. Crunchy peanuts, cool fruit jelly, soft white bread. I finish the first one in moments. I'm halfway through the second when it hits me.

The sun is bright. Blinding. Shining in my eyes as I sit at a table. I can feel the wood under my hands, rough, thick-grain wood, deep cracks and grooves, yet polished smooth by ages of wear. There is a groove under the index finger of my right hand, and I run my fingernail back and forth in it. I've done this a million times. Sat here, rubbing a fingernail in this groove, waiting. I smell . . . the sea. Brine. Ocean waves crash somewhere far away. A seagull caws, another answers.

Silhouetted by the sun is a woman, tall, willowy. Long black hair hanging loose down nearly to her waist. Her hips sway to music only she can hear as she stands at the counter, doing something. She is making a sandwich. Spreading grape jelly, thickly. Peanut butter, with lots of peanuts in it. Cuts it in half diagonally, sets it in front of me. On a white porcelain plate traced around the rim with delicate blue flowers.

She leans down, and the sun is blocked out by her body, allowing me to see her. I see her smile, spreading across her face like sunrise. Her eyes twinkle. "Coma, mi amor." Her voice is music.

She touches her lips to my cheek, and I smell garlic and perfume.

". . . Isabel? Isabel!" Logan's voice filters through to my awareness.

"My . . . my mother used to make me these sandwiches. When I was a girl. I think. I just . . . I saw her. I was sitting at a table. It was by the ocean, I think. That's all—that's all I remember. But I could . . . *feel it.*"

Logan is at a loss for words, but I don't need his words. He wraps an arm around me, tugs me close. "I'm here, baby."

It's all I need. There is nothing he can say, nothing to be said.

His heartbeat is a steady thump, a reassuring soft drumming under my ear. I have no idea what time it is, and I don't care. The world is spinning, and I feel disconnected from it. As if I could fly away at any moment, cast loose by centrifugal force.

"At Caleb's . . . I had a dream. A memory, I think. M'not sure. A car crash. But only maybe. All I knew was that I was hurt, and it was raining, and I was cold, and it was dark. So much pain . . . I was alone.

But then he was there, but it felt like I'd seen him before. And it wasn't a mugging. That's what he always told me. A mugging gone wrong. But that's not what happened. It's not. He lied to me. But why? Why lie about that?"

"Because maybe the truth of what happened is something he doesn't want you to know."

That makes far too much sense. And it makes my heart hurt. What could Caleb be hiding? There are simply too many possibilities, and I'm too dizzy to sort through them all.

I still have half a sandwich in my hand. I set it aside. I feel a cold canine nose nudge my hand, and I open my eyes to see a pair of Cocoas, blurred and overlapping, staring up at me hopefully. I barely manage to knock the remnant of my sandwich—just a small corner—on the floor at her feet.

She doesn't pounce on it, though, but rather looks at Logan pleadingly. "You're not supposed to have people food, but I guess it's okay this once." He scratches her affectionately behind her ear. "Go ahead, girl."

Cocoa devours it in one bite, licks her lips, and then returns to her place on the rug near the doorway between the living room and the hallway. Her tail taps the floor rhythmically—*thump, thump, thump, thump.*

"I like Cocoa. She's a good doggy."

A laugh from Logan. "I know. She's my girl."

"I thought *I* was your girl," I say, sounding a bit too petulant for even my own taste.

"Are you for real jealous of my dog right now, Isabel?" Logan asks, a laugh in his voice.

"No. Shut up." I can't hide the smile in my voice or on my face. Don't try.

The silence between us then is easy. I am content to let the world spin around me and beneath me, to lie against Logan and listen to his heart beating under my ear, and not think about Caleb or the lies or the mysteries or myself or anything.

"I have a confession to make," Logan says.

I wobble my head on his chest, a gesture meant to be a negative, but which ends up being more of a sloppy flopping of my head. "I can't handle anything serious right now."

"Nothing like that. It's just that I had an ulterior motive behind getting you drunk."

I twist and gaze up at him, but I have to shut one eye so there's only one of him. "Oh really? And what would that be?"

"So I'd be less tempted by you. I won't take advantage of you when you're wasted, especially not when you're as vulnerable as you are right now."

"That isn't what I expected you to say."

"I know." He rubs my arm. "I want it to be right. When it happens with us, I want it to be right. And you're just not there yet."

I shake my head. "No. I wish I were, but I'm not. He has answers I need, and until I get them, he has a hold on me I just can't break. It's not fair to you."

"Life isn't fair," Logan says. "It never has been and never will be. If it were, my best friend wouldn't have died, and I wouldn't have gone to prison. If life were fair, Caleb would have gotten arrested instead of me, and you wouldn't have amnesia. If life was fair, we'd be able to be together and there wouldn't be anything standing in the way."

"But life isn't fair."

"Not even close." A sigh. "I'm not saying I regret what we did together, but I just . . . it makes it all the harder for me right now. Because I've tasted you. I've gotten a little glimpse of what it'll be like when we can be together with nothing between us."

EXPOSED 219

"But I'm weak, so there is something between us." I choke on my next words. "Caleb is between us."

Once again, Logan is left with nothing to say. It's true, and we both know it.

"What time is it?" I ask.

"Why?"

"Because I have no idea, and I'm curious."

Logan tilts his wrist to glance at his watch. "It's two thirty in the afternoon."

"I'm tired." I want to open my eyes, but I can't. They won't cooperate. "I'm sorry. I'm no fun right now. I'm just . . . so tired."

"I'm here, Isabel. Just relax. Let go. I've got you."

I'm always falling asleep around Logan. Maybe because I feel safe with him.

I dream of Logan. Of being naked with him. Nothing between us. And then I dream of shattering glass and twisting metal, and darkness and rain. And then Logan is in the darkness with me, in the rain with me, standing just out of reach.

Just out of reach. In the dream, as in life.

wake alone, terrified. Sweating. Crying. Dream residue coats my mind with fear, fragments of nightmares flapping in the spaces of my soul like bats in a belfry. Hungry eyes, red in the darkness. Bright lights blinding me. Ice in my veins. Loss. Confusion. It's all there, in my mind, disordered and wild and jumbled and visceral but meaningless.

I try to breathe through it, but I can't. I can't breathe. My chest is compressed by iron bands, preventing me from breathing. My hands shake. Tears track down my cheeks, flowing freely, unstoppable. I ache to breathe, but I cannot. Terror batters at the inside of my skull and squeezes my heart so it beats like fluttering sparrow wings.

Where is Logan?

Where am I?

I'm in his bed. The mattress is wide, and empty but for me. The blankets are kicked back to the foot-end of the bed, the sheet tangled around my thighs. I'm drenched with sweat. It's dark outside. A digital clock on the bedside table near to hand reads 1:28 A.M. All is dark. Lights are off. Moonlight streams in through the window, a river of light silvering the floor and my skin. I am naked but for bra and underwear. I don't remember undressing.

I manage a thready gasp. Another. My voice rasps. "Logan?"

Nothing.

"Logan?" A little louder.

I tumble out of the bed, feet hitting the floor. The hardwood is cold under my bare feet. The bra is too tight, constricting me. I can't breathe. I fumble at the clasps and rip the garment off, toss it aside.

I'm still dizzy. My mouth is dry. My head aches. Pounds.

I can't breathe.

I can't breathe without Logan.

I find him asleep on the couch, clad in a pair of loose shorts and nothing else. A laptop computer is on the coffee table, open, screen dark, and his cell phone is near it, along with a pad of paper and a pen. There are several phone numbers written down, all local New York numbers, 212 area codes. Scribbles, things crossed out, doodles. Abstract designs, swirls of ink, squares merging with triangles, becoming trees of curlicues and arcs. He's written something at the bottom of the page, underlined it several times.

Jakob Kasparek.

Underneath that are two more words, connected to the name above by a darkly inked arrow: *Signed out.*

What does all this mean?

Just seeing him calms me. But he's restless, tossing and turning. I lower myself to the couch near his head, feather my fingers through his hair. He murmurs something unintelligible, shifts forward, closer to me. I pull his head onto my lap, and he makes a small, boyish sound of contentment that melts something in me. His hand rests on my thigh, and I scoot lower on the couch and prop my feet on the coffee table, and his arm wraps around my waist, between my back and the couch.

I do not fall back asleep, but I am able to rest, to close my eyes and relax and let a sense of peace permeate me.

I need this man so much it hurts.

TWELVE

doze through to dawn.

At some point past sunrise, Logan wakes suddenly and immediately, blinking up at me. "Isabel?"

I smile down at him. "Hi."

His eyes flit over my breasts. He struggles to pull his gaze away from them. "What . . . um. What happened?"

"I had a nightmare. Woke up and you weren't there. So I came looking for you."

"You had a nightmare, but I ended up asleep on your lap?" He doesn't seem inclined to move off my lap, however, and this is just fine with me.

"When I have nightmares, they usually leave me in a panic attack. I can't breathe, can't move. It's hard to even think. But when I saw you asleep here, it just . . . calmed me. Having you sleep on me like this . . . it was perfect. It was what I needed."

"I'm sorry I wasn't there when you woke up."

"But you were."

"You know what I mean." He rubs his eyes, wipes sleep out of them. His eyes constantly return to my bare breasts. "God, you're gorgeous."

"So are you," I say.

And he is. I spent a lot of time between drowsing examining his tattoos, trying to parse out the various images. Tracing the contours of his muscles with my fingers, watching him breathe.

"You need to put on a shirt. Or I need to be in a different room." His voice is thick, low. He sits up, and I see that I've affected him. He twists away in an attempt to hide it, but I saw the erection in the tenting of his shorts.

"Do you have my dress somewhere?" I ask.

He stands up. "Yeah, I took it off you when I put you in bed. Thought you'd sleep better that way."

"Very thoughtful of you," I say, watching him. "But I don't typically sleep in my bra. Rather uncomfortable. Maybe next time you can take that off me, too."

He vanishes into his bedroom and returns with my dress. "I don't know if I have the restraint for that." He hands the garment to me. "I'm gonna take a quick shower. You want one before I do?"

I shake my head. "No. Thank you. I'm fine."

He glances at me one last time, his gaze raking over my body with blatant desire and appreciation. And then he's in his bathroom and I hear the shower going. It isn't until a few minutes have passed that I remember the note he wrote himself and the questions it left me with. I decide to ask him. I prod open the door to the bathroom, smelling steam and soap. The shower has glass walls, so I can see him clearly, obscured only by a thick veil of swirling steam. His naked body is glorious, perfect, beautiful. I stare at him, watching him. He is facing the stream of water, one hand propped on the wall, the water beating down on his head and the back of his neck. He is leaned forward, spine concave.

It takes a moment to realize what he's doing; his hand moves slowly up and down his massive erection. He's masturbating. He doesn't know I'm here, and I'm watching, silent, enthralled. Aroused. His eyes are closed, his jaw clenched. His posture speaks of internal torture, some great conflict. He is squeezing himself roughly, tightly. I watch, and think about how much more gentle I would be. I watch, and feel absolutely no guilt in this voyeurism. I should, but I don't. Only pleasure. Heat billows through me, and wetness coats my core. I want to touch him. I want to peel off my underwear and slip into the shower with him, replace his hand with mine. I want to wrap my thighs around his waist and feel him inside me. Feel him take me, plunder me, ravage me. Ravish me.

I remember something he said, just outside this very bathroom: *"Get dressed, X, before you discover how much self-control it's taking to not . . . ravish you senseless."*

I want him to ravish me senseless.

But I dare not allow it. Not yet. Not with Caleb's scent so fresh on my skin. I want Logan. Need him. Desperately need him. But I cannot have him. Not until I've broken Caleb's hold on me.

God. Logan's hand is a blur now, and his body rocks, straightens. His fist plunges around his cock, down to the root, and then back up once more. I'm mesmerized by this, watching the taut bubble of his buttocks flex as he thrusts into his fist, and the head of his cock turns almost purple with the brutal force of his grip. I couldn't look away now even if I wanted to.

He groans, a quiet, constrained sound. And then his fist resumes its blurring pumping and he leans all his weight against the marble wall, face resting on his forearm, hips pushed forward. His body is bowed inward, spine arched. He is a vision of masculinity, all muscle and tattoos and hard flesh and angles.

I nearly come when he releases. It is a geyser of semen spouting out of him, splashing onto the marble and sluicing down the drain, washed away, and he continues his rough abuse of his member, pumping until another gush spurts out of the tip of him, and then he grips himself at the base and rubs there as a third fountain of white viscous liquid leaves him. And then he's rubbing his palm over the head and squeezing, pumping, squeezing. Finally, he's done.

And that's when he looks at me.

His eyes narrow. His jaw flexes. "Isabel."

His gaze flicks over my breasts, down. Fixes on my core. I glance down as well, and see that the silk covering my opening has darkened with dampness.

I meet his gaze unapologetically. Tilt my chin up.

And then I flee. Return to his bedroom and throw myself on the bed. God, what did I do? I watched Logan masturbate. Is he angry? I don't know. Surprised, at the very least. Confused. He saw how aroused I was, watching him.

Oh god. Oh god. I close my eyes and I can see it still, his thick shaft in his hard fist, the head broad and plump, dark as he squeezes himself mercilessly. I can almost feel his cock in my hands, can almost feel his lips on my breasts. I moan and slide my fingers under the waist of my underwear, slip two fingers into myself. Delve into the juices and smear them against my clit. Bite my lip and let out a groan as lightning sizzles through me.

I hear the door and know he's there. I don't open my eyes yet. I arch up off the bed and shove away my panties. Kick them off. Spread my legs open and touch myself once more, let my fingers find a circling rhythm.

When I've found it, I open my eyes and stare at Logan through slitted lids. He's leaning back against the closed bedroom door, a thick black towel wrapped around his waist, clutched closed in one hand. I don't stop. I keep my eyes on him as I fondle my clit, slip my fingers into my slit and smear wetness over myself once more, circle, circle. I'm breathing hard, and my hips flutter. My throat closes, and then I groan involuntarily, heat tightening my muscles, tension coiling inside my belly, low.

The towel around Logan's waist does nothing to disguise the evidence of his renewed erection.

What are we doing? Why?

I have no answers, but I know I'm not going to stop. And I know he won't either. But he'll get no closer, either. If he did, this would all change in a moment. A single touch, and it'd be over. He'd be here in this bed with me. And I want that, but like he said yesterday, I want it when it's right. And this may be wrong, or maybe it's not. I don't know. I just know I like his eyes on my body, and I wish it were his hands but I know if it were we'd be here for days and days, naked and tangled up and sweaty and getting so dirty together doing all the things I've wanted with Logan for so long it hurts, it seems, and yet after we emerged blinking and sore from this bed, I'd still have questions and problems and nothing would be different and nothing would be solved.

So I choose to wait.

And torture both him and myself with this intimate, voyeuristic display. I'm on display for him. Heels drawn up to my buttocks, slit open wide for him, wet and gleaming with my juices, heavy breasts weighted to either side of my body. I blink and glance at him, and he's naked. Towel dropped. Cock in hand. Impossibly hard again.

"Pinch your nipples, Isabel." His voice floats to me. I pinch my nipple between finger and thumb, and a whimper leaves me. "Harder. Make it hurt."

I squeeze hard, and lightning sears through me, and my hips lift involuntarily.

He's jerking himself roughly.

I meet his gaze. "Softly, Logan. Gently. Not so rough." He gentles and slows his touch. "Yes. Like that."

"Wish it were your hand," he murmurs.

"Or my mouth," I say.

"Or your pussy."

"That would be so perfect. I'd squeeze around you. I'd squeeze you so hard you wouldn't be able to pull out of me."

"If I were in your pussy, I'd never leave. I'd bury myself so deep . . ." He's pleasuring himself slowly, gently. But not the way I'd do it.

God, I want to touch him.

I remember the way he felt in my hands. In my mouth. His come on my skin, on my tongue.

I'm crazed. At the edge of my control. Ready to abandon the pretense of all this and just pounce on him like a lioness leaping for her prey.

"Why are we doing this to ourselves, Logan?" I ask, my voice ragged, desperate.

"Fuck if I know." He's close. His eyelids are heavy, his motions jerky and rough.

"I need you."

"Need you too, babe." He's grinding his teeth, his muscles are tensed, eyes narrowed and laser-focused on me.

I'm there. On the edge, riding the crest. Falling over, watching him. "Gonna—gonna come, Logan."

"Me too."

I don't dare look at him now. If I look at him, I'll leave the bed and sink to my knees in front of him and take all his seed in my mouth and on my face and on my breasts. I'll jump on him and ride him until I can't walk. God, I fucking want him.

"I want you so fucking bad too, Isabel," Logan says, and I realize I said that last part out loud.

"Oh . . . oh god. Oh god." I'm exploding, seeing Logan in my mind, against the backdrop of my tight-shut eyes.

And then I feel him. Am I imagining this? His mouth on my nipples, suckling them hard, flattening them, biting them, his fingers on mine, circling madly with mine?

I don't dare open my eyes and shatter the spell, I just go with it, moan and whimper and now I'm near to crying with the bliss blasting through me, wet tongue warm on my breasts, lips smearing and stuttering across my skin.

"Logan . . ." I whisper.

"Ssshhhh." He's close. Too close. I need him, and if he's really here, really in this bed with me, then I'll take him. He won't stand a chance against my desperation. "Hush, baby. Let me take care of you."

"But—"

"Hush." And then his mouth is there, at my core, over my clit, and my fingers are buried in his thick long hair and I'm tugging at his head, jerking roughly to get more of his mouth on me, to urge him for more. More. God, more.

I writhe against his face, and I come. So hard, I come. Stars burst in my eyes, and my breathing is ragged gasps and near-sobs of ecstasy.

"Logan . . . god, Logan."

I accept the inevitable. I cannot stop this. I want it. I will have it. I will have him. I can't resist. It's futile.

Again, his tongue lashes me to orgasm. I hurt from the potency of this climax, so hard on the heels of two other furious releases. He's punishing me, I think. Making me come again, and again. I can't stop. He won't let me stop. I didn't know this was possible, to just come and come and come, like a string of dominoes knocking one into the other. His fingers delve into me and his fingers are tweaking my hardened nipples and I'm crying, crying, sobbing, with guilt and with bliss. An agony of ecstasy. He incites this in me, he's done this to me before, we've been here before.

So close but so far.

I jerk free of him, scoot up and away from his eager nimble devouring mouth, and his eyes follow me. I lunge for him, crash into him, my mouth smashing against his.

"Erase it all, Logan," I whisper, my breath merging with his. "Erase everything. Please. Make it all go away. Take it all away."

"I can't, baby," he says, his voice a low rumble. "I can't change anything."

"Yes, you can. You've changed me."

I have to have him. I have to feel him. I can't do this anymore, this futile childish pretending that we're not going to have sex, this notion that we can edge closer and closer and not really go all the way.

We're kneeling on the bed, in the center, up on our knees, wrapped up, mouths crashing and slashing and mashing, his arms around me, fingers dimpling my spine and scraping lower to grab my ass with fierce strength, and I'm up against him, breasts flattened against the hard wall of his chest. I feel his cock between us, a thick hard hot ridge against my belly. I grip a tangled fistful of his blond hair and force him closer and reach between us to clutch his erection and smear the messy leaking fluid on my palm and down his length. He moans, and I eat that sound. I taste and swallow it, and stroke him again and suck down his breath and devour his sigh.

I lean into him, and he falls to his back. "Isabel—"

"I can't—Logan, I'm dying without this. I'm dying without you."

I whimper this admission to his jaw near his ear, and then I kiss where the words were.

His legs flail on the bed, and I know he feels the desperation too. He's fighting this, fighting himself, fighting me. I'm fighting it all too, but we're both losing.

I'm on him, straddling him, knees in the mattress beside the trim wedge of his hips, my ass in the air, need oozing out of my core. I angle, and his erection nudges my opening.

"Isabel, oh fuck, Isabel. Is. God, goddamn it." He is a tortured soul. He can't resist now, either. "God . . . *damn it.*"

We are doomed to this sin together. Slaved to this, chained to this.

"Look at me, Logan," I beg. He wrenches his eyes open, fiery indigo spearing into my soul. "Don't you dare look away."

We both know why we're not supposed to do this. Why it feels wrong, even though it feels so right.

I was just with Caleb.

I force the reminder upon myself. It shows in my eyes, I'm sure, and Logan sees it.

"I'm with you, baby." His gaze is bold and strong and unwavering.

We are frozen in this moment, him about to pierce me so perfectly, our eyes locked. Tensed, taut. Neither of us looks away.

My hands are flattened on his chest, my hair loose and draping in a thick inky black curtain, and now it blocks out the whole world as I lean down and kiss him.

Oh, heaven, the beauty of the kiss is endless and wild. It makes my heart soar to tangle my tongue against his and to taste my essence on his lips and lick it away; it makes my soul sing to feel the raging need in the power of his mouth on mine, makes my entire being vibrate with pure and ecstatic joy to give myself over to this, to him, to us.

I don't give him a warning. I don't give *myself* a warning.

I sink down on him as we kiss, plunge my tongue into the warmth of his mouth as he surges up into me and fills me and spreads me to stretching aching burning beautiful fullness. I can't help but weep at the glory of this.

"Oh my god, Logan, *Logan* . . ." I sob.

"Fuck, oh my fucking god in heaven," he breathes, and his hands fly to my hips, soar over my ass, my thighs, my back, scouring every inch of my flesh he can reach, "Isabel, my Isabel, god, you feel so fucking perfect."

There is nothing but this. I am impaled by him, seated fully upon him. I can't move. I can breathe, for once in my life I feel like I can finally breathe. He is my breath. He fills me to stretching and I am mad with delirium from it. It burns, the way he fills me. There is nothing like it, has never been anything to match the utter perfection of his body inside me. We are mated, made for each other.

"Isabel . . ." he groans.

And I remember he was so close to coming *before*, when he was on the other side of the room; he's held it back, and now he has to be in pain from the need to release, the need to move.

"I can't hold back much longer," he whispers, his grip on my body slipping and shifting from hips to buttocks to waist, as if he can't decide where he wants to touch me hold me feel me more.

"Don't hold back. Never hold back. Give me all of you, Logan."

I drive my body down his, letting the aching tips of my breasts trail down his chest. My hips flex until my thighs are flush with my torso, and he's crushed so deep into me it almost hurts. My lips touch his chest. My tongue flutters over his nipple. I nip at his throat. Cup his face in my palms and kiss his chin and the corner of his mouth and I lick his upper lip, taste the sweat there.

"Make love to me, Logan." I say it out loud, not whispering it, not hiding the crazed needy desperation in my voice, not hiding the pain and the conflict and the self-loathing.

I glide up his body, slipping him out of me almost all the way, and I don't pause, don't wait for his response; I pull his face to mine and kiss his mouth with all the starvation-fervor I possess, and I sink down on him. He groans into our kiss and thrusts up, and our hip bones collide like ships crashing prow to prow. His hands grip hard into the meat of my ass, a double handful of my buttocks, and he pulls me against him, even though I'm as fully seated on him as I can get, but we both need more, need him deeper.

I plant my feet against the outside of his thighs and let my weight rest on his chest, and I cling to his shoulders for balance, and I pull back, like a rubber band stretched to its apex, and then I crash down on him and I scream his name—"*LOGAN!*"—like a curse, like a blessing, like a prayer, like a benediction, and his voice is raised as well, raised with mine, shouting with me. He takes control then, without flipping me or switching positions. He takes my hips where they crease to meet thigh and plunges me down and pushes me up and sets the rhythm. He's shiny with sweat, a glistening sheen on his tan skin. His eyes bore into mine. We do not look away. I stare into him as he thrusts up to fill me, and my eyelids flutter with pleasure when he slides out but I do not close them, do not look away.

Sustained eye contact with another person is very hard. The mind, the soul, they want to look away after a while. To meet someone's gaze without looking away, without flinching, even allowing natural blinks, to just stare into them and receive the stare in return, it is nearly impossible.

Because it is too intimate. It is to bare one's very soul, one's vulnerable heart.

I give Logan every corner of me, I don't look away, I let him look into me, and I take that same from him. It is a gift.

We move in sync now. We find our rhythm. The music of our bodies uniting is dulcet, palpable. This is what each of us was meant for; we were meant to be this way, together.

"Isabel, god, Isabel." He sounds as if there is a world of words waiting on the other side of his teeth, and he's just barely holding it all back.

"Say anything, Logan."

We move madly now. I am coiled on top of him, legs pulled up beneath me, hips circling, breathing his breath, kissing him now and then, sipping at his lips.

"I love this," he says. It is ripped out of him, it sounds like.

I bury my face against his neck. "Me too. So much."

"I feel like I've been waiting for this for my whole life."

"I know. I have been, too," I say.

"I—" he starts, but breaks off.

I push up so I can look down at him, not daring to break our rhythm. This has been my entire life, I think. There has never been anything but this, but us. Nothing else exists. Only now. Only this heaven.

"Say it, Logan." I bite his lower lip. Suck it into my mouth. "Say everything in your heart."

"Scared before battle has nothing on what I'm feeling right now, Is." He murmurs this against my cheek.

"I know. I feel it in you."

"If I say it out loud, I'll never be able to go back."

"Me neither. I don't *want* to go back."

He sits up and tucks his legs beneath his buttocks, and I wrap my legs around his waist. He cups my bottom and holds me up. Lifts me, lets me fall down to impale him in me. I clutch his shoulders and lift myself up, relax down. This way, he drives up into me so deep it takes my breath away, sends stars bursting behind my eyes, novas of amazed ecstasy detonating inside me.

I surge against him. Drive against him. Cling to him and breathe against his skin and smell him and go wild on him, around him. Let go, let the madness out, growl and whimper and scream as my climax builds with his.

"Logan, god, Logan . . ."

"Isabel. Fuck, oh god." He bites my earlobe and then speaks to me as we love each other with mad abandon. "If I tell you I love you and then you go back to—if you go back, I'll break. I've survived a lot . . . rebuilt my life more than once. I can't do it again, not after you. You're everything to me now. I don't know how it happened, but I'm fucking gone for you, baby. I don't want to take this back, but I'm fucking scared to goddamn death that I won't be enough for you, that he'll still have his fucking hooks in you, and—" He rhythms his words to his movements.

"Never, Logan," I cut in. "Never. I won't do that to you. I won't go back. I won't take it back. I'm yours, Logan, please please *please* believe me. I'm sorry, I'm sorry, I'm sorry—"

We still move together, and he's still going somehow, still holding back, some kind of superhuman control keeping him back from the edge until he's ready to let go.

"Sorry for what?" he asks.

"For going back. For letting—what happened, happen." Neither of us is willing to say it out loud, not now, not in this moment. I give him all my truth. "I didn't mean to. And I hated it. Every moment, I hated it. And I hate myself for letting it happen. I was yours then. I was yours from the moment I saw you in that bathroom, from the first time I heard your voice."

He's losing it now. His movements are ragged, lurching, and his breath is coming in gasps, and his grip on my buttocks is so strong, so powerful.

I'm there, too, ready to come apart all around him.

He can't let go, though. I can tell, I can sense it.

I touch my lips to the outer shell of his ear, sunk down on him, fully pierced by him, his cock throbbing inside me, his hands keeping me aloft. I let go, let him hold me, let our joined bodies hold me. I cup his head, feather my fingers through his hair and writhe on him, inhale his scent.

I whisper to him. "I love you, Logan. God, I love you."

He arches his spine and pushes up into me and his voice rises in a wordless shout of release, and I feel him explode inside me. He flings us over so my back hits the mattress and he's above me and pushing into me wildly, his mouth on mine, and he's coming and coming and coming, driving into me so powerfully my breath is stolen. I'm with him, riding this with him, and now I'm coming apart too, and like I promised I clench around him as hard as I can and I scream his name and rake my fingernails down his back.

"Isabel . . . I love you, Isabel." He says this as he sags against me, his hips moving furiously. "I love you so much. So fucking much."

We collapse, I go limp, and he sinks against me, his face on my chest between my breasts, my hands smoothing in gentling patterns on his back, tracing the lines I gouged into his skin, both of us shuddering still.

Our sweat commingles.

Our breathing synchronizes.

I feel complete, for the first time in my life. I need nothing. Nothing but this. Nothing but him. Nothing but us.

And then Logan rolls off me, goes into the bathroom, and returns with a wet warm washcloth. He parts me and cleans me, gently and tenderly. Tosses the cloth into the bathroom and lies beside me.

That act alone means everything to me. The fact that he never looked away from me.

That each moment we just spent together was each of us giving, and thus each of us receiving exactly what we needed.

He climbs into the bed beside me, gathers me in his arms, cradles me against his chest.

I listen to his heartbeat. "Can this be forever?"

"Yes, Isabel. This is our forever."

"Promise?"

"On my life."

And that is all I need.

THIRTEEN

ogan is asleep; I am not. I cannot. His digital clock says it is 4:30 in the morning. I should be exhausted. I should be sore. I *am* sore, but not at all tired. Deliciously sore, perfectly achy. I feel delicate.

On the inside as well as the outside.

I lie on my left side and watch Logan sleep, gaze at the boyish innocence on his face. Absorb the beauty in the slack weight of his muscles as he rests. He's drooling a little, and I've been stifling a giggle at it for an hour and a half now. I half want to wipe it away, but I don't want to wake him, and it's just so cute I can't.

I'm fighting tears. Warring with a maelstrom of emotions. I'm so happy, deliriously happy. Vibrating with joy. Overwhelmed with incredulity.

He *loves* me. He loves *me*.

ME.

Logan Ryder told me he loves me.

Tears prick the corners of my eyes as I consider this, as I relive over and over and over the wondrousness of that moment, hearing those words.

But then I think of . . . everything else.

Caleb.

Caleb's lies.

Caleb's truths.

The complicated, labyrinthine tapestry he's woven of truth and lies, and how I'm not sure I'll ever untangle the two.

How, forty-eight hours ago, a little more now, I was pressed up against the glass of Caleb's high-rise penthouse window, being fucked by him from behind.

How I felt that happening, felt him strangling me with his toxic sorcery, his manipulative magic. How I seemed powerless to stop it. I always have the intention of refusing him, denying him, but I never actually am able to, and I do not understand why. What hold has he over me, that I cannot control my own body? What torture have I put Logan through, with this weakness? What kind of future can we have together, if I am so weak?

How can I ever face Caleb again, now that I've slept with Logan?

Not slept with—made *love* to.

I've fucked Caleb. Been fucked *by* him. Had sex with him. Been used by him. I've *never* made love to him.

I had sex with two men in a forty-eight-hour time frame. What does that make me?

It doesn't really mitigate things that I enjoyed it with Logan and did not with Caleb, nor that with Caleb it was . . . not forced, not involuntary, but—I don't know. I don't have the words for it. It felt involuntary. It *felt* like he was forcing me. But he was not holding me down, was not technically raping me. But yet I wasn't entirely will-ing, either. I didn't *want* to want him. I didn't want to be used by him.

I don't want to be his plaything anymore. But whenever he's around, that's how things end up.

I belong to Logan. I've chosen that, chosen him, chosen to belong to him.

But Caleb feels as if he owns me.

What do I do?

I can't stay in bed any longer.

I need to move, need to do something. Anything.

I slip out of bed, tug on my underwear and Logan's VOTE "NO" ON DALEKS T-shirt. Pad out of the bedroom, tiptoeing softly, shut the door behind me. There are four doors in this hallway: the bedroom, the bathroom, Cocoa's room, and one more. I try the one room I haven't seen yet: an office, a simple but beautiful dark wooden desk with a large flatscreen desktop computer, stacks of envelopes and papers, file folders, a white mug full of pens. The mug has a stylized bear paw print on it, surrounded by a red ring slashed top and bottom and both sides with vertical lines, like a rifle reticle, I think, and the word *Blackwater* across the top. There are photographs on the walls showing Logan in combat gear, wearing a featureless black ball cap, an assault rifle hanging by a strap, held casually in one hand, barrel pointed at the ground, his other arm around another man similarly dressed; another photograph shows him in more traditional-looking army fatigues, a camo-print cap on his head, surrounded by half a dozen other men posing in front of a mammoth truck. All the photographs are of him from his combat and military days, in pairs or with groups, smiling. Looking younger, harder, and sharper. There is one photograph, though, that stands out. It's in a little frame on his desk, all by itself. A tiny picture, smaller than my palm. It's a much, much younger Logan, barely into his teens, I'd guess, with his arm slung around a Hispanic boy the same age, both of them holding surfboards larger than they are, sporting huge, happy grins. His best friend, the one who was murdered by the drug dealer.

I leave the office; it feels sacrosanct.

Upstairs then.

I pause to stare at the print of the Van Gogh painting on the landing, *Starry Night*. I feel like I should be moved by this, but I'm not. Or, not as much as I once was. It still has meaning, but it doesn't cage my heart the way it used to. I wish I knew why.

I tread quietly up the stairs and find exactly what I'm looking for: a workout room. The whole upstairs has been opened up, every wall torn down, the load of the ceiling held up by a couple of thick square pillars running the center of the huge room. Every kind of exercise equipment available lines the walls, with free weights in the spaces between the pillars in the middle, and a black punching bag hanging by a thick chain from the ceiling in one corner.

I start with the free weights, doing stretches and lifts in several sets of reps to warm up. I'm not wearing a bra, so my workout will have to be low impact, as my breasts are far too large to run or anything like that without one. I lift free weights for a good thirty minutes, then move to the machines, starting in one corner and working my way around until I'm so weak and tired and sore I can barely move. But it's a good sore, a good tired. I'm drenched with sweat and smelly, so I limp downstairs and rummage in Logan's refrigerator until I find a water bottle, and I take it into the bathroom with me, drinking it as I close the door behind me and run the shower.

I peek in on Logan, who is still asleep, curled up on his side now, one hand under the pillow. I want to slide into bed with him, but I need space and time to sort through my feelings. Not to mention, I stink of sweat now.

I take my time in the shower, running it so hot my skin tingles and aches from the heat, letting it beat down on my shoulders. I try not to think of Logan in here, try not to think of his hand stroking his huge, hard member. To no avail. I can't think of anything else, and I know I'll think of that scene every single time I take a shower here now.

As I'm drying off, I think of my conversation with you. That story. It smacked of truth. If there are lies being told, it's not overt lies, but lies of omission, I think. I'm not sure. The story *felt* real. Felt true. And you seemed affected by the retelling, distraught remembering. Could you be telling the truth? I don't know. You could be. You very well might be. But there are undeniably elements you are either lying about or leaving out. There was no mugger, of this I'm sure. It was a car crash, as Logan claims. My memories, such as they are, jibe with that story, the car crash. My dreams, too. My dreams do not speak of violence, not the sort perpetrated by a criminal, but the violence of an accident. There is bloodshed, yes, but not drawn by a gun or a knife or a fist.

You lie, but speak truth.

You saved me. Stayed with me. You were there when I woke up. You were there every day after that.

I have to sit down on the closed lid of the toilet, as a memory hits me. Not of precoma, but of my recovery. Of you, on a treadmill beside me. You ran, dressed in a sleeveless black shirt and black shorts, earbuds in your ears. You ran, ran, ran. You didn't encourage me with words, but with action. I was walking. I wanted to give up. Holding on to the railings for dear life and struggling to merely put one foot in front of the other, to manage a slow walk. I wanted to give up, but then I would look at you and you were still running. As long as I was walking, you were running.

You helped me dress. I remember this, too. When I was released from the hospital, I was still working on coordination, regaining fine motor skills. Dressing myself was a slow, laborious affair, and you were there to help. Never touching inappropriately, never behaving awkwardly at my nudity. But looking back, I do remember you stealing looks, carefully avoiding my eyes and avoiding my skin. Curbing your desire, I now realize.

You helped me eat. Even fed me, in the hospital. And at home, on hard days. On my feet, staying upright, talking, it was all taxing. Just holding a normal conversation was tiring. So at the end of the day, feeding myself seemed like an impossibly hard task. And you would feed me. You never complained. Never showed impatience. You were always there.

You became my world.

The daily exercises to help me regain my mobility became a daily regimen of exercise to build my strength and shape my figure. I lived—not with you, but near you, and you provided everything for me. Food, clothing, entertainment; life. I never questioned it, because I had no idea what I'd do without you, where I'd go. I was so dependent on you. Utterly and completely helpless. I remembered nothing. I was no one. Knew nothing. You never claimed to be a boyfriend or family member. You never explained who you were to me, you were just . . . there. Stocking my refrigerator and cabinets with food, my closet with clothes. Showing me exercise routines and techniques, bringing me books, by ones and twos at first, and then by the armful, and then by the box load as my voracity for books grew.

And then one day, seemingly out of nowhere, apropos of nothing, you crept up behind me and I felt your not-quite touch like electricity. And that began a sexual exploration that didn't really qualify as a "relationship." You retained all the control. I was . . . not quite a slave, but nearly. And, if I am being honest with myself . . . a willing one. You would use one finger and stroke me to near orgasm, and you would keep me there for . . . so long. Tickle my clit until I was thrashing, begging, and you would tell me to wait, order me to not come until you told me I could. And if I came before you said I could, the next time you would bring me to the edge and not let me go over it for even longer. You would pin my hands over my head and torture me with near-orgasm for long minutes, what felt like hours. Until I swore I would do better next time.

I never got to touch you. I never watched you come, face-to-face. You were always behind me. I was always facing away. Face down, stomach to the bed. Knees spread apart. Or on my hands and knees, a pillow under my stomach. Pressed up against the window.

You really enjoy that. Pressing my naked body up against the window, taking your pleasure in me while I'm exposed for anyone to see. As if displaying your trophy, your prize, bragging, saying: *Look at what is mine, look, and want, and know that you cannot have her.*

I cannot count the number of times I've been taken by you, pressed that way up against the window, breasts flattened against the cold glass.

Why never face-to-face?

I wondered, but never asked.

It's like you were always hiding from me. But what were you hiding? There were a couple of times, especially more recently, before I left and found Logan, that I got a glimpse of the man you could be. The man who could perhaps be . . . not gentle, not tender, but very nearly. A man who could *almost* be intimate. Not merely a conquest-driven sexual dominant, not merely a predator, not merely a primal force of nature. But a man. Not a lover, perhaps, but at least a sexual partner.

I was never your partner. I was your subject. Your possession.

I remember you talking, a few days ago, in your home, about wanting me, about how even when I was a shaved-headed thing, frail and weak and lost, you wanted me. I remember thinking that if I want to truly leave behind Madame X and all that I once was, if I want to assume a new identity, I need to change my appearance.

I don't give myself time to think about it. I hunt in Logan's cabinet under his bathroom sink and find what I'm looking for: electric clippers.

My heart is pounding, hammering in my throat. Can I do this? My hands shake.

I click on the clippers, and the bathroom echoes with their humming buzz. My hand vibrates. I grab a fistful of my thick black hair, which when loose hangs to the middle of my spine. Pull it back and gaze at my reflection, try to imagine myself with no hair. I'm almost ten years older than in that photograph I saw on Caleb's phone. It would be such a drastic change, and part of me rebels against the idea of sliding this device over my scalp, feeling my hair fall away, having *no* hair at all.

But I need to change. I need to look different. I cannot resemble any longer the creature created by Caleb Indigo.

I fight my breath, blink away tears of I-know-not-what emotion. Bring the clippers closer and closer to my scalp. I feel the teeth whispering against the skin of my forehead.

And then, a mere eyeblink away from contact with my hair, Logan's hand encircles my wrist and pulls the clippers away. Tugs the device gently but firmly out of my hand.

"Isabel . . . baby . . . what the hell are you doing?"

I swallow. "I—I was—"

"You were about to shave your head?" He sounds almost panicked.

"Yes."

He tosses the clippers onto the lid of the toilet tank. "Why? I mean . . . god, your hair is so fucking gorgeous, Is. Why would you shave it all off?"

How honest can I be with Logan? My mouth vomits the truth before I have a chance to really think it through. "I can't be his creation any longer, Logan. He *made* me. He *invented* me. I had no choice in what I wore, how I looked. I was a persona; I was Madame X and she was always perfect. My clothing is all designer gowns, dresses, skirts, blouses. Sexy, but modest. And my underwear, even that was chosen by him, *for* him. You've noticed this before. My hair . . . he had a woman come every few months to trim the ends of my hair, but I wasn't allowed to cut it. I was given no say in this. She came, she trimmed the ends, and she left. I asked once if she could take a few inches off, and she just ignored me. I have no money of my own, so I cannot buy a new wardrobe. I don't even have a home. But my hair? I can change that. I can take ownership of that."

"But why cut it all off?" Logan threads his hands through my hair, the silky locks slipping like water through his fingers. "I would never tell you what to do with your life or your body or anything, but shaving it all off is just . . . it seems a little extreme."

"In order to operate on me, the surgeons had to shave my hair off. Caleb showed me a picture of me with no hair. I don't remember this. He says they operated on me and I seemed fine initially, I woke up, remembered myself. But then I started bleeding cranially, my brain started swelling, and they had to put me in a coma. When I woke up from that I'd lost my memory. But that picture? That was me, the last and only photo of me before I lost my identity. That was me as . . . as Isabel, as the Isabel I once was. The Isabel I used to be. And I want to—I don't know. I want to be her again. I know I'll never get that back. I've had a few minor memories return, but I'll never get everything back. I know that. But I just . . . I guess I thought by cutting my hair off, I could . . . regain some of who I used to be."

"I guess that makes sense. You want to identify with who you were. I totally get that. But what if—"

I cut in over him. "It's not just that. It's making myself different. Choosing how I look, for me. To be who *I* want to be. To look how *I* want to look, not how Caleb made me. That's what I want, more than anything, I think."

"And I get that too. But . . . shaving it like that is so extreme. There's an in-between. A way to change your look drastically without going to that extreme." He sighs, frowns. "I've known a few women who have shaved their heads. And I just . . . I don't know how to put this without sounding a little like an asshole. It tends to take away an element of . . . femininity. Not that you can't be totally woman, all woman without long hair, but to totally shave it off like you were about to . . . I don't know. I have a friend who owns a fancy, high-end women's salon. I can take you in to see her and you can get a professional haircut. Go pixie short, even. I just feel like if you shaved it on a whim, you might regret it. And that's not something you can undo."

"I—" A million thoughts batter at the insides of my head, each clamoring for expression. "I want to do it myself."

"Do you trust me?" he asks.

I swallow hard. Do I?

"Yes," I say.

Logan seems to sag with relief after that single syllable. As if he knows how huge that is for me to admit. "Then let's head out. I have a plan."

"But my hair?"

He smiles at me. "Just trust me, Isabel. I'll take care of you."

Then, suddenly, we are both aware that I am standing in front of the mirror, a towel wrapped around my torso. The end is tucked in at my cleavage, and now I have to clutch the thick cotton to keep it from falling open. And a glance behind tells me that he is nearly naked as well, wearing only a pair of loose shorts that hang at his hips, showing his sharp hip bones and the V-shaped indent of muscle low on his abdomen, teasing me with an almost-glimpse of his privates.

Our gazes lock in the mirror. My heart thrums. My gut tenses. My thighs clench, and heat rushes through me. Digit by digit, my fingers loosen their grip on the towel. This is déjà vu: me in a towel, Logan shirtless. This time, however, I know what lies beneath his shorts, and how it feels.

I release the towel, an intentional gambit. Stand naked in front of him. My breasts ache, my nipples harden. My flesh pebbles, tingles.

"Jesus, Isabel."

"What?"

He shakes his head. "Just you. You are, literally, perfect." His hands rest on the upper swell of my hips. "I'm standing here, staring at you, and I find it hard to believe that I get to touch you. That I get to kiss you. Make love to you. That I get to even look at you."

Palms skate lower to cup my bottom, graze over the backs of my thighs, circle around front. I cease breathing as his touch drifts upward then. Misses my core by millimeters, carves over my hip bones to my belly. Up, cresting my diaphragm, and then his hands are full of my breasts, lifting them, kneading their softness and hefting their weight, and I'm not breathing still because his thumbs brush almost idly over my nipples. I have to gasp then, because he tweaks and twiddles my nipples until I'm thrusting my chest into his hands, and lightning seems tied by a live wire from my erect nipples to my core, each touch sending blazes of heat and lust coruscating through me.

"Your tits, Isabel. Fuck, they're so goddamn incredible. I can't . . . I can't get enough of your tits. All of you, but especially your tits." He squeezes them, almost roughly. "What would you say if I told you I wanted to fuck your tits?"

The sudden and unexpected vulgarity has me panting with need.

I love his dirty words. Even if it's hard for me to speak that way, I love hearing it. "I would say . . ." I have to swallow my embarrassment. "I would tell you to do it."

"You would?"

I lick my lips, because they've gone dry with need. All the liquid in my system has gathered between my thighs. "Yes. Do it, Logan."

I spin in place. My eyes lock on his groin, on his erection outlined in his shorts, and it's so large and prominent it's nearly protruding from the elastic waistband. I reach out, slide a forefinger under the waistband and tug it away from his body. Expose him, inch by inch. Tug the silky, stretchy material away, tug it lower and lower. Until his entire massive erection is bared for me. Testicles tight and heavy, dark, nestled at the junction of his thighs. He leans down, lifts my breasts—lifts my tits . . . I like that word, the dirtiness of it, the lustful juvenility of it—and mouths my nipple. I watch, stare down at him, at his loose, tangled hair and my dark Spanish skin splashed by the golden of his fingers and the pink of his lips. Watch him capture my nipple with his lips and tug it away.

God, his mouth.

I bury my hands in his hair and bring him up to my face, take his mouth with mine. Demand his tongue. Devour his breath. When we cannot either of us breathe, I release him, and then we both watch as I finish baring him. He toes away the shorts, and we are nude together. Dark flesh and golden occupying the same space. I cradle his heavy testicles in my palm, and his breath catches. He watches me now, as I fondle him. Caress him. This is not to bring him to climax, but to show affection. It's for me, selfishly. To feel him, to memorize the sensation of being able to touch as much as I want, to absorb the beauty of his body and know that I can *have* him, that he is for me. I spread my fingers around him, and my hand seems so small, so tiny, so delicate against the size and thickness and iron-hard rigidity of his member. My fingers do not meet when I wrap them around him, thus. I curl one hand around him, place my other above it, and there is ample flesh above my fingers and below them. I plunge my hands down, and he lets out an involuntary-sounding moan.

"Isabel, fuck. What are you doing to me?"

"I'm just touching you, Logan."

"You touch me . . . I don't know how to put it." He pauses to think, and to watch as my fists slide up and down his length. "You touch me as if you've never touched anyone before. Like you might never get to again."

I wish I knew how to express the truth to him. I contemplate the most tactful wording, how to put this in a way that won't require using a certain mood-killing name. "That is . . . pretty much exactly the truth, Logan. I've never had an opportunity to just . . . touch. Experience. Feel. To just . . . enjoy. And my life being what it is, I really do not know what the future holds. For me, for us . . . so I just want to savor every moment." I sink to my knees in front of him. "I want to taste you, and remember the way you taste forever. I want everything with you."

He gazes down at me, his eyes betraying lust, confusion, antic-ipation, wonder, tenderness. He just watches for a moment as I kneel in front of him and stroke his beautiful penis, and he watches as I taste him, run my tongue up from root to tip. Kiss the broad head, and taste leaking essence. I tilt my head to look at him, watching his reaction as I wrap my lips around him.

His chest expands, and his eyes narrow. His hands flex into fists, and then he threads his fingers through my hair. Gathers it in his fist, wraps my long thick black locks around his palm until he's gripping the mass of my hair at the base of my skull. I think for a moment that he'll take control then, plunge himself roughly into my mouth. I tense in anticipation, and my heart thrums—my physical heart hammers in a nervous drumbeat, and my metaphysical heart clangs and jangles with equal parts glee and fear.

Instead, however, he lifts me to my feet. Pulls me closer, so my body is pressed flush against his, tits crushed flat against his warm hard chest, his cock a thick rod between our bellies. Tilts my head backward. His indigo gaze is fraught with so many emotions I cannot name them all. But they're all there to see.

"No, Isabel." His lips scour mine. His tongue dances in my mouth. "It's me who should be on my knees before you."

There is a wildness within me. A crazed beast that howls for release. A madwoman who rages against the cage of demure propriety that has so long defined me. How, though, do I express this? I want so much. Being with Logan has shown me a glimpse of what I could be like, of the Isabel I could be. The sensual, feral, sexual animal I could be. That I *want* to be, if only I could be brave enough.

"Logan." I feel like I'm gagging on the tumult of words and emotions. "I want—"

"What, Isabel?" He releases my hair, cups my face in his two large and rough but gentle hands. "Tell me what you want."

"I want to . . ." I struggle for coherency. "I want to be—I want . . . so much."

"Like what?" He brushes his thumb down my chin, toys with my lower lip. "Tell me, baby. Don't be afraid."

"But I am afraid, though."

"Afraid of what?"

I blink, and breathe, and think. And then let myself be honest. "That you won't like who I am, anymore. I'm changing. Every new experience with you shows me something new. About myself. And . . . in terms of this, you and I—"

"Let me stop you real quick." He leans in, bites my lower lip, the one he's been playing with, and I'm kissed into silence. "Maybe this will help: You're . . . I feel like you're a butterfly, just starting to come out of her cocoon. I've fallen in love with you already, Isabel, and that won't change. Nothing you could ever do or say will change that. And . . . the more you emerge, the more I'll fall in love with you. So just . . . *be you*. Be bold. Be brave. If you want something, just fucking *take* it, Is, and don't apologize."

I've already fallen in love with you.

That sentence is jarring. Seven words, and I'm shaken to my core. He says it so casually, so easily. Yes, of course, I remember our moment together pressed naked and sweaty together, whispering words of love into the intensity-laden, rarefied air of his bed. But that was in the moment. Words are drawn out during sex. Things are said. But to hear him say this in a moment of quietness between us, my heart swells to aching, expands to breaking.

"You spoke, before, of worshipping me. And you did." I have to swallow my nerves like saliva. "Now . . . I want to sin with you, Logan. I want to do bad things. I love it when you're gentle. I need that. But—I also like it when you're a little rough with me. We talked about—what happened. With—you know. When I called you. How I felt about that. And . . . I know, with you, it would be different."

His jaw flexes. "I just—I know you've been through a lot. And it's not that I think you're delicate, or fragile, but I don't want to ever be anything like *him*. I don't want to do things that would remind you of anything that happened with him. I hate even talking about him at all, much less in intimate situations like this."

"You're not. You're not like Caleb. Not at all. Even if you did something he did, it wouldn't be the same. Because your intentions are different. What you want, with me and from me and for me, they're diametrically opposed to everything he is, everything he wants."

His erection is subsiding, the heat of the moment dissipating. I'm not sure I want that exact moment back, because we've progressed.

Spoken truths. But I do want to retake this time with Logan, make it mine. Let myself have what I want. Give in to my desires. Explore myself.

What do I want? Right now?

My gaze moves out of the bathroom, to the hallway. I remember the first time I truly felt the full force of Logan's lust for me. That hallway, months ago. Me, naked. Him, in nothing but rain-soaked blue jeans. Being lifted, wrapping my legs around his hips and wondering in the deepest corner of my heart what it would feel like to be held aloft that way and have him sink into me.

Be bold. Be brave. If you want something, just fucking take it, Is, and don't apologize.

I take his hand and lead him out of the bathroom and into the short hallway. "Do you remember?" I stand, facing him, naked. Breathing deeply. "The first time I was here, in your home. This hallway."

"It's burned into my brain," he says. "I was so close to just . . . taking you. A flick of my fingers and my jeans would have been off, and I'd have been inside you."

"That's what I want, Logan."

His eyes bore into mine, and I can almost sense his erection burgeoning. I don't look down to see it, but I can just . . . sense it. I wait for him. He pushes his body against mine, but instead of stopping when we're flush, he keeps pushing. Until I'm forced to step backward. God, yes. His cock is thick and full. Digs into my belly. Warm, and soft, yet so *hard*. He keeps walking, and I'm pushed backward another step, until the cold plaster of the wall touches my shoulder blades and buttocks. My head thumps gently. His hand finds mine, right on left, fingers tangling. Left on right, palms mating. He lifts my hands over my head, presses the backs of my hands against the wall. He dips at the knees, feathers a whisper-soft kiss against

my lips, another, and a third, and then he bites my upper lip until it
hurts. I gasp, and he nips my lower lip. Pulls back, and I lean in to
seek a kiss, but he dodges, grins at my mewl of frustration. When I
think he won't kiss me, he does, surging closer and claiming my
mouth with sudden ferocity. Yet once I find the rhythm of the kiss
and sink into it, he pulls back. Bends at the knee, nudges the plump
softness of his cock against the juncture of my thighs. I spread them
apart, gasping with willing need. He stares into my eyes, hesitates a
beat, and then gives a roll of his hips. I feel him punch against me,
glans rubbing deliciously against labia. I pant, wanting him in me.

"God, Logan," I breathe.

"How do you want it, Isabel?"

He keeps my hands pinned over my head; our fingers are mated,
turning this intimate and loving rather than controlling. I am alive
with excitement, wired with need. He rubs his chest against mine,
and his chest hair scratches my sensitive skin, my nipples stuttering
against his pectorals. Rubs his belly against mine, his cock an iron
bolt between our bodies. Kisses my throat, and I tilt my head up to
welcome more of that, which he gives me, lips on my throat, just
under my jaw, down the outside of my neck, over the pulsing hollow
at the base. He bites my earlobe and works his hips, and I feel his
erection find my slit. I gasp, lean my shoulder blades against the wall,
and widen my stance.

"You want it like this?" He slides into me with exquisite gentility,
masterful slowness. Once, twice. So slow, so tender. "Or . . . like this?"

He pulls out. Straightens. Palms my cheeks and kisses me, desperately, fiercely, unendingly. I cannot breathe for the demanding
eroticism of the kiss, the way he owns my mouth and dominates
my breath and takes over my entire soul and mind and body with
just his mouth, his lips and tongue.

I am abruptly airborne. There is no warning, no transition. Just a release of my hands, and his palms under my buttocks and my legs winding automatically around his trim waist.

"FUCK!" I scream. The vulgar epithet is ripped out of me.

He is in me, crashing into me. The moment I left the ground, his cock slammed up into me with sudden power and I was left utterly breathless at the sudden onslaught, his erection stretching me to a sweet burn. He lifts me again, and then lowers me. This time, it is gentle. A reminder, I think.

"Like this?" he asks. Demanding an answer.

"No," I whisper.

His teeth nip and pluck at my skin, biting the flesh on the slope of my breast, at the side of my neck, worrying my nipple with searing roughness. He grips my buttocks in his hands and spreads me apart and lifts me up and lowers me, once more, gently. Thrusting into me, gently.

He slams his mouth onto mine with a sharp slash of teeth on lip and his tongue slashes mine and he . . .

There is no other word for it:

He fucks me.

His hips flex and his cock pounds into me roughly. His hands grip my ass with bruising force, splaying me wide so he can fuck deeper. And then his mouth leaves mine and finds my breasts. My tits. He laves them, licks them, not just my nipples but the slope and the undersides and my areolae, licking and kissing. All the while, he plunders me roughly, almost savagely.

"Like this?" he asks, his voice dark and guttural. Rougher than it has ever been.

"Yes, Logan, god yes." I cling to his neck, his shoulders. "Don't stop. Keep—keep fucking me just like this." I feel a bolt of embarrassment when that slips out of me, but then Logan makes a low grumbling growl and suckles my nipple harder and his cock drives into me harder, and I feel a blast of pride.

Oh, so perfect. This. I bury my hands in his hair, grip it tight and hold on. I ride him. I let myself go. Lean back to brace against the wall and moan wantonly, drive my hips against his, seek more and more and more. Ride him furiously, fingers tangled in his hair, tugging his mouth against my tits, encouraging him to suck and bite and lick them yet more. When his teeth pinch sharply at my nipple, I yelp breathily, and he does it again, taking my nonverbal encouragement for what it is.

I savor each fragment of sensation: his mouth wild on my tits, his cock sliding into me, stretching me, his hands clenching my buttocks so hard I'll have marks later—which I'll treasure, I must be sure to tell him—lifting me up and lowering me down, doing so harder and harder with each thrust, until my clit is bumping against his base just so, and I'm crying out nonstop, whimpering in his ear, sobbing my ecstasy to the ceiling.

There is no stopping my orgasm. It is a freight train barreling through me, the earth splitting open under me. I cannot tamp the scream that erupts. I writhe on him, grip his hair so hard I know it must hurt but he only growls like the wolf he is, hard and lean and primal and fierce.

"Logan—Logan . . . oh my fucking god, Logan . . ."

"Touch your pussy, Isabel. Right now, while you're coming all over me." He growls this into my ear.

I wrap one hand around his neck and lean back. He does the same, allowing some room between our joined bodies. His hands lift me, press my ass up and forward, and he continues to surge up into me, demonstrating incredible, breathtaking power and stamina. I reach between our bodies and touch my middle and ring fingers to my clit, just a touch at first. I groan and feel my still-undulating, clenching climax twist and ratchet higher, hotter, harder. God, this. I know exactly how to make myself come hard and fast. So I do. I find the perfect pressure, the perfect circling rhythm. Logan thrusts into me, and I'm whimpering now, sweat sliding down my temple and between my breasts.

Electricity, lighting heat; there are not enough synonyms for the power that flows through me. I come immediately, and it is as if I am being turned inside out, ripped open and spread apart and tangled up. I feel Logan beneath me and in me and around me, his teeth on my nipples and his hands on my ass and his cock inside my pussy and his hard body blocking out anything but him, anything but us, anything but this climax like a galaxy of stars going nova all at once.

I don't slow or stop, and neither does he.

I didn't know orgasms could exist thus, one after another until each explosion is part of the last, a chain of detonations. I didn't know my mind could splinter from the magnitude of this physical and emotional experience, my soul bursting into fractal shards so the soft vulnerable essence of who I am is exposed and melted and merged with Logan's.

Because he too is fragmenting. Coming apart. Going mad, in this moment. Letting loose all that boils within. His eyes fly open at the moment of his release, and I do not look away, I stare into his very heart as he pours himself into me. I see moisture pooling in his eyes, even as his voice is growling with predatory ferocity, even as his purely male and powerfully masculine body unleashes his orgasm. I feel him break apart.

And I am there to catch every piece and puzzle them together with mine. I kiss him as he comes.

I feel something break inside me, something hot and wet squirting out of me at the exact moment Logan cries out. It is almost embarrassingly involuntary, as if something literally broke open inside my core, drenching both of us where we are joined. I know Logan felt it.

His thighs tremble, and his knees give out. I find my feet as he crumples, and I am so desperate to remain connected to him in this moment that when he lies down on the floor right there in the hallway, I lie on top of him and take his manhood in my hand and play with it as it softens, cradle his heavy balls in my palm and caress those too. Kiss his chest and his chin, his cheek and his lips, his throat and the outer shell of his ear.

"Jesus, Isabel." He is breathless, gasping, pouring sweat. "I didn't know—I didn't know anything could feel like that."

"Me neither."

After a few minutes, he shifts beneath me. "As much as I love having you on top of me, babe, this floor isn't exactly the most comfortable thing to lie on."

I slide off him, stand up, and offer him my hand. He takes it, grinning, and I put all my strength and weight into lifting him off the floor. He's shaky still, sweating, breathing hard.

"Good thing I never skip leg day," he says.

I am reminded, now that the adrenaline and sexual high is wearing off, that I'm sore from my own workout. "You amaze me, Logan."

He shakes his head. "It's you, Isabel. It's all you."

I'm not sure what that means. Only that the way he says it makes my heart melt all over again.

"Now we're both all sweaty," I say.

"And you just took a shower." He twists on the hot water, steps in.

I step in after him. I wish I had something cute and quippy to say, but I don't. I can only lean under the hot spray and let my hands soar over his body, let my eyes close and let him wash me. Let him scrub me, taking far more time than is really needed to get me clean. And when he's done washing me, it's my turn to run the bar of soap over his wet, slippery skin and take all the time in the world to simply appreciate the beauty of his body with my hands.

"We'd better get out soon," he says, "or this is going to turn into round two."

The water still runs hot, and I am still afire with barely sated need. He's woken something in me, I realize. An insatiable voracity.

I lean my back against the marble under the shower head, spread my stance wide, feet far apart. Urge him to his knees. Tangle my hands in his hair and pull his face against my core, writhe my slit against his mouth and keep him buried there until I come.

Again and again and again.

There is no end to the number and the ways that this man can make me come.

And when I'm limp and panting, I let myself collapse to my knees. I remember what he said he wanted to do to me, when this all started. He's hard, by this time. Wonderfully, gloriously hard. Swaying in front of me, wet with shower water. Wet with need. I lick the water away, swipe after swipe of my tongue up his length. Sink my mouth onto him and suck until he's gasping, and then back away. Cup my breasts with both hands and lift them, lean against him. Fit his cock into the narrow space between them and then press them together. He thrusts, and the tip protrudes from between the taut globes, and I take it into my mouth.

"This is what you wanted before, right?" I ask, glancing up at him. "Like this?"

"Fucking hell, Is," he groans, tipping his head back.

"I'll take it that's a yes?"

He looks down at me, his eyes heavy-lidded. "Fuck yes."

I move with him, rising as he pulls back, lowering myself around him as he thrusts up, and at the apex of each thrust I capture his glans with my lips and suckle the tip, lick him, flick my tongue over and around. He's barely even blinking, watching this.

His fingers go to my hair. I'm glad he stopped me from shaving it all off, because I love his hands in my hair, the way he holds on. I'll have to make sure when I do cut it, I leave enough for him to hold on to.

"Mmmm," I moan, when he pulls at my head, urging me to take more of him, "Yes, like that. Take it, Logan."

He surges between my crushed-together tits and into my mouth, harder and faster, and his hands clutch at my hair, gripping the damp mass and holding me in place. All I have to do now is hold on to my tits and take his cock into my mouth. I do so eagerly, loving each taste of him, the slide of his hardness between my teeth and over my tongue. Not going deep, just enough that I can taste him.

I moan now at each slide of his cock between my lips. I moan for him, because when I do his lip curls and he thrusts harder and his cock throbs thicker, and I moan for myself because giving him pleasure and seeing him lose control is bliss to me, is its own form of sexual pleasure. Not the kind of pleasure that leads to orgasm, but the kind of pleasure that can only come from giving something beautiful and incredible to one's lover.

He is my lover.

This revelation stuns me, sends my heart into palpitations. Little things like that have the power to shock me, for some reason.

He takes me. Takes my mouth. Takes my tits.

"I'm about to come, Isabel," he grunts in warning.

I moan around him, humming. Release my tits, and take his cock in my hands. Stroke him slow, gazing up at him. Lips around the broad springy head, tongue fluttering over the very tip.

It's a whim, a last-minute decision to retake ownership of something done to me. To choose something for myself and in so doing erase the ignominy and violation I felt.

I feel him tense, feel him throb between my lips. The decision hits me, and I pull my mouth off him and sink down onto my haunches on the wet marble, shower splattering warm on both of us. He comes, a thick white jet of seed shooting violently out of him and onto my upturned face. I feel it on my mouth, lips, chin. My mouth is open, so it lands on my tongue, salty and musky. On my cheek, running down to my jaw. I stare up at him, blinking through the spatters of water and strings of come, and see that I've shocked him.

I'm up on my knees again, his cock between my tits, and I accept another splash of his come on my lips, licking it away with a glance up at him, feeling powerful and seductive. I did this for *me*, not for Logan. As a "fuck you" to Caleb and everything he did to me that I didn't choose. It's not something I would want on a regular basis, but I need it in this moment. I am retaking myself. Assuming ownership over my sexuality.

I take Logan's cock into my mouth and wrap both hands around it and pump hands and mouth on him until he's groaning and grunting and his knees are dipping and he's hunched over me. Until he gently tugs me away, up to my feet. Finds the washcloth and wrings it out. Curls his arm around my waist and tucks me to his side, tips my face up, and washes away his seed, kisses me.

"Wasn't expecting that," he murmurs.

"I know. Neither was I. But I wanted to . . . remove the stigma and negativity of how that felt."

"I don't want you to ever feel—"

I twist off the water as it's starting to go cold, then cut him off. "Logan. I did what I *wanted* to do. For me. Letting you"—I work up the courage to say exactly what I mean, the way he said it—"letting you fuck my tits . . . that was for you. Having you come on my face, that was for me. Not because I got any kind of weird sexual satisfaction from it, but . . . well, you know what happened. I told you. I did that for me. To take it back."

He helps me out of the shower, unfolds a dry towel, and wraps it around me, and another for himself. We each dry off, and then I turn to him as he cinches the towel around his waist.

"Logan? I do wonder, how did it feel, for you? What did you think?" I don't bother with the towel, once I'm dry. I like his eyes on my body.

He lets out a breath. "There's nothing you could do that wouldn't be incredible. But . . . it was hot. I'm not gonna lie. Seeing you, watching you, watching you take my cock in your mouth, between those big beautiful tits of yours . . . it was hot as fuck. I swear to god I'll never forget it as long as I live. It's a mental image I could jerk off to until the day I die. Coming on your face . . . that's a little different. That's not something I've ever really wanted to do before. Just not my thing. I never wanted to make anyone feel like I got off on . . . something that to me smacks of degradation, I guess. It's a common theme in porn, the come-shot to the face. But I never saw the eroticism in it. Sex, for me, to be really amazing, is about mutuality, mutual satisfaction. And that's what's out of this world about our connection, is that we just . . . we have this incredible, fucking *amazing* chemistry together."

He turns it back to us. God, I love him.

Is he real? Or am I dreaming? Is this just a fever dream?

"Do you masturbate very much?" I ask.

He bobbles his head. "Depends."

"On what? Be honest."

He moves into his bedroom, and I follow him. We each dress, and he speaks as he tugs on underwear and then jeans. "Before I met you, I had a few flings. Nothing serious. Not one-night stands, exactly, but . . . somewhere in between, I guess. Short-term. But . . . between flings, yeah, I'd jerk off regularly."

"And since you met me?" I don't know what answer I want to hear.

He tugs a T-shirt on, a slightly morbid one, black with a white skull near the bottom, the lower mandible fading into tree roots. A crow perches on the skull, and a red rose grows out of it, and the words *Bullet for My Valentine* are printed across the top. I eye it with distaste, and he catches my expression.

"No? Too much, huh? Okay." He flips through a drawer stuffed full of T-shirts and pulls out a different one, exchanges them. This one features a man with long shaggy hair, a bandana across his mouth and nose, and a crossbow on his back, with *The Walking Dead* in large red block letters. "Better?"

I nod. "Yes, much, thank you. That other one was . . . gross."

He chuckles. "Yeah, metal band shirts tend be a little gnarly, I guess."

"You didn't answer my question," I prompt.

"You really want to know the answer?" He waits until I've tugged my dress on and tied my hair back.

"Yes, I do."

He leans back against the edge of the bed. "First, there's been no one else since I met you. I hope that's obvious. If not, there it is. I've not so much as spoken to a woman who isn't an employee since the day we met at that auction. And—" He sighs, glances at me, and then away. "Every day, sometimes more than once a day, thinking of you, yeah, I jerk off. After we first met, it was just . . . *you*. That kiss in the bathroom. I've never gotten so hard from just an innocent kiss before. And you were so fucking sexy, it tormented me. I pictured you in this very room, sliding that dress off . . . shit, this is kind of embarrassing. I feel like a teenager all over again, talking about this."

"Don't be embarrassed, Logan. Tell me more."

He swallows hard, rubs the bridge of his nose. "And then, after that scene in the hallway there, and we almost—yeah, I thought of that a lot. I thought of just . . . sinking into you. I'd imagine how fucking tight you'd be. How soft you'd be. I felt guilty about it, too. Dirty. Like I was . . . defiling you somehow, whacking off thinking about you. But I couldn't help it. I'd try to think of something else, but nothing . . . turned me on. Not like you. I even tried porn a couple times, which I'm not generally a big fan of, but it just seemed . . . stupid. Empty. Nowhere near as fucking erotic as you, in my hallway. The way you dropped that towel, practically begging to be shown how beautiful you really are."

"Not practically, Logan. I *was* begging."

"I couldn't, though." He looks up at me. "I hope you got that."

I nod. "I did, and I do. Doesn't make it easier, but I understood."

"It was self-protection. I felt myself falling for you, and I couldn't let myself get too attached too soon, not knowing how things would shake out between you and Caleb." He ducks his head. Speaks to his shoes. "Even still, I have this . . . fear. That you'll still go back to him."

"Logan—" I want to reassure him, but he speaks over me.

"I don't fall easy, Isabel. But when I do, I fall hard and fast." He stands up, strides over to me, takes my hips in his hands. "There's no going back for me now. I wouldn't want to, even if I could. This is it, for me. I don't—I don't see anyone ever being able to match you. So just keep that in mind, okay? Do what you have to do. I'll never hold you back if your path leads you away from me. But just—just don't do so lightly, okay?" Logan is an articulate man, not given to stumbling over his words or hesitating. That he does now paints a picture that leaves me near tears. He is a warrior, a man who has seen and delivered death, and narrowly escaped it himself. A man who has been to prison and come out the other side a better person.

A man who has been betrayed and can still find the courage to show himself to me, who can allow himself to be vulnerable.

Knowing what I know, knowing what I've done to shake his faith in me—more than once . . . what courage must it take for him to say these things? It is unfathomable.

"*You* are my path, Logan."

"I sure as hell hope so. And believe me, Isabel, I won't take a single moment for granted. Not even if we have a fucking thousand years together."

He palms the damp knot of hair at the base of my head and tugs so my face is tilted up to his.

Kisses me,

and kisses me,

and kisses me.

Love is a painful emotion, I'm realizing. It cracks open the walls around my heart. Demands honesty of me. Courage. Vulnerability. Humility. It is not a light, frilly, easy, storybook thing, where the hero and his lady can ride off into the sunset together. The lady must be a warrior as well, willing to face the darkness with him; she must be brave enough to face the demons and dragons alongside her hero if she wishes to see sunrise, let alone the sunset.

FOURTEEN

My heart is in my throat, thick coil of black hair in one hand, scissors in the other. I blink and let out a breath, stare at myself in the hairdresser's mirror, at Logan's reflection. He's standing behind me, hands in his pockets, watching. His friend, Mei, the stylist—who actually owns the entire salon—has my head in her small, delicate hands. Holding me steady. Soothing. Stroking nimble fingers over my scalp.

She understands, I think, even though I've told her nothing of myself, nothing of my story. I told her only that I needed to change my appearance drastically, and she met my eyes, stared at me knowingly for a long moment, and just smiled at me. Sat me in her chair, stroked her fingers through my hair, fanning it out, billowing it, pulling it back severely to assess the shape of my face, folding it up and under to get an approximation of what I might look like with shorter hair.

And then hands me her scissors. "You make the first cut," Mei says.

Despite having been moments from shaving it to the scalp mere hours ago, now that I have my hair in hand and scissors ready to make the first cut, I'm having a moment of doubt. Of hesitation.

Logan says nothing. Just watches.

Mei takes the scissors from me. Moves to stand in front of me. She is short and slight, hair dyed lavender and clipped close on the sides, left longer on top, twisted and pulled back over her head. She speaks English fluently but with a pronounced Asian accent. "It's your choice. You do it, you don't do it, only one who matters is you. But I think you want to do it. We donate it to Locks of Love." Her fingers run almost compulsively through my hair again. "You make first cut, I make you beautiful. Make you *more* beautiful. You already beautiful."

She hands me the scissors again, lifts my hair bound between her fingers in a thick rope, a small gap between her two hands. "Cut between hands."

I breathe out. Snip the scissors open and closed—*snicksnick-snicksnick*—and then, before I can second-guess myself any further, I open the scissors wide and cut between Mei's hands. I feel weight float free from the column of my neck. My head feels lighter. Mei takes the scissors from me and moves around to stand in front of me, blocking my view of myself in the mirror. I shake my head, and the sensation is bizarre. No thick sheaf of hair waving at my back, no long strands tangling around my ears, draping over my shoulder. There is nothing. I want to cry, yet also laugh. I'm not sure which.

"Let me see," I say.

Mei just shakes her head. "Not until I'm done. Close eyes." I close my eyes. She spins me around, pats me on the shoulder. "Okay, open, but no peeking."

She buttons a black cape around my neck, and her fingers run through my hair several times. Oh god. It's short. So short. There's so little up there for her fingers to even move through.

And then she starts cutting. *Snick . . . snicksnicksnick . . . snicksnick.*

I feel bits of hair flutter down and land on the black cape, on my shoulders and sliding down to my lap. A bit here, a bit there, my hair going shorter and shorter and shorter. Her scissors are so fast, moving unerringly, never hesitating. As if she has a vision and knows exactly what to do to make it reality. Like a painter utterly sure of her brushstrokes. I'm staring at Logan, who is just standing in the middle of the deserted salon, legs spread wide, arms crossed over his broad chest, eyes on me, on Mei, watching intently. His expression is inscrutable, which makes me nervous. What does he think? Does he like it? Hate it?

What will *I* think?

I have no idea. I like the way it feels, though. Loose, light, free. Everything I want to be, everything I'm striving to be.

After what seems like an eternity of cutting, she steps away, gestures for me to stand up. "Come, come. Almost done. Wash, style, and then you see." She leads me to a sink with a U-shaped divot in the front, puts me in the reclining chair, and settles me backward, so my neck rests in the U. Warm water, strong hands. She doesn't just wash my hair, she massages my scalp, powerful fingers digging into my scalp and the back of my neck, loosening tension, relaxing me. Kneads shampoo into my now-short hair, rinsing it away. Towels me dry.

"Okay, back to chair." She sprays a little foam into her palm, rubs her hands together a few times, then works the mousse into my hair. "It will take time to remember, but you only need a very little product now. Shampoo, conditioner, mousse, only a little. Before, so much hair, you need a lot. First few showers, you will squirt too much. Just laugh, every girl who cuts all her hair away does it. I had long hair, like you, once. Cut it all off, dyed it purple like so." She gestures at her head. "To make my father angry. I use too much shampoo for weeks. Never remembered."

She uses a blow dryer on my hair, brushing stiffened fingers through it, working it forward, smoothing it down on the sides. I feel it tickling my forehead, my temple, brushing my eyebrow.

It took her perhaps fifteen minutes total to wash, dry, and style my hair. It feels miraculous. It took me fifteen minutes just to shampoo all my hair, another fifteen to rinse it. And it would still be sopping wet for at least twelve hours after washing it. Sometimes a full day, or more.

Now, it's washed, dried, and styled in fifteen minutes. No hours of brushing.

This alone makes me giddy.

"Yes, very good." Mei places her hands on my shoulders, squeezes, leans down close to my ear. "Ready?"

I have to let out a nervous breath. "I think so." I straighten my spine. "Yes, I'm ready." I close my eyes as Mei spins the chair around.

"Okay," Mei says, "now look."

I open my eyes, and my breath leaves me in a whoosh. Short, messy. *Perfect*. It's boy-short. Pulled forward into my eyes, long narrow V-shaped points draping down in front of my ears. The cut accentuates my exotic features, makes my already large, dark eyes appear dramatically larger, highlights my high, sharp cheekbones, heart-shaped face, my lush, kissable lips.

"Can I do makeup on you?" Mei asks.

"Sure?" I shrug. "I don't usually wear much."

"Not much. You don't need much." She opens a cabinet under her station and pulls out her purse, lays cases and tins and brushes and tubes out on the counter of her station.

Spins me away from the mirror yet again, brushes blush on my cheeks, runs eyeliner under my eye, smears eye shadow on my eyelids, lip stain on my lips. I don't wear much makeup, never have. I was always told that I don't need it, that natural beauty such as mine is best appreciated with little or no adornment.

When Mei is done, she turns me around, and yet again I am left breathless, speechless. My eyes are enormous, their natural almond shape and dark irises emphasized and highlighted. My eyes are . . . hypnotic, this way. My cheekbones look razor sharp now, my lips even fuller, darker red. The overall effect is subtle, but dramatic. Smoky, mysterious. Sultry. Sensual.

"My god, Mei." I am near tears. "I look like . . . I don't even know. Not even myself, anymore."

"Is it good? You are crying, but I don't know if it is a good cry or not."

"No, it's perfect. I love it. It's perfect. I can't believe this is me I'm looking at, right now."

I turn my head this way and that. Examine myself from different angles. I really, truly do not even recognize myself. I look edgy, modern, sexy, exotic. Nothing like the formal, Old World aristocratic beauty I used to look like. Used to *be*. I love the messiness of it. The wind could ruffle it and muss it, and it wouldn't ruin the look. I could run my hands through it, and it wouldn't look worse. I do so, feather my fingers through my hair, marveling at the lack of weight sliding through my fingers. I push all the hair to one side, draping it all over to the left, and my look changes slightly. To the right, the same, a subtle change in the way the look sits on me. Brush it forward again and mess it up.

"See? You get it." Mei smiles at me. "Mess it up. Play with it. You could slick it back, too. That would look badass, very dramatic, very different. It makes you look beautiful, a new you. Still woman, not butch at all, just short, and edgy. Different." She unbuttons the cape and pulls it off me so the loose hair falls to the floor at my feet.

JASINDA WILDER

I rise to my feet and lean into her, wrap her up in a hug. She stiffens at first, clearly not comfortable with such affection, then somewhat awkwardly hugs me back.

She pushes me away after a second. *"Oh*-kay, hug time over now."

"Sorry. I'm just . . . thank you, Mei. Thank you so much. I love it."

"I'm very glad." She glances at Logan. "Any friend of Logan is a friend of mine. You come back any time. We have girl talk, drink too much wine, and bitch about stupid boys."

"I'd like that."

"Good. You come here Friday night. I close at seven, we have a good time together." She gathers her makeup into her hands, glances at me. "You have your own makeup?"

I shake my head. "No, like I said, I've never worn much makeup. Some eyeliner, lipstick, that's about it. Nothing this dramatic." I don't mention that I don't own *anything*, much less something so frivolous as makeup.

"It's a good look for you. Makes you look mysterious. A little intimidating, I think." She yanks a plastic grocery bag out of a cabinet in her station, dumps the makeup into it. "For you. I have more. You practice. Come Friday, I teach you, if you want."

"Thanks, Mei. I—"

She ushers us to the door, waving her hands as if herding chickens, cutting off my thanks. "Now, go. Go. I have another client soon, and I have to clean up."

We're outside in the late-morning sun, walking to Logan's SUV. When we're in his truck and waiting at a stoplight, I turn to him. "So. What do you think, Logan?"

He looks at me long and hard. "It's an incredible transformation, Isabel. You are absolutely gorgeous. There's nothing you could do to ever make yourself look anything other than stunning. But this look? It's perfect for you. Like Mei said, it makes you look even more mysterious than you already are."

"How do you know Mei?" I ask.

"Oh. Um. Well, I hired her to do some programming for me. She's actually an insanely talented computer programmer too, like seriously one of the best I've ever met. So she worked for me programming our website and debugging some of our systems as a freelance contractor. But then when that was done, we stayed friends."

"Just friends?"

He eyes me. "Jealous?"

I blush. "Maybe a little. It's an unusual emotion, for me. I don't know how to process it."

He just laughs. "We went out once. I went to kiss her at the end of the date and we were both just like . . . nah, it's not there. We've been friends since." A glance at me. "Jealousy is totally natural and normal, by the way. Just be honest about it with yourself and with me."

"It's just new for me. I never . . . it never occurred to me to be jealous until I saw Caleb with someone else. He did it on purpose. He was mad at me about . . . well, that's a long story. But he was mad at me, so he arranged for me to see him kissing another girl on the street below my apartment. My old apartment, I mean." I try not to remember. I don't want those memories crowding out my new sense of self. "As far as tactics go, it was effective. But that was the first time that I can remember feeling jealous. I thought he was . . . I don't know. Not mine, because it didn't work that way between Caleb and me. But it just . . . it never occurred to me that he'd have other women in his life. It wasn't a good feeling."

"I don't suppose so." It's all Logan says on that subject. Smart of him, I think. Nothing good could come from his opinion of Caleb. I know how he feels and why, and there's no sense discussing it.

Miles pass under the tires, past the windows. The radio is off, silence is thick. I don't know where we're going.

"What do you want to do, Isabel?" Logan asks, abruptly breaking the silence.

"I was wondering where you were going."

He shakes his head. "No, that's not what I mean. Right now I'm taking us to lunch, this great Mediterranean place I know in Brooklyn. I meant with your life. With yourself. What do you want? How will you live?"

Optimism leaves me in a rush. "I don't know, Logan."

"I only ask because I know you well enough by now to know you'll only be content if you're making your own way." He reaches out and takes my hand, glances at me briefly. "You can stay with me. I'll support you. Everything I have is yours. If that's what you want, you'll never have to work another day in your life. I'm not as wildly rich as Caleb, but I'm doing pretty fucking well for myself. You'll never want for anything. My point wasn't that you're not welcome, or that there's some kind of expiration date on you staying with me. But I feel like you need your own space. Your own thing. So that's what I'm asking. What do you want for yourself?"

He's right. I would feel owned all over again if I relied on him. Even if that was not his intention, even if he went out of his way to make sure I didn't feel that way, it would seep in.

So what do I want?

I have absolutely no idea. What am I capable of? What am I good at?

I spend a long, long time thinking. And I can only come to one sad conclusion. "I've only ever done one thing. I only know how to be Madame X, and I cannot be her anymore. But what else can I do?" I am near tears, but I keep them down. Force them away.

"What if you don't have to be Madame X anymore, but still

perform that same basic service, just . . . on your own? For yourself. Not as Madame X, but as Isabel de la Vega."

I breathe deeply and slowly, carefully. "I . . . I don't know. Could I? I don't know. Why would I do that? What was it I really did?" I trace the stitching in the leather at the edge of my seat. "Looking back, I find only dubious value in the service I performed."

"See, I disagree. I think you performed a *very* valuable service. When you're dealing with people as rich as your former clientele, parenting often gets left at the wayside. Pursuit of wealth is the only thing that matters to many of them. So . . . you end up with spoiled rich kids who have no conception of reality, who don't value hard work or money, who have no sense of self or decency or morals or anything. And I think your real value was in taking them down a few notches. Making them realize that the world wasn't always going to revolve around them. That it didn't, doesn't, and never will." He pulls to a stop on a street, I have no idea which one or where we are, and parallel parks in front of a restaurant. Doesn't get out, pivots in his seat and looks into my eyes. "I think you could open your own business doing the same basic thing, but maybe take it a few steps further. You'd probably make a fucking fortune, *and* you'd be doing the world a favor by taking the douche out of some of the spoiled assholes out there."

I consider it. "You really think so?"

He nods. "I really do. But the thing here is that you'd be doing it on your own terms. No persona. Just you being you. You'd do what you did before, meet and assess each client, and come up with a treatment plan or whatever you want to call it. Teach them manners. Like, basic manners. Make them wait tables. Make them do charity work, like at a soup kitchen or something. Whatever you think necessary to enact the change in them."

"Where would I find clients? I—I don't even know where to start."

He smiles at me and squeezes my hand. "I can help. It's sort of what I do, you know. I can even float you a startup loan."

"I need to consider."

He nods. "Of course. It's a big step."

I put it out of my mind as we exit the SUV and sit down to eat. The food is delicious, of course. I let him order for me, and thus do not know the names of any of the dishes. I just know that everything is heavy in garlic, features rice and olives and lamb and chicken and thick crispy pita bread. It is flavorful and filling, but not heavy. As we eat, Logan brings the conversation back around to the idea of me starting my own business.

"One thing I'd say for sure is that you wouldn't work out of your home. You need a separation of work and home. Unless you're, like, a computer programmer or something, you need your own space that's just for you. Especially in the line of business you're considering. You can't have clients coming and going from your living room. That just invites familiarity, and you need to remain aloof. Untouchable. Imposing. The atmosphere would still have to seem informal, comfortable, but separate from your personal space." He shovels a few forkfuls of rice into his mouth and then stabs a green olive, gesturing with the fork and the olive. "I think—I think . . ." He eats the olive, and I'm noticing that the more he discusses this, the more effusive he becomes. It's endearing and adorable and inspiring, seeing his excitement over this idea. It's contagious. "I think if you bought a town house kind of like mine, we could renovate it to suit your needs. Make a front room, a deep comfortable leather couch, a little kitchenette and bar, a bay window overlooking the street. And then make a separate entrance leading to your space, which would take up the rest of the house, use both upper and lower levels. Maybe make the bedroom a loft over the rest. Keep it open, you know? The door to your space would need to be really secure, though, maybe use biometrics. Thumbprints and whatever, right?"

I interrupt his flow. "Logan. This all sounds wonderful, but . . ." I cannot help a sigh of defeat. "I don't have a single dime to my name. I don't own a single article of clothing of my own. Nothing. Where am I going to get the money to buy a town house in Manhattan, much less capital to open a business?"

He waves my objection away with his fork. "Told you, I'll help you out. Run you a business loan."

"I'm not taking your money, Logan. That would only—"

He sets his fork down, his gaze serious. "I didn't say 'give,' Isabel, I said 'loan.' I'll have my banker work up the paperwork for you. I know you wouldn't take money from me, and that's not what I'm offering. I'd have no stake in your business itself, other than the hope that you're profitable so I see a return on my investment. I'm not looking to make a profit myself off this, so the terms would be pretty forgiving, low interest, make it easy for you to pay it off. This is to help you. Get you started."

"Why, Logan?"

He makes a funny face. Sad, tender, loving, and confused all at once. "Because everyone needs help sometimes. And because I love you. I want to help you. I'd just give you the damn money if I thought you'd take it. I have more than I'll ever be able to spend, even with giving a shitload away to charity. I want to see you succeed. I want to . . ." He sighs and leans back in his chair. "There's selfish motivation at work here, too. If you're successful, if you're working for yourself, then you're more likely to be happy. And if you're happy, that just means things between us will be that much better."

I can't help a smile. "So even your selfish motivations are centered on my happiness?"

A grin. "Well, yeah. I mean, think about it. If you're happy, then your focus can be on me. If you're happy, my chances of being able to keep you naked in my bed for entire weekends are that much better. And after last night and this morning, Isabel honey, I've got plans to keep you naked and sweaty for as long as you'll let me."

"I like the sound of those plans."

His eyes heat up. "We could buy a little place in the Caribbean, stay naked on the beach for weeks on end."

I close my eyes and dream. Pretend I'm successful. Making my own money running my own business. Logan is mine, all mine. There is no one else. I imagine being on a beach somewhere. With him. Lying naked on a blanket in the sand, the sun hot above us. His mouth all over me. I squirm, desire flushing through me at the idea.

"You're picturing it, aren't you?" He's leaning toward me over the table, whispering in my ear. "You and me, naked on a beach?"

"Yes," I breathe.

"Picture it, babe. Keep that image in your mind. We'll make it a reality."

There are a few moments of silence then, as we finish our food. My mind wanders, back to his bedroom, to us. To him, asleep on the couch. The notepad, the scribblings.

"Logan?" I have to know. I have to ask.

He glances up, eyebrows lifted in query. "Hmmm?"

"Who is Jakob Kasparek?"

He freezes. "You saw that."

"Yeah. I saw. What did that note mean, Logan?"

He chews, swallows, breathes. "I did a little more digging. I managed to get a peek at the discharge papers from the hospital. The signature on your discharge sheet is Jakob Kasparek."

"Not Caleb Indigo?"

He shakes his head. "No. Jakob Kasparek." A lift of his shoulder. "I looked for that name, but I found nothing. Not a single thing. So

I don't know anything except that whoever signed you out of the hospital was named Jakob Kasparek, not Caleb Indigo."

I swallow hard. Try to breathe evenly. "I . . . I don't mean to doubt you, but . . . are you sure?"

"One hundred percent. I'm sorry, I know that . . . probably doesn't make things easier for you."

"I just . . . I remember the day he signed me out. I remember him signing the paper. I—I didn't see the signature, but . . . it just makes no sense. I don't know. I don't know."

My head spins. Whirls. Aches. Nothing makes any sense. Nothing adds up. Nothing is true.

I feel panic boiling under my skin, gripping my throat and my mind. I have to shut it down. Think of something else. Don't go there, not now. Not here.

"You said you give money to charity?" I ask, just to shift the conversation.

He shrugs, recognizing my gambit for what it is. "Yeah. I mean, my business is worth . . . well, a lot. Thirty million, last time I checked. I spread it around, make sure my people are raking in their own personal fortunes, because they do the lion's share of the work. But even if I only kept thirty percent of the company's profit, that'd be nine million a year, something like that. And I'm just one guy, you know? What does one guy do with nine million dollars a year? I keep my life simple. I own one home, and I stay around Manhattan for the most part. Take a few vacations here and there. But I like working, so I work a lot. Means I don't spend a lot. I only have the one car, because driving in New York is a bitch so there's no real point in owning a bunch of fancy cars. Not my thing anyway." He waves a hand. "So I give a lot to various charities."

"Like what?"

He's clearly uncomfortable with this line of conversation.

"There's one that does a lot of work with combat veterans, guys coming home from Iraq and Afghanistan. Therapy, retreats, shit like that. It's a nonprofit I started with a couple other guys from Blackwater. They do a lot of really amazing work with guys that have PTSD, outside-the-box stuff, not just sitting in a fucking room talking about our emotions with a shrink. Soldiers hate that shit. We hate talking about what we did. We just want to put it behind us and not have nightmares, you know? So the focus is PTSD treatment that's not just talking. Equine therapy, canine therapy. Art, music, sports. Stuff like that. Then there's the education fund. That one directs money past all the red tape of bureaucracy and directly into school districts that need money, inner-city schools here in New York and all across the country. They're expanding all the time, getting into new school districts with every check written. No testing requirements, no bullshit, no politicians skimming off the top. Just cold hard cash going into schools so kids can learn." He opens up as he speaks, and his eyes and his expression reveal his passion. "I love that one especially. When I was a kid, my education wasn't all that important to me. I was more concerned with getting high and into trouble with the fellas. But even if I had been, where I lived, I wouldn't have gotten much of an education anyway. And San Diego is a lot better off than somewhere like L.A. or the schools in somewhere like Queens, you know? There's just not enough money for the schools to do shit about shit for anyone."

"That's amazing, Logan," I say.

He rolls his eyes. "It's not. I just donate money. I've got it coming out of my fucking earholes, and charity is somewhere to put it so it's not just sitting there. And besides, it's a tax deduction."

"What others are there?"

"Lots of little ones here and there. Helping at-risk teens, 'cause I've been one, women's shelters, food banks, drug recovery clinics."

"Don't downplay what you're doing, Logan. It makes a difference."

He smiles at me. "I know it does. That's why I do it. Warrior's Welcome, the one that works with soldiers . . . I host retreats every year for that one. Get a whole bunch of rotated-out soldiers and Marines and security contractors, take 'em to a farm in upstate New York, and do a bunch of fun stuff. Trail rides, paintball games, basketball tournaments. The whole point of the retreats, though, is the Bonfire Bullshit. Make this huge-ass bonfire, tap a keg, and trade war stories. It's a judgment-free zone, you know? That's the point of it. You don't tell stories to friends or family, 'cause they won't get it. They *can't*. When it's a bunch of other dudes who've fuckin' *been there*, it's different. Some guys don't want to talk, and they don't have to, but even listening to other guys' stories, hearing the truth that there are people who know exactly what you're going through, what it's like, that's cathartic as anything else ever could be."

"You never cease to both surprise and amaze me, Logan." I cup his cheek. "Every time I think I know you, you reveal something new."

He shakes his head and laughs softly. "Yeah, I'm a real puzzle."

"You are, though. You're a successful businessman, yet you came from urban poverty and an at-risk childhood. You were in a gang. You watched your best friend get murdered. You've been to war. You've been to prison. Yet despite all that, you're successful and well adjusted." I give a lock of his hair a playful tug. "And you're the sexiest man I've ever met."

"You're gonna give me a complex, babe," Logan says.

We're outside, standing on the sidewalk near his SUV. For once in my life, things feel . . . normal. I've got hope. I feel like I am a new person, becoming someone complete.

My heart feels full.

I love Logan. He loves me.

The world is afire with possibility.

And then my blood runs cold.

I see Thomas, first. Tall, frightening, skin black as night, teeth white as piano keys. He has something long and thin and dark in his hands, not a gun, but a stick of some kind. A bludgeon. I don't know where Thomas came from. He was not there, not anywhere, and then in an eyeblink, there he is. I don't have time to even open my mouth.

Thomas's hand flashes in the bright golden light of early afternoon. There is a dull *thud*, and the stick connects with Logan's head, right behind his ear, just so. Precise. A practiced move. I see Logan collapse, the light instantly bleeding out of his eyes.

I inhale to scream, but a hand covers my mouth. Len. I twist, kick.

"You think I wouldn't find you?" This isn't Len's voice in my ear. It's yours.

I feel tears of despair prick my eyelids. No. No. Not this. Not you. Not again. Not now.

I feel motion, feel the whispering breeze of your passage from behind me to in front of me. There you are. Perfect, handsome. Calm and collected. Cool. I smell your cologne. Black suit, crimson shirt, top button loose, no tie. You have a pistol in your hand. Flat black, small in your large paw.

You glance at me. You do not smile. "I thought I could let you go," you say. Your expression is . . . almost sad. Regretful. You glance at Len, behind and above me. "I was wrong."

I feel something sharp touch my neck. A needle. It pricks me, and something cold rushes through me.

Darkness rises from the shadows at my feet. Reaches up for me. I fight it.

You point your gun at Logan.

No!

No! I scream, but it comes out a faint whimper.

I watch in slow motion as your finger tightens on the metal crescent of the trigger.

NO!

I want to scream and cry, but I cannot. I can only fade into darkness.

I don't see it happen. I only hear a loud *BANG!*

And then there is nothingness.

Only cold and black and empty.

FIFTEEN

Consciousness eludes me. I seek it, struggling up through darkness, wallowing in silence, floating in absence of sound and sensation. Near consciousness. A slow, delicate sliding across the cusp of wakefulness. Where there is awareness of self, but no ability to truly perform higher functions.

I struggle. But it is like being wrapped up in a cocoon; it is a fight I cannot win. I succumb.

There is a fist in my hair. My head is tugged back. I'm moaning. I'm faking the sound, though, because the grip on my hair is painful, but the moans are expected.

I'm on my hands and knees. On a bed. In the dark. Silence, but for my moans, and the low male grunts behind me.

It hurts. Too big, too much. Too hard, too rough.

I've been here on my knees for an eternity. Taking the punishing, driving thrusts for forever. I'm raw.

I want it to stop.

But I'm not allowed to talk. Not allowed to make a sound but for the moans. I know the rules. I know the punishment if I break them.

I am expected to orgasm. But the breath washing over my neck smells of whisky, and orgasm seems to be out of reach.

A hand smacks across my buttock. "Say my name." *The order is a rough, slurred growl.*

"Caleb . . ." *I whisper it.*

Another smack, to the other side. "Say it again."

"Caleb."

"Louder." *A harder smack.*

The pain sears through me. These aren't playful, sexual spanks. They are meant, they are punishment for a failing. They hurt.

But the pain at least is a distraction from other discomforts.

"Caleb!" *I say it loudly.*

"You're going to come now." *Despite the whisky breath, the words are clear and lucid and not slurred.*

I cannot. But I do not dare say this. Nor do I dare fake it as I do the moans. I am very bad at faking orgasm, I've learned. I am always caught out.

"Come, X. Come hard."

"I—"

Upright now. Still behind me, the thrusts continue unabated. Fingers steal around my waist and between my thighs. It's only a sizzle at first, but it's something.

The fist in my hair tugs hard. Pulls my head back so I'm forced to stare at the ceiling. Whisky breath on my face, in my ear. "Come for me, X."

The fingers at my core move swiftly, precisely, and lightning lances through me, hot and sudden. I do not have to fake it, thank god. The pleasure is a dull throb next to the anticipation of being released.

But I'm not released. The presence behind and within me pulls away, moves to sit at the edge of the bed. I remain kneeling, hunting for breath. My scalp tingles.

But I'm not done. A hard hand grips my wrist and tugs hard. Pulls me roughly across the mattress, shoves me to the floor, to my knees. Fingers curl into my chin-length hair. Guide me to the waiting member. Hard, but not completely.

"Finish me."

I do as I am ordered. With my hands, with my mouth. It takes a long time. I am tired. So tired. My jaw aches. My forearms ache as well from constant up-and-down motion. When the release comes, it is much less forcefully than usual.

I am allowed to climb into my bed then. I curl up on the mattress, in the center, and a blanket settles over me.

I note the absence of footsteps, feel the presence beside me. Standing. Watching me.

I allow my body to go limp. Even my breathing. Let my mouth fall open. After many long minutes of pretending to sleep, I smell whisky, hear breathing. I am not entirely faking this descent into slumber anymore. I am nearly asleep now.

"Isabel." This is whispered, so low it is nearly inaudible. "My lovely Isabel." Sadness. Regret. Longing. Misery. The whisper is fraught with these things.

Who is Isabel?

Lips touch temple. Gently, so softly it could have been a whisper of air, a figment of my imagination. "It wasn't supposed to be this way."

What wasn't?

"I'm so sorry. It wasn't supposed to be this way."

I am losing the battle to stay awake. I fight it. This close to sleep, nothing seems real. I am delirious with exhaustion. I am imagining this, surely. I've fallen asleep and I am dreaming. Surely. Surely.

The man I have come to understand over the past year would not speak thus, does not experience such emotions. It is a dream.

Just a dream.

Only a dream.

W ake up, X." The familiar rumble in my ear.

I blink. Open my eyes, and experience a debilitating disorientation. Am I awake? Am I dreaming, still?

Where am I? *When* am I?

I am in my room. My blackout curtains are in place. My noise machine shushes with the sound of soothing crashing waves. My bed. The door to my bedroom is cracked, emitting a sliver of light. Through it I can just barely make out a slice of my living room. My couch. The Louis XIV armchair, the coffee table with its antique map.

What is going on?

Have I dreamed everything?

I am near tears. No. No. I didn't dream Logan. That was *real*. He is *real*. It wasn't a dream.

It wasn't.

Was it?

I still have the fragments of memory floating in my head, you in my room, the aching, the exhaustion, the numbness. The near-sleep fantasy of a Caleb who experiences real emotions, for someone named Isabel.

Isabel.

I sit up. You crouch at my bedside, and when I sit up, you rise to your feet. You are imperious, cold, distant. Tan suit, dark blue button-down, top button undone. You fasten the middle button of the suit coat.

"Time to get up, X. You have a client in thirty minutes. I've prepared your breakfast."

"Wha—um. What? Caleb? What am I doing here? What's going on?"

You turn. "What do you mean, what's going on? You have a client. Travis Mitchell, son of Michael Mitchell, founder and CEO of Mitchell Medical Enterprises."

I shake my head. It aches. Feels thick. Memories jog and tumble with fragments of dream.

It wasn't real? Logan, his town house on the quiet street. Cocoa. Naked in bed with Logan, savoring every touch, every kiss. I remember every moment. I can picture every scar, every tattoo.

"No." My voice is raspy, hoarse. "No. Stop, Caleb."

"Stop what?" You seem honestly confused.

"You're fucking with my head. It won't work." I slide my feet out of bed and stand up. I am naked.

"Get in the shower, X." A step toward me. "Now."

I back up. "Stop. Just . . . stop."

I run my hands through my hair, and that's what shakes everything loose. My hair is short.

Mei.

Logan. *Oh god*, Logan. "You shot him!" I lunge forward, smash my fist into your cheekbone as hard as I can, suddenly full of fiery rage. "You fucking *shot* him!" I swing again, my other hand, connect with your jaw.

You rock backward, stunned, and then you catch my wrists and easily overpower me. A moment then, as I resist you. But you are far too powerful. You grunt, and throw me aside.

I land on the floor between the bed and the wall, and in a blur you are there, kneeling in front of me. Your hand latches onto my chin, gripping my jaw in a crushing vise grip.

"You . . . belong . . . to *me*." Your voice is the venomous hiss of a viper. "You are mine. You are Madame X, and you are *mine*."

I lash out with my heel, catch you off guard, and my foot impacts your chest, sends you toppling backward. I lurch to my feet. Back up. Catch against the corner of the bed.

"Fuck you, Caleb!" I spit. "*Fuck . . . you*. My name is Isabel Maria de la Vega Navarro. I am *not* Madame X, and I am not a possession. I do not belong to you. I will never belong to you again."

You collapse backward against the wall, lying where you landed after I kicked you, as if you meant all along to lie there. "You *are* mine. You will always be mine. You've been mine since you were sixteen."

"What? What does that mean?" I think of what Logan told me.

"I thought you had all the answers. I thought your precious Logan knew everything."

"Don't be petulant, Caleb." I hunt in the darkness for some way to cover myself without having to pass you, since you are between me and the closet.

I end up tugging the sheet off the bed and wrapping it around me, letting the end drape behind me like the train of a wedding dress. After a moment, you stand up, brush off your suit. Glance at me. The cold hard mask is in place.

"You might as well have breakfast." You exit my bedroom without a backward glance.

I follow. Everything is as it was. My books. Empty mantel, no TV, no radio, no computer. My library, the case with my antique books and signed first editions. The paintings—*Portrait of Madame X; Starry Night*. The breakfast nook. A single simple white porcelain plate, half a grapefruit, vanilla-flavored Greek yogurt, a mug of Earl Grey tea imported from England, a single square of organic wheat bread toast with a thin scrim of farm-to-table butter. I stare at the food, and my stomach rumbles. I want scrambled eggs with cheese, a Belgian waffle piled high with whipped cream and strawberries drowning in processed syrup, crispy brown bacon, white toast slathered thick with jelly.

I ignore the breakfast you've provided. Put four pieces of bread in the toaster. Find a container of cage-free eggs and an unopened rectangle of Dublin cheddar cheese. I set about making scrambled eggs, and I'm not sure how I know how to make them. But I do.

I crack four eggs into a bowl and whip them while the pan heats.

I'm struck by a memory:

Mama is at the counter, a white bowl in one hand, a fork in the other, whipping eggs in a smooth circular motion of the fork. Music fills the kitchen from a small radio on the counter near the stove, guitar and a man singing in Spanish. Mama's hips sway and bob to the rhythm. The morning is bright. Waves crash. I sit at a table, running my thumbnail in a crack in the aged wood, watching Mama beat the eggs. I wait for my favorite part: the liquid bubbling hiss when she pours them into the pan.

A seagull caws, and a boat horn goes BWAAAAAAAANNNNHHHH! in the distance.

Mama smiles at me as she scrapes the fluffy, cheesy eggs onto my plate, and then kisses me on the temple. Her eyes twinkle. "Coma, mi amor." Her voice is music.

The memory is so visceral that I can smell the eggs, and her perfume, the salt of the sea, hear the seagulls and the boat horn. Tears slide down my cheek, and I hide them by ducking over the bowl as I finish whipping the eggs. I pour the beaten eggs into the pan, and the bubbling hiss makes the memory roar through me, making me feel as if making these eggs somehow connects me to my mother. A simple but powerful thing.

I add a generous amount of cheese as I fold and stir the eggs, soaking in the memory of Mama, eggs, and a breakfast by the sea.

The toast pops, and I spread butter thickly onto the squares of toasted bread. When the eggs are cooked, I slide them onto a plate, pile the toast onto the plate, retrieve the still-steaming mug of tea from the table, and take my breakfast to the couch. I am careful to make sure the sheet remains tucked around me, keeping me covered.

You watch from the kitchen, anger boiling in your gaze. I ignore you and eat my breakfast.

As I eat, I remember the note I saw beside Logan's laptop.

When I finish, I set the plate on the coffee table and lean back on the couch, sipping at the tea. "Caleb?"

You saunter toward me. Take a seat on the Louis XIV armchair, cross one ankle over your knee, drum fingertips against the armrests. "Yes, X?"

You are trying to rile me, and it won't work. "Who is Jakob Kasparek?"

You pale, your eyes widen, your lips thin. You cease breathing. "Where—where did you hear that name?"

"Who is Jakob Kasparek?" I repeat.

A hesitation. "No one. I've never heard of him."

I eye you across the rim of my teacup. "Liar."

"X—"

"Tell me the truth, Caleb." I am proud of how even my voice is.

"I told you—"

"Lies, you bastard! You've told me nothing but fucking lies!" I lean forward, shouting. *"TELL ME THE TRUTH!"*

You seem rocked by my spittle-spraying scream.

I feel feral. Violent. "Just tell me the goddamn truth. Tell me what happened to me. Tell me who you are. Tell me how long I was in the coma. Tell me what year the accident happened. Admit there was no mugger. Tell me—just—just fucking tell me, Caleb!" I sob the last part. "I need to know. Why do you feel like you own me? Why can't you let me go? Where is Logan?"

You shoot to your feet. "You sit there demanding answers. But I owe you nothing. Nothing!" You stalk toward the door.

I hurl the teacup at you, tea dregs spraying across the room. The delicate porcelain smashes against the door beside your face, and you halt, spinning in place.

"Are you crazy? You could have hit me!"

"I was aiming for you, you fucking asshole." I clutch the sheet to my chest. Stand behind you, seething. "Who . . . the *fuck* . . . is Jakob Kasparek? Because Caleb? That's who signed me out of the hospital, not Caleb Indigo."

Your shoulders slump. "Fine. I'll tell you." A glance at me. "But go put on some clothing."

"I'm not going anywhere. Start talking." I fear that if I leave for a moment, you'll be gone and the door will be locked and I'll be a prisoner all over again.

You perhaps understand me better than I thought. You vanish into my room—my *former* room—and return with underwear and a matching bra, a dress, and heels. You hand it to me and wait expectantly.

I stare at you. "Turn around. I'm not changing in front of you."

You just blink at me. "Seriously? After all we've—"

"After all you've done *to* me, you mean? Yes. Seriously. I'm not yours. You don't get to watch me dress anymore."

With a sigh, as if to protest the ridiculousness of the situation, you turn in place. I dress quickly, hating the uncomfortable, confining lingerie and the modest, formal dress. I ignore the high heels. Grip the front of the dress at the bodice and rip it open down the center an inch or two, so it gapes open, revealing a bit more cleavage. And then grip the sleeve on one side and rip. The delicate seam parts easily, leaving my arm bare. I do the same to the other side. I smile. Much better.

You turn around. "What the hell did you do? That was a ten-thousand-dollar dress custom made for you."

"I do not care, Caleb. I will not dress in *your* clothing, I will no longer look how *you* wish me to look."

"And your hair—"

"You don't get a say."

You sigh. "Fine." You sit once more in the Louis XIV chair. Hook a knee over the other. "What do you want to know?"

"Who is Jakob Kasparek?"

A silence. You stare past me. Your expression softens; your gaze goes distant.

"Me."